THRONES
OF DESIRE

THRONES OF DESIRE

EROTIC TALES OF SWORDS, MIST AND FIRE

EDITED BY
MITZI SZERETO

FOREWORD BY
PIERS ANTHONY

CLEiS
PRESS

Published in the United States by Cleis Press, Inc.,
2246 Sixth Street, Berkeley, California 94710.

Printed in the United States.
Cover design: Scott Idleman/Blink
Cover photograph: Cevdet Gokhan Palas/Getty Images
Text design: Frank Wiedemann

First Edition.
10 9 8 7 6 5 4 3 2 1

Trade paper ISBN: 978-1-57344-815-4
E-book ISBN: 978-1-57344-829-1

Contents

FOREWORD

In my observation, women generally crave reassurance the way men crave sex: often. So when it comes to erotic fantasy, male-written stories feature myriads of phenomenally luscious young virgins throwing their eagerly naked bodies at the man's rock-hard erection so he can rapidly fill them all to capacity and move on, looking for adventure. Female-written stories feature demure young women yearning for the handsome prince with the seductive curve of his eyebrows who must marry soon or lose his heritage, and he must somehow not only notice his worthy handmaid as more than a sex object, but satisfy her repeatedly that he now realizes that he always secretly loved her and must have her as his queen. No, of course they aren't all quite like that, but for generalities these will do. I always hoped for well-plotted stories that included sex and magic and realistic action and characterization, but seldom found them. So when I became a writer, I tried to write stories that merged the male and female elements, and got nowhere, finding no market. They had to be one or the other, not both. Parnassus—that is, the traditional publishing establishment—had spoken.

But there has been progress, notably in the past decade as electronic publishing developed, because it opened the market wide for both what authors wanted to write, and readers wanted to read. The bottleneck of hidebound traditional publishing was getting bypassed, and erotic fiction flourished. Now the uncensored market, rather than the censorious editors, governed. Along with this revolution came a crossing of boundaries as men like me wrote fantasy with real penis-and-vagina sex in it, and women wrote erotica with blunt cock-and-cunt action. The traditional viewpoints have crossed over and overlapped and we are no longer required to be typecast. No longer does fantasy romance have to consist of a chaste kiss followed by an ellipsis and perhaps later a stork delivery, the limit of what a maiden aunt thinks is appropriate for children, never mind that this is not being marketed to children. Those ellipses drove me crazy. Consider what other fiction would be like if the same technique were applied. The hero girds his sword and marches forth to fight the dragon...afterward recovering from his grievous wounds. The sorcerer waves his magic wand and...our friends are relieved to have escaped his power. The sphinx says "I will pose you a riddle"...after which they gaze on its dead body. The hero knows he must destroy that nefarious magic ring...and thus the world is saved. Or the movies, when *Star Wars* might start with print scrolling grandly across the screen, consisting of one huge ellipsis. Do these ellipses improve the stories? No? Then why use them at all? Today we don't have to. The old repressive editing can go...itself.

Still, merely having magic, adventure, and sex in the same story isn't enough. Each element needs to be integral to the whole. The test for this is that if you can take it out without destroying the story, it's not integral. It takes some writing skill to meld the several elements. Which is the point here: we have stories that do merge not merely man and woman, or on occasion woman and woman, but the divergent aspects of the narrative. I was delighted to read a story wherein it is the woman who craves the sex and the man who is desperate for reassurance. In this one he is deliriously ill from combat wounds and she tends him devotedly, even clasping his chilled body to hers when there is no other way to warm him. In the course of that he recovers enough to get sexually aroused, and blindly forces sex on her. When he is completely well he realizes that he has raped her, and is horrified and refuses to touch her again, despite her interest, until she asks him which of them he is punishing. That leads to a slow clarification of motives and guilt until it can be worked out. We have to see the sex occurring in order to understand the state they both are in and how they finally come to terms with it. Or the one wherein a woman with erratic fathoming has to mind read the secret name of a hostile sorceress, and that comes only when she is in the throes of illicit sex in the presence of that sorceress. Or the problem of a blood-bond to a dragon steed that must exist if that dragon is to be ridden into battle. But semen is like blood, and when the female squire has sex with the dragon rider she partakes of his essence and can now ride the dragon. Sex is integral and vital to the story.

These stories seem to be mostly by and for women. But I as a male reader enjoyed them, and believe that you, the reader of either gender, will too. They are magically complete.

Piers Anthony

INTRODUCTION

The fantasy genre has a long and distinguished history in literature, evolving within the last two centuries into the form of fantasy we know today. Although the genre has always remained popular with true aficionados, it's experiencing a renaissance in today's contemporary fiction, particularly that of high fantasy or, as it's commonly referred to, "epic fantasy." Epic fantasy works are set in worlds that are often timeless and strangely familiar, yet at the same time completely alien to us. These worlds can exist within our own primary world or in a parallel one. They are worlds that draw us in and make us *believe*, even though we know such worlds cannot possibly exist.

Or can they?

Legendary authors such as J. R. R. Tolkien and C. S. Lewis helped hone and refine the epic fantasy genre, inspiring generations of future writers to craft their own works. Although many of these works were initially intended for younger audiences, the genre began to change and evolve as more adults picked up these books, especially in recent years. The stories became darker, sexier, as did the characters. Indeed, these were no longer books targeted for the eyes of children and adolescents. These books were instead being targeted for the eyes of adults. The film and television adaptations of novels such as those from *The Lord of the Rings* trilogy and their sexier cousin *A Game of Thrones* (adapted from George R. R. Martin's epic fantasy series *A Song of Ice and Fire*) have buoyed the genre to the bestseller list. And it is here where it happily remains.

Thrones of Desire: Erotic Tales of Swords, Mist and Fire is a place where lust and legend abound, and adventure, passion and danger entwine. Think mystical lands and creatures, kings and queens, knights and renegades, heroes and villains. Think battles and danger, honor and dishonor, good and evil. Most of all think hearts filled with passion and secret desire. This is a place where romantic chivalry is alive and well, but so too is romantic wickedness. This is a place where the good do not always win, and the bad are often more captivating and desirable than their altruistic counterparts. In these timeless lands, the battle for flesh is as important as the battle for power.

Intrigue, sorcery, revenge, lawlessness, love and redemption, dark secrets and mysterious trinkets, evil spells and entanglements with supernatural beings—everything is possible in these mythical landscapes. This anthology brings these elements together in a collection of original stories penned by an international cast of writers that have embraced the true spirit of epic fantasy and created their own special worlds for us to visit. You'll find it all right here: corrupt kings, lusty queens, handsome princes, virginal princesses, randy knights, wicked sorcerers, kick-ass heroines, vengeful witches, mysterious shapeshifters...and we're definitely not short on a few dragons either!

I've set out the welcome mat, and I invite you to step into these magical and sensuous worlds to experience them for yourself. Be warned: you might not wish to return to this one!

Mitzi Szereto
London

HOT AS A DRAGON'S BLOOD

Eric Del Carlo

U nder the moons' pale luminescence and beneath the crushing
weight of his own disappointment, Caffax wandered the
long stony plateau where the dragons waited in their ranks for
the dawn, and for the great battle that would decide this war.
Here was the brink of history. The Three-Cornered War had
prevailed for generations, a gruesome wasteful stalemate; but
tomorrow the dragons would fly in such numbers against the
Kekkelati Empire of the east that the deadlock would break.
One side or the other would be left victorious.

But Caffax would not be a part of that awesome bloody
mayhem, even though he was a dragonmaster, even though he
had brought his family's salt dragon from his home village of
Uebimmo's Point to the designated staging area in the easternmost reaches of the Realm of Vahcray. This crucial battle would
have to be waged without him.

Caffax had committed an...indiscretion. But what was, to
him, far more damning was that he and the brawny Vahcray

supply clerk had been *caught* at it.

His eyes trailed along the rows of tethered, resting dragons, and his heart swelled with sorrow. Here were the finest mounts he'd ever seen: sinuous spiral dragons, plump water dragons from the Sapphire Sea, ink dragons nearly invisible in the moons-lit nighttime, tusked and ferocious pike dragons, the huge purple shell-backed rock dragons, and dozens of other varieties. Truly, there were dragons here he knew only as rumor, breeds which came from the Kingdom of Mavvan.

The Realm of Vahcray and the Kingdom of Mavvan, long-time enemies, were boldly joining forces to vanquish their mutual adversary, the Kekkelati Empire.

Caffax approached his salt dragon and raised a hand. The white-whiskered face lowered and brushed his palm with a huge warm nostril. The creature knew him the way all such beasts did: by his blood.

The large, dignified beast to whom he had been blood-bonded since his thirteenth year was also anticipating tomorrow's historic battle. Caffax was certain of this, though he and the dragon didn't communicate verbally. The mare had a large troop saddle buckled to her back. Caffax would have delivered soldiers eastward, either archers trained to fire while in flight or infantry he would have dropped at a designated site.

Now, tragically, that wouldn't happen. He stroked the salt dragon's throat, where he felt her heavy pulse beneath the scales. The mare would be confused when, as the dawn arose, he steered her westward, back toward Uebimmo's Point and the terrible explanations he would have to make to his family.

All his life he had wanted to do his part to bring an end to the relentless Three-Cornered War, which had taken the lives of men and women from his village as well as throughout the Realm.

With the thump of the mare's hot blood beneath his hand, Caffax hung his head and let the first hiccupping sobs jerk his narrow chest.

Then he heard the cry for help, and the cruel laughter that followed. His feet fell hard on the ground as he started toward the disturbance. Ahead he saw torchlight and shapes moving against it.

"What goes on there?" he called out, surprised by the strength in his voice.

He came up to a trio of guards, and one individual who was not a sentry. He saw the sneers on the faces of the guards, and he recognized that look of frolicsome cruelty. The three were terrorizing the fourth person on the scene, laughing and shoving. Caffax remembered occasions like this from his own childhood, when he had been the object of sport, the outcast, the *strange* boy who didn't take a proper interest in girls.

The guards stopped what they were doing, for the moment. A torch flickered in the hand of one of the sentries. Caffax was still wearing his dragonmaster livery. He had meant to go to battle in this finery. Perhaps, though, the costume still had a use. These guards might mistake him for an officer.

"Stand away from him," he said in that same commanding tone. Hopefully they didn't know of the scandalous events of earlier today. "Release him!"

In the unsteady light, he saw a hand touch a sheathed sword's pommel. Caffax himself wasn't armed, and his flesh prickled, anticipating the bite of cool lethal metal. Still, he stood his ground.

Then a chuckle from one of the guards was followed by another muttering amusedly, "*Him*, he says." But the trio did step back.

The dark, sturdy Mavvan woman raised luminous yellow

eyes toward Caffax. She smoothed her exotic scarlet robes and said, with a tentative smile, "My thanks to you. I should like to stand you a drink for your bravery."

He had figured she would take him down the broad cut-stone steps to the plain below, to one of the hundreds of campfires or tents. Instead, she turned up a trail toward a small craggy peak. As she climbed, her shape was revealed where it pressed against the fabric of her robes. This was a taut, almost brawny individual. Caffax had difficulty convincing himself that this was indeed a female.

The Kingdom of Mavvan lay southerly. A different people, with their own customs. Recently, the inhabitants of this faraway land had been the ancestral enemies of Vahcray. Too recently, in fact. It was why the guards had been bullying her.

Halfway up the peak, she stepped off onto a broad ledge and he came after, surprised to see a structure here. Or the remains of one.

"It's the old lookout," she said, indicating the small roofless building, its rough walls half razed.

"How did you know this was here?"

"I reconnoitered the area yesterday when my unit arrived. I am squire to my dragonmaster. Ours is the locust dragon, the large gray colt."

Caffax had no squire, seeing to his own mount and supplies. "Mine is the salt. Blue leather saddle."

"I am sure I must have seen it."

"She's a fine mount."

"As is our gray," she said. "Won't you come inside?" Her accent lent the words a melody.

Caffax didn't know if he wanted company this night. But this place was peaceful and isolated, and he would only have spent his time weeping with his dragon, after all. Besides, she had mentioned a drink.

She said, "My name is Rhoishko."

"Caffax." No need to identify himself as a man of Vahcray. Just as her Mavvan dress and speech distinguished her unmistakably, to say nothing of her skin's pigment.

He followed her into the tiny ruin.

She struck a flint and lit a candle. The wax smelled of autumn breezes. The structure's interior was empty of furnishings, but the accumulated powder from the crumbling walls made the floor soft as he sat down. Rhoishko lowered herself opposite. A dark-glassed bottle of strange curving shape sat nearby, along with two small matching brass cups, which gleamed in the candlelight. She poured equal measures.

Caffax lifted one of the cups. The liquid inside appeared purple. He raised it to his lips.

"Shall we toast?" Rhoishko said.

His cup still hovering, he asked, "Shall we what?"

Arching brows drew together over her yellow eyes. "A toast. A salute. Something said over a drink. You do not have this custom in the Realm?"

"I'm afraid not."

"Well, then." She posed a moment with her cup upraised. "We drink to the defeat of the Empire. May a lasting peace follow."

"A lasting peace," he repeated, truly meaning the words. Then they both drank. What a charming practice—the *toast*. He would have to pass it on when he next had the chance. Of course, the customs of Mavvan and Vahcray might blend and blur even more should the alliance endure after the Empire's fall. Caffax, though, had his doubts. There would always be people in the Realm like those bullying sentries, full of pointless hostility.

The liquor was warming and sweet. He liked it. They talked of the war, and agreed how costly and useless the stalemate had been.

They talked of tomorrow's epic battle.

They spoke of dragons. Breeds, training, technique. Her knowledge was very impressive.

And they drank more of the purplish liquor.

Caffax had undone several catches on his elaborately embroidered jacket. He was experiencing a deepening peace, which some part of him knew to be merely the onset of drunkenness. Still, it was better than facing his present reality. And, truly, Rhoishko was good company.

Something occurred to him belatedly, however. He sat up. Gazed at the candle. Eyed the dark-glassed bottle that had been waiting here, as well as the *two* cups.

He looked across, focusing his gaze on the scarlet-robed woman. She too had loosened her raiment with the heat of their drinking. She was a dragonmaster's squire, she'd said. But she was also Mavvan. Caffax didn't want to distrust her solely on the basis of that. But—

"But," he heard himself saying aloud, "what, may I ask, were you in fact doing on the plateau so late amongst the dragons?" Now that there was no retrieving the question, he wished he had made it sound more casual.

In that melodic tone Rhoishko said, "I didn't come to see the dragons." She carefully set aside her brass cup. "I sought you. And I have found you."

Softly he asked, "What do you want from me?"

"I wish to ride your salt dragon into battle tomorrow."

He found himself blinking repeatedly and rapidly. For a time he couldn't stop as he tried to make sense of her statement.

Finally, all he could do was bleat, "*What?*"

"I was duplicitous earlier. I have seen your salt mare with the blue saddle. I can ride her."

She was saying these outrageous things in so matter-of-fact a manner. "But you're not a dragonmaster," he sputtered. "You said—you're a squire."

"I am a woman. In the Kingdom of Mavvan that means I can never become a dragonmaster, even though I know how to fly, even though I am the equal of the dragonmaster I serve."

"Because you're...a woman?" It only added to his confusion. "That doesn't make any sense."

"It is a cultural intolerance."

"It's barbaric."

"More so than the prejudice which has banned you from tomorrow's fight?"

It landed like a blow. Caffax flinched. She knew. Of course she knew, this snooping squire. He lowered his head between his knees, raked fingers through his long tangled blond hair.

He heard her slide across the powdery floor. She laid an arm over his bony shoulders. "You have been unfairly excluded," she said, and the sympathy in her voice sounded quite authentic. "In Mavvan, we don't have this strange bias. Men may mate with men, women with women. It makes no difference. So, perhaps we are not so barbaric after all."

"I'm sorry I said that." He squeezed shut his eyes. A tear dripped down his nose.

She dotted his temple with her lips. "I want your dragon, Caffax."

"You can't take her."

"So, you mean to simply fly off home with that salt mare, then?"

"I have no choice. I've been stripped of privileges."

"It's a waste," Rhoishko said.

"I haven't a choice," he repeated.

"Let me fly her into battle. I think you know I am capable."

He believed that. Her knowledge of dragons was extraordinary. But still... "You can't have her."

"That seems selfish to me, Caffax."

"No." He raised his head and looked into her eyes. "I mean, you *can't*. I'm blood-bonded to her. She won't respond to anyone else. Don't you bond with your dragons in Mavvan?"

Her arm was still about his shoulders. She had drawn him tight, practically into an embrace. "Of course we do. A dragon-master's mount knows his scent. But when a master wishes to sell a beast to which he is bonded or give one away to, say, an apprentice, he simply passes his blood to the other. The practice is commonplace."

Confusion whirled anew in Caffax's head. What was she talking about? "How can one...*pass blood*?"

Rhoishko told him, in frank terms. It was the carnal act. And since only males flew dragons in the Kingdom of Mavvan, this sexual deed occurred—routinely!—between men.

"Granted," the Mavvan squire said, "it is not blood, per se. But the essence is contained in the primal fluid. One body absorbs what the other delivers."

As his mind continued to twirl alarmingly, a remote part of Caffax considered what she had said. Transferal of the blood bond: it sounded plausible; so much so, in fact, that he wondered why he'd never heard of the procedure before.

"That I am a woman," she continued, "should not—*can*not—have any bearing on the process. This is your chance to contribute to the war's outcome, Caffax. Let me take your mare into the fight tomorrow."

There it was. The whole incredible conundrum, set forth in stark terms. Make love to this female, and the salt dragon he had spent much of his life training for this battle would still be a part of this war.

Rhoishko was kissing his forehead again. Her fingers weaved gently through his hair. He felt her muscular body pressing harder against him. The purple liquor was still coursing in his veins. Surely he could do this. Surely.

Her hands now worked on his clothing. His flamboyant jacket dropped from his shoulders. She caressed his flesh through undone catches, moving toward the fastening of his trousers where—Caffax was *very* surprised to discover—his manhood was straining toward hardness.

Plainly aware of this, Rhoishko moved to touch him there—

Which was the precise instant that a rebellion tore through Caffax's being. Suddenly and awkwardly, he launched himself to his feet and went lurching toward the doorway.

He couldn't do this! It was simply against his nature. He stumbled outside. His shirt trailed him, dangling by a sleeve. Rhoishko had succeeded in undoing his trousers, because they were hanging to his mid-thighs. He realized this only when he lost his footing and fell hard to the ground.

"Caffax."

Her voice carried tranquilly. He looked up and found her in the doorway, backlit by the candlelight. She had shed her scarlet robes and stood nude. Her body was robust. Was she really so different from the supply clerk with whom he had so foolishly dallied earlier today? Her breasts were smallish but as firmly molded as the rest of her. Yet there between those taut thighs was only the moist dark of her curls. It was an absence, or so it seemed to Caffax.

"I want you to take my salt dragon," he said. "I do, but..."

She came to him. "You are a brave man, Caffax."

"Maybe not brave enough." He blinked up at her. "Is there

some other way?"

She bent and softly stroked his cheek. "In Mavvan it is taught that a dragonmaster must give of himself completely in order to bond with his dragon. It is the same when that bond is transferred. You must give of yourself. To me."

Her mouth moved toward his.

Caffax closed his eyes. And felt the touch of her lips. They were moist and velvety, and they moved against his without insistence. She tasted of the liquor they had both been drinking. He let his mouth answer back, giving in to instinctive responses, not thinking of this person as a woman, a female, merely as a friend, someone who had been kind to him.

Her hands were in motion once more, tugging the shirt's sleeve from his wrist so that his torso was bared. He thought she would reach for his crotch again, and tensed; but she instead set about caressing his upper arms, his chest, even as they continued to kiss. Her fingers found his nipples and grazed them, which sent a shiver through him.

When those fingers caught his aroused buds and applied a mounting pressure, Caffax groaned against her mouth. At that same moment her tongue invaded him. Again he allowed himself to respond spontaneously. His body's deep instincts took over. After all, he was a human, and humans had been designed to reproduce. Some part of him, despite his own private proclivities, had to answer that primary urge.

He met her agile tongue, and the kiss deepened. It was strange to feel no rasp of beard or stubble against his face, but the strangeness passed and was forgotten. Rhoishko squeezed his nipples even harder, igniting a fiery pleasure. Her brawny body pressed his. Her own erect nipples brushed his flesh. He should raise his hands, touch her there, squeeze her breasts in the way of men and women. The thought was dizzying, almost giddy.

Then he stopped thinking, and took hold of her breasts. Rhoishko gasped. Her nipples were large compared to his, he realized as he rolled his fingertips across them. Her pleasure was evident as she swayed and stabbed her tongue fiercely into his mouth. Caffax was pleased to be pleasing her—yet, strangely, it seemed to be something more than that. He was *enjoying* this.

Once again, his manhood swelled. Pausing in their kissing and squeezing, he kicked off his boots and trousers. They were both naked now.

Rhoishko sprawled beside him. The night sky's light bronzed her bare body. She lay back now with elbows braced behind her, facing him. Her legs were spread, her knees raised. Caffax's breath hitched as he saw her exposed sex gleam in the dim light. He had never beheld a woman in this way before. He had never been in the presence of a female who so obviously desired him; or if he had, he'd been oblivious.

He chuckled out loud.

"Do I amuse?" she asked. But she wasn't offended. She fairly purred the question.

"No," Caffax said. Then he surprised himself by adding, "You arouse." He moved toward her.

She reached up and guided the proof of his excitation between her outspread thighs. They paused to kiss again, and he felt himself shivering. Out of fear, yes; but also from unadulterated lust. Arms outstretched, the heels of both hands on the ground on either side of her, he hovered over Rhoishko. For one brief frantic instant he thought he would climax right then, in her hand, but he was an adult and knew how to control himself, even in a circumstance as bizarre and unforeseeable as this.

Murmuring soft unintelligible words—maybe they were just sounds—the Mavvan woman set his swollen crown to her folds. The angle felt strange, and again he was keenly aware of her unfamiliar anatomy. But there was no rebellion in him this time. He lowered himself from his palms to his elbows, and as he did so, he slid inside her.

Her channel waited for him. He felt her warmth, the luscious grip her body took of his shaft. It stunned him. Somehow, he hadn't expected it would be this...easy. But how smooth the ingress, how graceful. He lay atop her, his manhood buried within. Her arms wrapped his shoulders, and her thighs pressed his flanks. Yellow eyes glimmered up into his. Her teeth were bared with pleasure. Neither of them seemed aware of the hardness of the ground on which they lay.

He moved his hips; hers worked against his: a deft thrust and counterthrust. With his every downward plunge, he felt her respond. He kissed her again, decisively now, jamming his tongue onto hers. Bliss spread through him, racing outward from his groin, awakening all his body. He ground against her. She writhed underneath him. Sweat had started to oil both their bodies.

Suddenly, Rhoishko was shuddering. Her fingertips dug sharply into his shoulders. He thought something was wrong; she was in pain. What clueless, clumsy thing had he done? But before he could begin to castigate himself, he saw a look of ecstasy clench her features as she broke off their kiss to bare those teeth once again. Her back arched, lifting him, driving him even deeper into her. Caffax felt a peculiar pride. He had given her this joy.

She ended with a long, hitching sigh. Then her squeezed-shut eyes sprang back open, and the predator's leer returned to her face.

Rhoishko was strong, as well as nimble. Before he knew what was happening, she had seized him and was twisting, rolling them as one. It was very nearly an acrobatic feat. Caffax quickly found himself on his back. She was now astraddle him. Somehow during this maneuver she had contrived to keep them coupled.

He looked up at her, at her damp skin glistening, at her lovely breasts, at the fierce grin splitting her features. He experienced a curious moment of helplessness, but it wasn't unpleasant, not at all.

Rhoishko, in the position of control, started to plunge herself on top of him.

Her firm but slick grip on him never faltered. She planted her feet on either side of his hips and rose and fell on him. He found he could do little more than jab himself up into her; but it was enough—more than enough—to sustain his excitement. She slammed down on him, far more violently than when he had been driving himself into her. He liked it. It was animal-like, primal. He imagined himself as a beast, performing the reproductive act, operating on pure frenzied instinct.

The thought almost made him laugh again. Instead, he reached up for her jouncing breasts, squeezing the irresistible flesh, mauling her engorged nipples. Her head whipped back and forth above him. Digging his heels into the ground, he thrust savagely up into her. She was thrashing about on top of him now, and he sensed, then saw, a new shudder move through her. Again her teeth were bared, spittle flying from between them. Her sweet, wet canal clutched him, the inner muscles tightening.

Poised above him, she froze in that bearing of rapture. Droplets of sweat spattered his chest. Caffax nearly climaxed with her this time. But not quite. Not yet.

He grinned. Then, abruptly, he was grabbing hold of her and moving her bodily, sliding out from beneath her. She followed his urgings, offering no resistance. Desire plucked at him, mighty ivory fingers twanging his nerves. He grappled her over onto her knees.

How beautiful she looked posed that way, reared up on hands and knees, her gorgeous buttocks thrust out toward him. He moved in behind her. And now, for the first time, the sexual act felt familiar to him. His knees rested between her splayed calves, his thighs pressed flush against the backs of hers. Eagerly, he closed his fingers around the curves of her hip bones.

Even the entering of her touched off a string of blurred memories, similar acts with males, deeds committed quickly and fearfully. And while this penetrative feat wasn't *quite* like those, its familiarity was comforting, and the last vestiges of unease left him.

Caffax made merciless love to Rhoishko, the squire from Mavvan. Their bodies smacked loudly together with his every thrust. His testicles spanked hard against her backside as she took him to the hilt at each impact. He gripped her hips, fingers practically gouging her flesh.

For her part, Rhoishko bucked back against him with perfect timing. Her muscled body gleamed and undulated. He wanted to plumb her deepest places, wanted to reach her innermost self. He felt their connection, the brutal primeval link, but it was tempered by affection, by the sympathy he felt for her and her plight—being denied her destiny as a dragonmaster merely because of her gender.

But that wouldn't happen. He would not allow it.

Her head turned. One yellow eye appeared, blazing. A fresh wave was overtaking her. She trembled on her hands and knees.

Shouting it, barking it, she commanded him, "Give yourself to me, Caffax!"

He did so. The crisis erupted. It seemed to rip through every part of him—bunching his toes, locking his knees, thundering his heart, spinning his skull. His pleasure gushed, vast violent jets, each one deposited deep inside her. The quaking of her body added to his bliss, milking his essence from him, taking everything he had to give.

After a long while he slid from her and lay down with her. She held him and dotted his damp temple again with her lips; and murmuring softly and melodically, she thanked him, again and again.

It was only the next day, in the bloodless first light perhaps a full watch before the sun's actual rise, that it occurred to Caffax to truly doubt that this undertaking would work. Could a blood bond really be transferred? Suddenly, it seemed the wildest improbability.

Nonetheless, he led Rhoishko down the steep trail to the plateau, where activity was already stirring. He was clad again in his fanciful livery; she wore her scarlet robes. They did not speak, but he felt a lingering connection, something beyond the merely physical.

Well, there had been nothing *mere* about it, he noted ruefully, glancing back to flash her a brief smile. She returned it, but he saw she was nervous. As was he. Last night had been a wonder, a thoroughly unexpected and joyous event. But today was the real challenge.

Dragonmasters and support crews were assembling, people gathered from all across the Realm of Vahcray as well as the Kingdom of Mavvan. Caffax saw the nudging, the furtive—and not so furtive—pointing. He caught muttered comments and sniggers meant for him. He ignored them all. He strode across the grounds.

How confused these snickerers would be, he thought, if they knew how he had passed the night.

The salt mare was awake and waiting as he approached. He smiled up at the creature as she lifted her head and quivered her whiskers. He gestured for Rhoishko to step up beside him. Biting her lip, she did so. Did she too doubt that this would succeed? If it was a commonplace practice in Mavvan, she shouldn't be anxious. Then he understood. Her status as a woman had planted a small inescapable seed of uncertainty in her. It was the prejudice of her Kingdom taking one last swipe at her.

Caffax raised his hand and let the salt dragon sniff it.

"Now you," he said.

Rhoishko put up her hand. Around them, others had paused to watch. Peripherally, he saw a Mavvan man dressed as a dragonmaster gaping as the scene unfolded.

The salt pressed her nose to Rhoishko's open palm. The dragon snuffled. Then she twitched her crusty white whiskers, sniffed again, and angled her head to let the Mavvan woman caress her jaw. It was done. It had worked.

Caffax had shed too many tears too recently. Dry-eyed, he smiled again, warmly this time. "What will you tell your dragonmaster?"

She shrugged, her yellow eyes alight once more. "He doesn't really need a squire. In Mavvan, that's a matter of prestige. He won't miss me." She reached for his hand and squeezed it. The gesture was curiously intimate, considering all that they had shared.

Caffax stepped back and watched as she acquainted herself with the salt mare. He harbored no doubts regarding her abilities. He didn't know what he would tell his family when he returned to Uebimmo's Point—or even *if* he would return. The future was unformed, but that didn't frighten him at the moment. He only wished Rhoishko and the dragon well and hoped for a speedy end to the war.

When he finally glanced away, he chanced upon the eye of a man in soldierly garb. He was a robust sort, with a fierce fringe of red beard and wide shoulders. Their gazes locked. Caffax saw the special twinkle there in his eye, the secretive sign, and he gave the man a shallow but meaningful nod. Perhaps this soldier would be coming back from the epic conflict. Maybe that was a reason to stay here, to wait, to see what happened.

OF HIGH RENOWN

Janine Ashbless

Gareth was gone from the bed before dawn.

Emlhi woke alone. She breakfasted and washed, then donned her chemise. And there she stopped. There seemed no point in dressing further; she had nowhere to go and nothing to do. There were no animals to feed now, no vegetables to weed. She sat back up on the big bed where no pleasure had been taken, her arms around her knees, and waited. She remembered the obdurate line of Gareth's back turned against her and the wasteland of mattress that had stretched between them. She let the tears leak out—tears she hadn't dared shed before him—and wiped them away with her skirt.

She remembered.

She remembered the arrival of the knights. The warning beacon on the hill had been lit, so every villager was barricaded into one of the stone houses about the square. Emlhi crouched beneath a shuttered window. The room stank of the sour breath of terrified people.

"A priest!" roared the voice from outside over the clatter of many iron-shod hooves. "Where's the bloody priest?"

Turo, Emlhi's cousin, peered through a crack in the shutter. "They look like knights," he said. "Lots of armor. There's something on their shields...."

"Damn your craven asses!"

"Yellow sun on a blue field," Turo muttered. "That means..."

"Where's your priest, when a man stands at death's door?"

"Helion?" Emlhi finished for Turo. "They're Knights of Helion?" She sprang up and heaved back the door-bolt. Voices were raised all around her in protest, but she took no notice. Blinking, she stepped out. There were horsemen gathered toward the seaward end of the square and one circling his mount in the center. She stood anxiously as he turned toward her. The knights looked barely human under their layers of plate and scale armor, with even their horses rendered unfamiliar by their heavy barding.

"You're Knights of Helion?"

"You're the priest?" the foremost horseman answered. His voice was hoarse from shouting and his surcoat was rusty with blood. She couldn't see his face because of his heavy helm. The other knights, equally faceless, sat at slumped, painful angles in armor that was dinted and filthy.

"His daughter," Emlhi replied. "Does that mean—?"

His voice cut across hers. "I need the priest, girl!"

She took a deep breath, the pain still raw enough to make her voice tremble. "There's no priest in Yeldersholme. My father was taken away by the Raptors last year and staked upon the—"

"Spare me. Have you any herb-lore from him, girl? Any healing?"

Emlhi swallowed. "Some."

"You'll do then." He swung his horse side-on to her and

Emlhi suddenly realized that there was a second knight behind
him leaning so hard on his back that their two sets of armor
seemed one mass of steel plates. "Come here. Take him down."
Emlhi took one step, then halted.

"Blast you, girl!" he barked, but there was exhaustion in his
voice now. "We routed the Raptors at the Stone Gate. This man
was wounded. We have to take ship across the sound, but he's
fevered from the injury and there's little chance for him unless
he's tended. Do you understand? Gareth, we're leaving you here.
These villagers will look after you. Take him down, girl!"

Gareth was a full-grown man in heavy armor and showed
no sign of consciousness; Emlhi stood about as much chance of
holding his weight up as she would have the horse's. When the
knight loosed the belt tying his wounded companion to him, all
Emlhi could do was help him slither in a controlled rush to the
hard-packed earth. He didn't fall flat though—he ended up on
his spread knees, slumped against her braced legs—so under all
the plating there must have been some spark of life.

"Does that mean the Raptors are gone?" Turo called. He'd
come out with some of the other villagers, though they were
hanging back at a distance. "Are we free?"

"For the moment," said the knight grimly. "They're
regrouping on Far Vinchor and we go to face them. Our vessel
will be here with the high tide."

"That's this hour, my Lord Knight."

"Then we're just in time."

Emlhi was appalled that these battered men should be about
to do battle again. The one at her feet stank of old blood.

"Girl," snapped the knight, wheeling his horse: "If he lives
you'll be well rewarded by the Knights of the Helionic Order. Tell
him where we went and that it will be too late to follow. Gareth!"
He bent from the saddle. "Gareth, the gods go with you."

The wounded man raised one hand in feeble imitation of his salute.

Then the riders gathered themselves into motion and poured away down the street toward the harbor. The rest of the villagers came streaming out of the houses to follow, their eyes wide, the first grins showing. The Raptors were gone, and now, for the first time in years, they knew hope.

When the square had emptied, Emlhi crouched down to her knight and worked the helmet off his head. His neck sagged. Emlhi grimaced—he was as gray as a corpse already. His hair was an unruly black mop and his beard was no longer neatly trimmed, but what caught her eye were the veins on his neck, slate-blue and clearly visible against his skin. *Blood-poisoning*, she thought. *He'll be dead within the day.* "Sir Knight. Where does it hurt?" she asked, without real hope of a reply.

"My shoulder." He waved a mailed fist at his left side. "One of their lizard-mounts got over the top of my shield. Their teeth are poisonous." She was surprised how lucid he was. There was a staining of blood around his shoulder, but it was impossible to see the wound under the complex welter of stiffened leather and beaten steel plates.

"Right, then," she said, starting to uncinch his breastplate. It was a fancy piece of work, inlaid with brass. "Let's get this off."

For a moment he didn't react. Then as she pulled the breastplate from him, he groaned and looked up at her. His eyes were gray, but so bloodshot it made her own water to look at him. "My armor," he protested through clenched teeth.

"If you live," she said curtly, dumping the sun-etched masterpiece on the ground, "you'll get it back." She found the strapping for a shoulder-piece and worked it loose.

"No," he muttered.

"You can't even stand up in this lot," she snapped. "Do you

think I'm going to carry you to my house? You're going to have to walk for me. And it's uphill."

The breath hissed between his teeth. It took a moment for her to realize he was laughing. He made no further protest as she managed to strip him down to his padded leather under-armor. Several bloody punctures described a wide semicircle across his shoulder. Realizing the size of the thing that had bitten him, Emlhi tried not to shudder. "Can you stand?"

With her help he managed, though he grunted with pain. She had to get under his good arm to brace him, and he swayed against her. She grabbed his wrist and found his skin was hot— really hot—and when she looked up at his face she could see sweat starting to run down his temple. *The fever's already on him*, she thought.

"Come on, Sir Knight. This way."

They staggered across the square. As they passed the plane tree at the first junction he reeled sideways, and she helped him turn and rest against a wall while she got her breath back.

Gareth looked down at her in surprise. "Perlanna?" he said. "What are you doing here?" Then he pulled her against him with a sweep of his arm and kissed her. Emlhi was so shocked that she didn't resist. His lips were burning hot. He kissed hungrily, without restraint, and his mouth tasted metallic. When he let her go she was gasping. Then the fire in his eyes guttered. "You're not Perlanna," he said, troubled. "She's dead." His eyes rolled up behind their lids until only the sclera showed, and then he slipped slowly down the wall, unconscious at last.

She remembered how she had misused him.

It was an unending struggle to keep him alive. The venom in his blood seemed to have destroyed his body's sense of equilibrium and threw him between burning fever and frigid tremors every few hours. Emlhi cleaned and bandaged the deep puncture wounds in his shoulder, but after that she simply tried to keep his temperature on an even keel—stopping the fever boiling his brains at one moment, piling blankets over him to maintain some vestiges of warmth the next. She fed and watered him, cut fresh bracken every morning for his mattress and, when she was not watching over him, tried to keep up the work of her small-holding. She snatched her own sleep during his chills, dozing in her father's old room.

Between fire and ice, the knight would have passages where he seemed to be lucid but completely exhausted. Then as the fever flared up afresh he'd begin to talk and sometimes try to rise from his bed. He stared at the ceiling and spoke to people who weren't there. He raved about battles and campaigns and the horrors he'd witnessed until Emlhi wanted to stop her ears for sorrow. Sometimes his hallucinations grew worse and in terror or fury he would lash out at her. If he hadn't been so weakened by his illness, he might have been really dangerous.

It went on for days, and there were times she couldn't under-stand why he did not die. She might have called in an older female relative to share the labor of care, but she guarded her sole right to Gareth possessively. Exhausted, she took strength from his stubbornness.

And she took more than strength.

The first time it wasn't her doing. She was sitting on the edge of the bed, tending him as he burned. She'd been wiping his face and chest with a damp cloth, dipping it in fresh water every few minutes and waving it about to cool it. He was twisting in discomfort, tossing in a delirious dream, his hands scrabbling convulsively across his belly. When she touched his cheek with the cloth he would turn his face toward it, like a baby seeking the teat. She ran it down the midline of his torso and he grabbed her hand, knotting his fingers around hers. Gently she freed the cloth with her other hand and continued to bathe him. He kept his grip on her. His head was thrown back, his larynx working. Then he pushed her hand into his crotch.

Until now she'd kept his hose on, unwilling to steal the last shreds of his dignity. It was a mistake, she realized; the fabric was sodden with sweat—and beneath it his cock was engorged, as hot and solid as the rest of him. He wrapped her hand around the thick length and squeezed hard, and, as Emlhi felt a blush flood her face, a great sigh of relief escaped his taut throat. Then he began to rub her hand up and down. She squirmed with shame but she didn't pull away. His cock grew harder beneath her imprisoned grasp, lengthening as it filled. She was clumsy, passive, too inexperienced to know what to do. He masturbated with her hand until he spasmed—and then he relaxed, falling almost instantly into a dreamless sleep.

Emlhi, trembling, pulled her cramped fingers away and plunged them into the bowl of water.

That was the first time; it wasn't the last. She began coming to him when he burned, the sheets thrown aside and his body— fully naked now, and cleaner and cooler for it—sprawled out across her bed. Then she would take his cock in her hand and stroke its velvet length, squeezing him gently at first and then with more firmness, her face rapt, her breath shallow in her throat, her pulse pounding in her breast and her groin. She thrilled at the catch in his breath and the wet kisses of his fore-skin and the noises of his pleasure. She delighted to see him stretch and shudder at her touch, to see his balls tighten and jettison their burden in spurts across his belly. She loved the peace that came across his features when it was done. She would sit and watch him even when he slept, enchanted by the simple rise and fall of his chest.

Because, if she could make herself overlook his suffering, he was beautiful. The heat had melted any fat from his body, stripping him down to muscle. His shoulders were broad, his hips tight, his thighs long and slab-hard. His nipples responded to the cold cloth by turning into little brown berries. Emlhi loved to touch him.

She knew what she did was shameful, but she couldn't stop herself. She was young, and she ached with loneliness.

All her life her irascible father had guarded her jealously. A widower with no other children, he'd had no desire to lose his housekeeper to another man. But when he'd been the only one to dare speak out against the occupying Raptors, they had come for him. No one, not even the other members of his family, had dared fight in his defense. Emlhi had been the only one to try and she'd been held back, weeping and raging, by Turo. She'd never forgiven them. Since that day she'd turned away from the village and her relatives, and turned in on herself. Her natural instinct for love had curdled and set like mortar.

Gareth—deaf and dumb and blind, the knightly embodiment of courage and completely at her mercy—was the man that, entirely without his knowing, opened her up anew.

She remembered the night she'd checked on him and found him curled in a fetal ball on the bed, with the blankets piled like fallen enemies on the floorboards. She put the candle down and touched his shoulder, finding his skin icy. He shook beneath her hand.

"Oh, I'm sorry," she gasped and grabbed up the blankets. He didn't seem to notice; he was whimpering very softly under his breath, like a dog in pain. Quickly Emlhi slid into the bed at his back. She was wearing only her shift, because she'd been ready for bed herself. She pressed her warm belly to his spine and felt the chill of his flesh soak into her own. She ran her hand down his ribs and hips and rubbed the rough hair of his thigh.

"Hush," she whispered, kneading the knotted muscles of his neck with her other hand, pressing her face to his shoulder blade. "You're all right. You're all right." She rubbed her thighs against his, willing the warmth into him. By tiny increments he relaxed, the shuddering soothed away as the covers trapped the heat. His limbs unknotted enough to allow her to slip her hand around his waist right into the pit of his belly where his pubic hair tickled her fingers. It took a long time though, and she was tired by the day's work. Gradually she fell into a doze.

Emlhi awoke when Gareth pulled the blanket aside. Sleepily she protested at the draft then realized that the man in her bed was no longer cold. He'd stretched out and turned to press against her and he was hot, his skin burning on hers. He put his hand on her thigh, and even through the rucked linen of her shift it felt like he was branding her. Emlhi surged into wakefulness. He wasn't just uncoiled—he boasted an erection that was pressed into her hip.

He's sick, she thought. *And weak as a kitten. If I want to stop him, I can.*

Moonlight through the window revealed little, only his bare calf, his knee pushing between hers. Higher up, their bodies were drowned in shadow. The guttering stub of the candle outlined only the peak of his shoulder. His head was on her pillow and he was panting. Emlhi put her hand up and felt his face; the rasp of stubble, the smear of sweat from his temple, the loose locks of his hair. His breathing was faster than any healthy man's and he was leaving a wet patch on her throat.

"Sir Knight," she whispered. The pulse in her belly began to beat. *He can't make me*, she told herself. *He can only do what I let him.*

Pulling up the last span of her skirt, he ran his hand up the inside of her thigh and pressed it into her delta. "Hsgood," he slurred. Emlhi juddered beneath him. His fingers probed deep into her slit, seeking her moisture. She whimpered, feeling his heat catch in her sex, flaring up through her belly. He parted her folds and dabbled his fingertips within, while his palm and thumb stirred her mound and caressed the rough hair. Her wetness was growing more marked by the heartbeat. She felt completely helpless, suffused by the ancient imperative to yield, to melt, to submit to him. She parted her thighs and he slid his hand up and down the length of her slot, drawing the juices up to the bud of her clit. She moved under him, pushing up to meet him, her shallow little gasps drowned by his fevered panting. The shadows shook against the wall. His thigh was growing heavier and heavier on hers. She slid her own hand across her belly, under his arm, and took hold of his shaft. It jerked in her hand.

Then without warning, just as she was rising to her crisis, he pulled from her grasp and shifted his weight, heaving on top of her. The black silhouette of his head and shoulders loomed over her. Bereft, she caught her breath but spread her thighs willingly, thinking that she knew what must happen next—but she was completely unprepared. Pressure and slippery motion suddenly became a stabbing pain, an unbearable rending. She arched under him, expecting it to be over in a flash. It grew worse.

"No!" she cried. "You're too big!"

He swooped to mash his face into her throat. His entire weight was on her now, pressing her flat, grinding into her belly, crushing her ribs. She could hardly breathe. At that moment she realized with a sick jolt that she no longer had any power to deny him what he wanted. She had far underestimated his strength. And still the pain grew.

"Please, no!" she cried. "Stop!"

He took no notice. The burning heat in his flesh erupted into an agonizing fire as he thrust into her. She bucked beneath him and he grabbed her wrists and pinned her. Then suddenly, miraculously, the pain slackened and she was through to the other side, blinded by tears, pummeled beneath his thrusts, the breath forced out of her with every surge of his hips. He was groaning, too feverish to censor himself, his aching muscles driven into the territory of pain. His deep cries mingled with her sharper ones, and she felt like she was drowning in his sweat and his strength and his mindless need as their cries and their bodies fused.

She remembered the day he'd finally come out into the sunshine, wearing clothes she'd had to beat so hard on the river boulders to clean of his blood that the fabric was worn thin. He looked almost translucent himself, his eyes sunk in dark hollows and his garments hanging loose upon him. Above the neck of his shirt his collarbone stood out sharply. He had a blanket wrapped about his shoulders.

She motioned him to a place upon the porch. He sat slowly, like an old man, but when he smiled at her the sunshine seemed to grow warmer. "You look so much better," she said.

"I feel like a flag worn ragged by the wind." His voice was softer and deeper than his thin frame would predict; dark like his hair. He looked around at the little yard in front of her house and at the trees beyond their fence. Chickens were scratching in the dirt. "It's a beautiful day. How are you, Emlhi?"

"I'm just sorting the last of the winter apples." She indicated the flat baskets around her feet. "Would you like a small cup of beer, Sir Knight?"

"Gareth," he reminded her gently. "Beer would be good."

She fetched him a mug full from the crock behind the front door and he took it from her hand carefully, using both of his. She sat herself nearby, but he took her by surprise when he stretched forward and brushed the corner of her mouth with his fingertip. "What happened there?"

She touched the deep scab and blushed. "You were... When you had the fever you used to think you were fighting your enemies. You managed to smack me one with your elbow. It's nothing." It was kinder to say that, she thought, than tell him the truth: *You punched me, Sir Knight, thinking I was a Raptor sorcerer.* He looked upset enough by the bowdlerized version.

"I'm sorry!"

"It's fine. You didn't mean to hurt me."

"Nevertheless." His brows were knitted. "I will make reparation."

"It's no problem," said Emlhi, smiling. "You weren't to know."

"I'm a Knight of Helion," he corrected her. "We must take responsibility for what we do."

It was hard not to mock him. "Even in your dreams? You must be forever doing penance."

He smiled wryly, then his gaze slipped away and a shadow tainted his expression. "I had such terrible dreams." He looked into his beer as if scrying through the dark surface. "About the battle of the Stone Gate, the lizard-riders there, the dragons..." He shivered. Emlhi patted his foot, though she thought maybe she shouldn't do that, not to a knight. Gareth didn't seem to notice. "And there were dreams that weren't dreams; I saw things. They seemed so real at the time. I remember snakes crawling out of the walls and terrible faces leering at me from the angles of the roof..."

"It was only fever visions. You shouldn't worry now. It's all over."

His face, pale to start with, was ashen now. His scrubby beard, which she'd patiently clipped with her needlework shears back to a stubble, stood out like it had been drawn on his face with charcoal. She bit her lip, wondering if he was going to faint. It could take a long time to recover from an infection of the blood.

"There were things, too, that seemed like dreams at the time, but now..." He lifted his gaze to meet hers, his eyes dark and filled with dread. "I hope that they were dreams."

She could feel the blood running out of her own face and she looked away across the yard.

"Emlhi..."

"Fever makes you imagine all sorts of nonsense."

"Emlhi... Did I...?" He struggled for the words, and when they came out he spoke so softly she could barely hear them. "Did I despoil you?"

The color seemed to drain from the bright day. "Don't worry about it," she said creakily.

"Oh, gods. Look at me, Emlhi."

She obeyed. She felt dizzy. There were two burning patches on her pallid cheeks. "It was nothing," she said.

"Really? That's not how it looks."

She had no reply. *It was everything*, she thought. *It was the moment I will carry all my life.*

Slowly, Gareth put down his beer, pulled himself up against the nearest pillar and walked away back into the house.

She remembered the day of their wedding. How the sail of the small boat waiting to take them on board had snapped impatiently behind them in the breeze. How Gareth had held her hand on the quayside as he spoke his vows, with the whole of the village as witnesses. How he had never touched her again, not once, since that moment.

Gareth returned to their chamber in the Citadel of the Knights, in High Elerath, while the morning was still young. He'd clearly been out in the practice yard; he laid his sword aside and stripped off his damp shirt to reveal muscles standing proud from exertion. He'd started putting more bulk on, Emlhi thought; the gauntness was lifting from his face. But he didn't turn that face toward her, and he didn't speak.

"Are you feeling stronger?" she asked huskily from her seat on the bed.

"A little better every day." He tipped water from a bucket into the wooden tub and unlaced his hose, deliberately turning his back on her.

"That water will be cold. Let me send for more."

"It's fine."

He washed standing up in the tub and she watched as he poured water over his hair and shoulders, scrubbed his neck and underarms and crotch, then scoured his feet. She wanted to ask if she could help wash his back, but she didn't dare face his chill rebuff. When he'd finished he wiped himself off and then took an apple up from the platter and went out onto the terrace, into the sun. He ate it, core and all, while he waited to dry, the light picking out his well-defined musculature and the contrasting black sheen of his hair. Damp locks loosed stray droplets of water to trickle down his back. Emlhi felt her stomach clench with yearning. She imagined how those long, strong legs and those hard forearms and that taut belly would feel under her hands. Gareth paced back and forth, his eyes roving the city below. She wondered who he was looking for. There were few knights left in High Elerath; war still raged across the islands.

When he'd devoured the apple, Gareth came back in from the terrace and poured himself a cup of wine. He'd seemed unselfconscious of his nakedness, but he drank with his back to her, looking at a blank patch of wall. His bare ass was as hard and discouraging as two clenched fists.

"My Lord," Emlhi said humbly. "May I ask you a question?"

"Of course."

She slipped down to the floor, feeling the sheepskins beneath her bare soles. "Which one of us is it that you're punishing?"

The flagon clinked on the edge of his metal wine cup. He took a moment before replying. "Why should I be punishing you?"

She could think of far too many answers to that. "For being of common stock, not fit for a Knight of Helion?" she suggested. "For being the daughter of a village priest? For bringing you neither dowry nor title nor renown?"

He looked over his shoulder at her, his black brows drawn together, anger snapping from his eyes. "Is that what they are saying in the Citadel? Don't listen to them. You're my wife and that's all the status you require."

"Then, my Lord," she asked, her heart in her mouth, "why is it that you don't treat me like your wife? You married me to make everything all right, but this is not all right. Why won't you even look at me?"

His mouth tightened. Then, as if acknowledging her words, he turned away again. She read the anger in the set of his shoulders. "It's not your fault," he said in a low voice. "I can't look at you without shame."

"Shame?"

"Not you. Me."

"But why?"

He pressed his clenched knuckles to the wood. "I'm a Knight of Helion. The order was founded to bring light and order and hope to the world. I've made my vows. I've always tried to be true to the standards set for us. To have fallen so low— to have taken a woman by force—do you think that's what I intended when I received my sword?" He snatched up his cup and smacked it at the wall; it rebounded, but left an indelible red smear across the plaster. "How am I supposed to live with myself?" he demanded.

"You were ill," Emlhi reminded him. "You had a fever."

Gareth laughed harshly. "A knight is judged by his deeds, not his excuses."

She took a pace forward, her heart pounding. "Please look at me. Please."

He shook his head, dismissive.

"Look at me!" she commanded, her voice cracking, and he swung around to face her. He was a knight, not used to peremptory orders from civilians and certainly not to taking them from a slip of a girl; barely curbed ire was visible in his expression.

"I tended you when you were ill," she said. "I gave you my own bed and fed you and dressed your wounds and cleaned you and helped you make water." She plowed on, ignoring the pain she knew she was causing his battered pride. "Do you think I did all that from my pure compassion? Do you think that when I washed the sweat off your naked body I didn't see what was under my hands? Do you think I am some sort of...saint?" Her face was burning. "In your fever you caught me and put my hand upon your pizzle. Do you remember that?"

"Oh please, gods, no more," he protested.

She pressed on. "Do you know how much I liked it: to feel your heat, to know the release you felt, and to know that I was giving it to you? I took such pleasure from you! Oh, I was a maiden and I didn't know how to get what I wanted, but I was no child. When you sweated I laid you bare, and when you shivered I'd get into bed with you and wrap my arms around your naked body and soothe your shaking. It wasn't pity that moved me to that." She was trembling with the strain of confession. "When you...when you lay upon me...when I felt you...I didn't try to escape you."

"You begged me to stop," he whispered. "I remember that much. And I did not stop."

"I was frightened. And it hurt; it was my first time with a man. You were...too rough, for a maiden. But I wanted you. I wanted you so much. You didn't force me. Believe me in that, my Lord."

"Then," he said, and his low voice was terrible, "you surely misled me afterward."

"No. Please don't. Why do you have to do this?" Emlhi's voice shook. "Why do you have to find someone to blame? I desired you and I thought that you desired me. Isn't that enough? I would have yielded to you a hundred times—or once, if that was all you wanted. You could have left me there. I'm sorry that your marriage is no joy to you, but I told you over and over that it wasn't necessary to redeem my good name."

"You *let* me wed you, out of shame."

"I was blind with love."

"Love?" He breathed the word incredulously.

"And I thought that you did desire me, at least. It would have been enough for me!" She was trying desperately hard to keep her voice under control but it was wobbling now and tears were welling in her eyes. "Of your pity, my lord, if you cannot desire me then repudiate me and send me home. I cannot bear this." There was a great hollow pain in her breast. "I am burning, and you will not touch me."

She shut her eyes tight, trying to hold back the tears. So loud was the blood in her ears that she didn't hear his bare feet on the sheepskins, didn't know he had crossed to her, until she felt his touch on her face.

"I never meant to hurt you." His voice was ragged. The brush of his fingertips made her heart leap painfully. She opened her eyes and the tears spilled out down her cheeks, and then he stooped to kiss them away. His mouth was gentle, but it didn't stray near hers. "Don't weep, Emlhi."

It was an easy role for him to play, she thought with tormented joy: he the rescuer, the comforter of her weakness. It was how he wanted to see himself. Elation and outrage crashed in her breast—but stronger still was the terror that he might stop, that he might be knight enough to resist, even now, the lure of desire. She took his hand from her cheek and laid it softly on her breast. Gareth the man responded at once; she could feel the lightning flicker of arousal as he stiffened. Gareth the knight was another thing entirely, and looking up into his eyes she saw the conflict raging there. In his mind there were only three kinds of people: victims, their oppressors and the heroes that saved them. He couldn't envisage a world in which these roles were confused. He couldn't understand how such categories were meaningless to her.

She touched his lips, her fingers trembling. *Let me show you*, she begged silently.

"You burn?" he whispered.

Couldn't he see it? She nodded and stretched up to kiss his lips. He responded cautiously, almost fearfully—but he did respond. His hand closed upon her breast, kneading the soft orb, finding lone resistance in the puckering tightness of her nipple. Emlhi let slip a helpless noise of nervous pleasure, but his mouth was on hers and he swallowed it. Then he released her just far enough to draw out the short lace at her neckline, looking all the time searchingly into her eyes, his disbelief and mistrust warring visibly with his growing urgency. With two hands he smoothed the shift over her shoulders. It fell to the floor and Emlhi, to her own confusion, blushed beneath his gaze.

Gently Gareth slid to his knees, naked before her nakedness. He kissed her breasts, then her navel, then knelt even lower to press his lips to her pubic fleece. His beard was soft on her skin. Emlhi wound her hands in his unruly hair and surrendered to the bliss of his embrace. His tongue swept her clit, describing exquisite circles until the wetness blossomed between her legs. She nearly overbalanced and he had to support her, his hands strong on thighs that suddenly felt as shaky as a new-born filly's.

"Forgive me," he whispered, pressing his temple and cheek to her belly.

What is there to forgive? she wanted to ask. But the words that came out of her mouth were, "I did. I did it the first time you opened your eyes and asked my name." And suddenly her own tears were falling, on her breasts and on his face.

He rose to his feet then, slipping his strong hands about her waist. But he didn't pull her against him as she hoped; instead, subtly, he held the distance between them. His eyes bored into hers, his expression intense. Suddenly Emlhi was seized with terror: he had, after all, got what he wanted from her—forgiveness.

He was going to send her away.

She put her hand to his groin. His cock, erect and burgeoning, nuzzled her palm. She pressed his shaft to her belly and he closed his eyes momentarily.

"Let me try again," he whispered. His mouth brushed hers. "Please. I want to get it right this time."

"Yes," she breathed, opening to his lips and his tongue.

The gap between them closed.

AT THE SORCERER'S COMMAND

Kim Knox

The air reeked of blood and tar, wrapping around me, mixing with the distant flared hiss of fire. I shivered. I should've been in my master's rooms, hunting through ancient scrolls for a defense against the sorcerer, Kiritan. Not here, lost in a sea of tents flapping in cold, night winds. The creak and thwack of the timber-framed mangonels ran ice through my blood. I wasn't a soldier. Far from it.

Panic whipped my nerves, my heart beating hard. I hadn't volunteered for this sortie. I was an apprentice, barely that, with the first swell of magic in my blood. But I'd also shown another skill in the first few weeks of my training. A skill the Duke's new paladin, Varun, commandeered as he fought back against the besieging army.

"Keep up, Miar."

Varun's low voice cut into my thoughts and he grabbed my arm. His strong fingers bit into muscle, heat bleeding through the thin sleeve of my shirt. The familiar scent of leather, metal and skin wiped away everything else. He pulled me close and his breath brushed my temple. "You know the drill. Concentrate. Stay close. Try not to be stupid."

I stiffened. "Then you should've left me behind."

His grin burned, the heat of his mouth taunting me. There was that hint of a growl that hollowed my legs. "I'm not letting you go, Apprentice Miar."

His words sank into my belly, shoving aside my fear for a much darker want. I'd lusted after Varun from the minute he'd appeared in the Hall of Magic. Not that I could have him. My untouched body was promised to my master when my studies were complete. Payment for his skill and time.

"I have a promise to keep to you. After this."

I frowned, even as my heart drummed. "What promise?"

His full, low growl pushed desire deep into my flesh. He wanted me to concentrate, whilst whipping my body with forbidden need. "Varun..."

"That's Commander to you, Apprentice Miar."

He tugged me forward, broke into a run and with swift signals, directed his squad as we swept through the maze of tents. The lust fell back and fear ran thick through my blood again. Every shadow was a threat and I strained past the snap of tent canvas for the slightest sound. Varun's men were silence itself, the soft thump to muddied ground the only sign that another Rahimani sentry had met his death—

A hand. A knife. I saw a face.

"Senecae," I gasped without thinking.

"What?" Varun turned as a man collapsed to his knees beside me.

"You know my—"

A dagger silenced the officer as he gave me his soul. I watched the man wilt to the ground. Watched his night-blackened blood ooze into the sand. I told myself that he'd been about to plant a blade in Varun's back, slit my throat. It was kill or be killed as we moved toward the sorcerer's tent.

It didn't help.

Varun frowned. "You used your skill. Now forget him."

One of his men appeared and dragged the body away, his boots kicking over the stained sand. Blood smeared his cheek. It was a jolt. So many were casually dying around me. And soon it would be my turn to kill.

"There," Varun muttered.

Grit blew in a whirl around the clear patch of ground separating the officers' tents from those of the nobility. Bored sentries stood outside each one, slouching on ornate spears.

The guards who crept up on them mixed with the shadows, silent and lethal. My heart was a knot of pain in my chest. I had to watch, even as I wanted to run and Varun's fingers formed a vise around my arm.

With muted grunts, the sentries were dead. His men dragged the bodies away into the darkness and three reappeared in the gaudy tabards of the dead soldiers. The guards leaned on their ornate spears, mimicking boredom.

The way was clear. My stomach turned over. I wasn't one of his men, trained in the arts of killing. I was a potion-stirrer, an apprentice ruining my eyesight as I pored over ancient scrolls by the flicker of tallow candles. I wasn't ready for this. Ready to kill.

Varun's gaze flicked around the deserted area, his mouth thinned, his body tense, before he ran, shielding me from possible attack. He stopped before the canvas of a darkened tent. With his hand tight around my arm, he parted the flap and peered within. With a final glance at his men, he dragged me inside.

Varun tilted my head up. "Do it. Find the inner name of the sorcerer."

In the heavy darkness, filled with the hot scent of ginger and turmeric, I froze. I'd worked with Varun for days, but he'd never listened, not once, as I tried to tell him I had no idea how my talent worked. My ability to find the inner name—the secret name everyone was born with—was something that simply appeared. A sudden bolt. I had no control over it.

"I don't—"

Light seared my eyes, blazing around the tent, fierce and white. I shrank back, only Varun's hard grip keeping me from running.

"Shit!" Varun's voice cut through the sudden panic biting at my flesh.

"Welcome." A woman's voice, warm and deep, flowed around me. The fierce glare of light dimmed to a lamp she held high in her hand. She was tall, pale with shining white hair. She looked young...but there was something about her. Perhaps it was in her light blue eyes, or the tilt of her jaw, or the way she stood. I knew she was old, extremely old.

She leaned back against a solid table, placed the lamp beside her and folded her arms. The deep red silk of her robe creased. "Well, isn't this nice?"

Varun pulled me to him, his hand snaking across my body to grip my hip. "Now would be good, Miar."

The heat of his strong arm, the way it crushed against my breast and belly, burned through my thoughts. An insane obsession, that's what it was. How could I be thinking of the way he held me against the solid muscle of his body when I was in such danger?

The sorcerer Kiritan's pale eyes fixed on me and a white eyebrow lifted. "Should I be afraid of this apprentice? She hardly has enough fire in her blood to light a candle."

"Focus." Varun's firm lips burned against the shell of my ear. "Find it."

I closed my eyes, wanting to follow his order, but feeling only the warmth of his skin, his hard body, the dark promise in his voice. I sucked in a breath. What was wrong with me?

"I lied, there is fire in her." Humor lined Kiritan's words. "Not magical. She lusts for you, Commander. Her untried body simply aches for what you'd do with her."

"Miar…" He growled my name.

I willed my eyes open and stared at the woman who'd taken a step away from the table. Varun unsheathed his sword, the long blade glittering in the lamplight.

"Iron can't kill me, Commander."

Kiritan waved her fingers, a careless almost contemptuous gesture and Varun's muscles stiffened. A heartbeat later, his sword flew from his strong hand, ripped away by an invisible blast of magic. He laughed. "Magic. Just ropes and mirrors."

He'd gone mad. He was *goading* the sorcerer. The paladin had always said magic was nothing more than trickery, that it would never, could never influence him. His confidence was insanity now. He had to be able to feel the surge of power in the air. It crackled over the dip of the canvas roof, the fire in the lamp hissing and spitting. Sparks danced across Kiritan's long fingers and a dark smile lifted her mouth.

"I've shielded this tent. You can't escape and your soldiers cannot save you." She paused. "Should I have fun with you? Prove that magic is all too real and bent totally to my will." Her smile deepened. "My whim."

"Miar, find her name!" There was a hard edge to his voice. I didn't want to call it panic.

"A soul-catcher? Is that what your little apprentice is? So

rare. So..." Kiritan stroked my cheek, her fingers light and cool. "Unpredictable."

Varun growled, but made no move to stop her. His lack of action twisted the growing knot of fear in my belly. I was his responsibility. For him to allow the enemy to touch me... Her magic bound him...and didn't that prove her incredible power, if she could hold someone like him?

"Well, little apprentice. Reveal my secret name. Drop me to my knees. Let me offer you my soul."

I stared at her, willing her name to burst across my thoughts. But it didn't. The gleam in her eyes mocked me, mocked my failure. She was right. My talent was unpredictable. "I don't want to kill you."

She laughed, the sound harsh, bitter. "I command a whole army of the reawakened." She waved her hand again. "They're mine, body and no soul." Her smirk made my heart beat hard. "They'll take your precious Duke and render him, devour him for his slight against my people." Her chin lifted. "Come dawn, your fortress will be mine."

Varun's soft laughter cut through my terror. She was going to throw us to the beasts that fought for her and he could laugh? "Nice words. Impossible, but well delivered."

Kiritan's mouth thinned and the spark of power thickened around her. "I know what you are. Does she? Should we let her find out?"

"You can't control me."

A sneer cut her mouth and she lifted both arms, her fingers stretched, her spine arching. White fire arced over her head, jagged and hot. Contained lightning. Not even my master risked drawing on so much power.

"I beg to differ, Paladin Varun."

She brought her hands together, the fire twisting, writhing,

AT THE SORCERER'S COMMAND

bending to her command until it became a shining ball of power. Strain showed in her face, her neck, her skin bleaching white under the brilliant light of the ball. And still she pushed...until the fire slithered into her veins, a living force, a fierce, white glow that spidered under her skin. Her blue eyes gleamed silver.

"Follow your nature, Varun. Take this untried woman for your own." She reached out with her finger and touched him. Her laughter was raw. "Now I can enjoy some entertainment before my army devours you and your people."

Varun jerked back, but took me with him and I stumbled trying to stay upright. "Varun...?" I fought to keep the fear from my voice. I knew his plan couldn't work. I'd said it so many times, and he'd simply glared at me and told me to trust him.

The ripple of his growl ran heat and panic over my skin. His fingers flexed against my hip before he trailed a slow line across my belly. His touch pricked unexpected warmth and I pulled in a quick breath, want pooling in my flesh. I cursed my insane want for this man. We were going to die and my single thought was the delicious fantasy of his bare skin against mine.

"Miar..." He filled my name with need and it wrapped around me, mixing with the slow stroke of his fingers over the rough linen of my breeches. He tugged at the cord that held them, loosening them around my hips. "Finally."

His fingers dipped inside, teasing, his fingertips featherlight across my skin.

"Showing her mercy, Varun?"

I ignored Kiritan, ignored the bite of sarcasm in her voice. Closing my eyes, I thought only of Varun's touch. The skim of him against my flesh, the circles he drew, his low rumble vibrating down my spine to add to the liquid heat. His finger pushed lower, finding the sweet nub that fired want through my veins. I bucked against him, my mouth opening, the push of air quick and hot over my lips. I'd ached for this, for him.

"Take her."

Varun snarled at Kiritan's command, but another finger pushed into my flesh and the quickened strokes, wanted but unfamiliar, stoked pain and pleasure. His other hand tugged at my breeches, baring me, and the chill air cooled my hot skin. My face burned. He'd exposed me to the sorcerer, but the thrust of his fingers, the play of his palm against my ass pushed back the mortification.

I wanted him. I would have him.

The prick of his days' old bristles was rough against my jaw. "You're mine to fuck, Miar. Should've taken you in your master's rooms, let him see how much you're mine. Not his."

The image caught me, of me bent over the potions table, Varun's fingers hot in my flesh. "He'd protest." I swallowed as his fingers brushed my ass, moving, and then the hot rub of his cock pushed between my cheeks. My heart hammered and the slick sound of his fingers in my sex flared the desire consuming my body. "My virginity is…is his prize."

I crushed my eyes shut. Fire burned on the edges of my mind, the fury in my flesh, the power of it surging through me. I shook. I wanted him, not my master—an ancient and twisted man— to be the one to have me. I ached to have him, the torment of his cock teasing me, flashing fire under my skin. I pushed back against him, finding a rhythm, working with the fingers buried in my flesh. Varun growled and the sound threaded through me, igniting the wildness.

Light and heat blistered over me, tearing out a cry as the fire of my bliss wrapped around and over and through me. Varun's fingers didn't stop and the quick strokes found the final flickers of my release, making me gasp and twist against him.

"That's it." His voice was a snarl and a heavy hand in the small of my back shoved me down. Bent at the waist, Varun's knuckles brushed my ass. "His prize is my prize now."

He surged forward and I cried out, the sudden flare of sharp pain, the strange fullness and the flutters low in my belly a rush through my flesh. He pulled back and the friction broke a pained groan from me. "Varun..."

"Did you think he'd be gentle?" Kiritan's question was strained and quick, her breathing uneven. She was watching us. Enjoying us. I could almost...feel her. Knew she leaned against the table, crushing the silk of her robe as she buried her fingers between her thighs. "It's not in his blood. Varun is Connvel, aren't you, Commander?"

Connvel. Shadowbeast. My heart turned over. I stared back at him, fear sudden and thick in my throat. Golden eyes met mine. The shadow of an animal held him, the flicker of lamplight revealing the outer shape of the mythic predator. Panicked, I tried to pull away, but his hands gripped me, yanked my body to him, burying himself deep.

"You..."

His growl rippled over my skin. "Look away, Miar."

My head snapped back and I grabbed at the heavy chair before me, my knuckles white. Varun was Connvel. I fought to breathe. Created beyond memory by dark magic, I'd never know his inner name. Shadowbeast...Varun was the same as the reawakened the sorcerer owned. He had no soul.

"Bent over for your master to see." Varun's roughened voice pricked my skin. "Fuck." He stroked into me again, hard and deep, and I bit my lip to deny the moan wanting to escape. I stared at the rug, my breaths too fast, the fire in my blood increasing. His laughter was quick, dark. "I wanted you then. To see the old bastard's face when I made you come."

My heart thudded, the thrust of him in my flesh weaving hot threads in my belly. I shouldn't want him. He was a thing of dark magic, caught in the bidding of the woman whose moans skittered across my skin.

I ground back against him, taking him deep and earning a snarl that danced light behind my eyes.

"She *likes* the beast. Maybe I should have my men play with her after..."

"I own those I fuck." Varun cut through the sorcerer's vicious words. The promise in his voice of endless nights with him, of him taking me, fucking me, twisted the raw heat in my flesh. I wanted him harder, faster—because I knew my time with him was an impossible fantasy—wanted him slamming into me, driving me screaming to my release. I needed to lose myself for one blistering moment.

"My master would be watching us." Fire flickered up through my belly, the cool night air teasing skin exposed by my loose shirt. "She's watching us."

Varun snarled and pushed deep, his pace quickening. His fingers dug into my hips, the pain mixing with the desire that pounded into me. "Magic..." He wrapped disdain around the word. "You're mine to enjoy. Not theirs."

Kiritan gasped and—again—I could almost feel her reactions. They slipped over my thoughts, twisting through the insanity Varun wrought in my flesh. The hotness of her skin, the slick way her silk robe rubbed against her legs, her hips, her sex as she...enjoyed our bodies.

"Fuck her, Varun. Find your pleasure. Because after, they'll have her." Kiritan's voice was thick, lined with the needs of her own body. "And I'll have you for myself."

Anger twisted through me. She wasn't getting her stained hands on him. He was mine. I didn't understand any of it. But

I wanted Varun—whatever he was—before my time ran out. Before that sorcerer bitch ended it with another wave of her hand.

"I will never take her like this."

Varun's vow whipped across my skin, driving out all worry, all fury, all thought. I sucked in a breath. My belly tightened, the promise of my release scorching, bound up in the fierce strokes of him into my flesh, in the flash of pain from my untried body and the hard drag of his hands as he made me meet every powerful thrust.

Almost there. Almost. The tightness; how my limbs shook, only the chair and Varun holding me upright. I had to—

Fire surged up through my flesh, snapping me taut, Varun's animalistic howl ripping the air, driving my release higher, harder, surging out, catching...

There. On the edge of the wild riot in my mind. The sorcerer. Caught in our desire, our release, her own flesh betraying her as it splashed hot light and joy over her mind. Varun's hands dragged me up, his lips to my ear. I quivered, the final pulses of my release pushing through my body.

"Find it. Find her name." And his teeth took my earlobe.

Pain flashed across my skin; I gasped. And it was there. Shining. Bright. Her name.

"Darut."

It burst from me. The sorcerer let out an inhuman howl and slid like a sack to the floor. She seemed to be shrinking, the red silk of her robe falling around her in thickening pools. The smooth skin on her face shriveled. Thinned lips, withering as she spoke, let out a broken voice. "You know my name. My life is yours."

I sagged and only Varun's strong arms held me up. His hot hands burned my skin and my heart turned over. "You used me."

"I wanted you." His hand brushed low over my belly, a tease

across my skin, reminding me he was still buried deep within me. His smile curved against my ear. "And you want me."

"This..." I waved a hand, not knowing how to begin to demand an explanation. Had he always planned to fuck me in front of the sorcerer? Aware that was how I'd find her name? "You knew."

"Fierce emotion," he murmured and drew back. He pulled up my breeches, turned me and retied them. "She's a full-blown sorcerer." He glanced at the curled woman on the floor. "Or she was. You needed something more than a quick burst of worry, of laughter." He ran his thumb across my parted lips and I tasted myself, sweet and musky. "I gave you that."

"By fucking me?"

Varun looked down as he rebuttoned his own breeches and straightened his tunic. "And revealing what I was." He held my gaze and the flicker of gold shone in the darkness. "Pain, fear, joy. A potent mix." He moved away to pick up his sword and sheathed it. He paused by Kiritan, his face a cold mask, and dropped to his haunches. "You never controlled me. Could never. Magic is rope and mirrors, exactly because it will *never* work on a shadowbeast." His smile was dark and I saw that flash of his other self. "They bred us *too* well."

A strange baying cut through the silence. The hairs on the back of my neck stood on end and a shiver raced through me. The reawakened were reacting to the loss of the woman who'd made them. I closed my eyes against their pain of dying a second time.

"Ease their passing." I glared at Kiritan curled up on the dark rug, the silk of her robe a spill of red around her spindly body. She writhed and groaned against my order, her skin cracking like dry paper. "Do it, Darut."

Skin and muscle retreated from her face, sucked away from the bone, the effort to return the dead using up all her power.

Pity twisted around my heart, but I remembered what she'd planned for me, for Varun, for the people terrified within the fortress and the dead she'd taken from their rest. What little I, or anyone else knew of my skill, was that to break word to me would leave a soul tortured. Kiritan had to obey me.

The baying faded and I stared into the woman's aged eyes. The sorcerer was broken...but I couldn't kill her. I wasn't Varun, bred, trained for death. "Go back to your islands. Forget sorcery. Live out what's left of your life." My gaze flickered over her curving spine and wrinkled skin. Kiritan wouldn't live long.

"Miar..."

Varun's growl of my name, the undercurrent of anger straightened my spine. I wasn't him. "I'm not killing her. It's enough."

His eyes narrowed and he stilled. I didn't move, didn't breathe. What I thought and felt for Varun twisted knots in my gut. He'd used me. Fucked me to break through the sorcerer's defenses. I couldn't deny I'd wanted him. Still wanted him. And that knowledge had the knot wringing tighter.

Varun gave a short nod. "We're leaving." He put out his hand and I stared at it. "Miar?"

I swallowed, my heart thudding. I could run, disappear into the night, a casualty of the siege. Or... "What's left for me? My master won't train me." The echo of pain between my legs reminded me why. I'd given my virginity to Varun. My body was worthless to a mage now. "I've nothing to offer."

"I did what had to be done." His mouth thinned and my chest hollowed. I was a...necessity. "How I did it." He looked to the floor and a muscle jumped in his cheek. "My promise to you. The Duke will pay your mage for training." A wry smile twisted his mouth. "You'll become a great mage. The Duke won't let a soul-catcher escape him."

They had my life mapped out, but a mage enjoyed his right to fuck his apprentice. There'd be no agreement. "My master will object."

A hint of gold gleamed in Varun's eyes and it caught my breath. "He won't object. He'll accept the Duke's offer. If he refuses, he forfeits and faces me." He took a step closer and the heat, the need in my body flared. He traced the line of my jaw, his touch light but sure. "No more of his sly gropes. No more pressing himself up against you...accidentally." A growl rippled from him and I swallowed. I focused on firm lips I'd yet to kiss. "He'll understand no one touches you but me."

"Varun..."

"Are *you* objecting? Is that it?" His mouth brushed mine, so warm and tasting simply of him. I sighed. I didn't want to fall for him so easily. He'd used me. "The only man you can't control."

"I..." My words dried and I covered my mouth with my hand. Suspicion whirled through my head. "You." My hand dropped. "You found me out. Waited. For me."

He stroked my cheek. "I came for you."

I froze. Varun had appeared a few weeks before the start of the siege. I hadn't paid much attention to the rumors surrounding him, why a soldier of his caliber would swear loyalty to a hinterland duke. Who found favor with the Duke wasn't my concern. Until now. "You came for *me*?"

"Soul-catchers must be guarded. Complemented." His lips touched mine again and my own parted, the heat of his breath a temptation. "And who better than a beast without a soul to catch?" He stepped back and laced his fingers through mine. "Time to go, Miar."

He tugged me forward and I stumbled after him. What was I doing? Did I want my life bound up with this man? I stared at him. Flickering lamplight touched his face, the hint of the monster that explained the darkness in him just there. Almost caught out of the corner of my eye.

"You can never tame the beast." Kiritan's cracked voice followed me and touched my fear. A hacking cough escaped her and she pushed herself up out of the mass of red silk. "My overconfidence broke me. I should've known that even with all my power, a shadowbeast cannot be wrought to anyone's will." A smile twisted across her withered lips. "Even yours."

Varun flexed his fingers around his sword hilt. He held my gaze. His voice was low and sure. "Miar doesn't need to control me. I made a promise to myself. To her. What I offer, I offer freely."

I swallowed. "Freely?"

"Commander." One of Varun's guards pulled back the tent flap. He squinted against the flare of the lamp, his gaze flicking over the wizened woman on the floor. He straightened and saluted. "The siege is over. Her magic is broken. The reawakened are so much dust. However, the mercenaries and soldiers— the live ones—are in chaos. We should get back to the safety of the fortress."

Varun gave a short nod. "Agreed." A smile cut his mouth. "Add to their chaos, Lieutenant."

"Sir." And he was gone.

Without a backward glance, Varun pulled me from the tent. Smoke billowed from dry canvas, the lick of flames chasing across the flaps of the surrounding tents. Shouts and screams filled the air. Through the darkness, shapes moved and I caught the gleam and flash of swords. Varun wanted total chaos? He had it.

He unsheathed his own sword. "Ready?"

He grinned at me, the shine of gold in his eyes tightening my heart. I wanted him, all of him, the man and the monster that wrapped around his flesh. Tasting me, fucking me. Bared skin and teeth and tongue, caught in a wild riot of need. My flesh ached. I would have him the moment we burst back into the safety of the fortress. I didn't question it anymore.

His gaze narrowed, but I caught his desire. "Keep those thoughts hot for me."

And with that, Varun pulled me into the night.

SILVER

Anna Meadows

M y mother married me off as soon as I was more woman than girl. She said it would keep me safe.

I did not ask what it would keep me safe from. I already knew.

Some women in our family called our blood a blessing, a sign that a star had loved one of our ancestors. My mother did not agree. She saw our streak of star blood as a sign that, generations earlier, a woman in our family had sinned. She hated our hair, black to the point of blueness. She cursed our skin tinged with gold, not pink like men wanted. She feared what might become of us if our cloaks fell away one evening and the town saw how our bodies glowed, mimicking the silver of winter constellations. Faint, but enough that it could not go unnoticed.

The Lucero family would demand that I marry their son by torchlight at midnight, their family custom. It was their place to make demands. When he was hardly more than a boy, their son Caspian had fought so bravely defending the town that the Prince had given him an estate.

The night of the wedding, my mother did not dress me in white. "You will wear green," my mother said, because green was the color of Caspian's family.

Then she produced a necklace I had never seen before, a thin cord of gold strung with a drop of opal. Pale and milky as a moonstone, it caught the light in flecks of coral and blue. My mother turned it, and it wore a shine of lightest green.

She fastened it around my neck and I stumbled, catching my breath. The moment it touched my collarbone, it felt as heavy as an opal thousands of times the size of the little gem on the necklace.

I reached to unfasten it, and my mother stopped me.

"Bear it," she said, and turned me to the mirror.

I startled to see the girl in the glass. Her skin was touched with pink, not gold. Her wrists did not glow silver. Her hair was no longer the color of the night sky, but as yellow as straw.

I looked like a girl that the Luceros would gladly see their son marry.

It would keep my star blood a secret. "The Luceros have never seen you uncloaked," my mother said. "They know nothing of how you truly look."

The moment I met the Luceros' son on the hillside, I whispered a prayer of thanks for my mother's gift. Fair-haired and ruddy, Caspian still had the blush and health of boyhood. But his height and the look of his back through his shirt reminded me he was not a boy. He was a man who would not care for a wife whose lineage bore the streak of a falling star.

As the priest spoke, Caspian took my hands, his fingers warm. When he shifted his weight, I shivered at the way that I could make out the shape of his thighs through his trousers.

Even the scars on his forearms were like cold water at the small of my back. The flinch in his eyes, which were green as his family's crest, gave me hope that he was becoming hard as I grew wet beneath my petticoat.

I kept the opal around my neck when he lowered my cloak from my hair, now pale as lemon pith. I kept it on when we undressed, backs turned, on either side of our marriage bed.

That night, my skin did not shimmer like moonlight on water. My hair did not darken.

But my new husband did not want me.

He blew out the bedside candles. "Good night," he said, and the cut in his voice told me he would not have me, even as I cringed under the weight of the opal. Even with fair hair and pink cheeks, my face and body did not stir in him what his had in me.

My shoulders and back grew sore from the impossible weight of that small opal. My fingers stung with the memory of my hands in his. The space between my legs brightened and faded like clouds crossing the moon.

Then I wished, as children wish on stars, as women in my family have many times.

The next night, my new husband began to suffer.

He raved as though the house was full of specters. One minute he was delirious; the next, alert as a startled animal. When asked why, he wouldn't speak.

No one else noticed the hardening between his thighs.

The next morning, he recalled the night before like a fever dream, and he was sheepish at the memory. But that night he again grew skittish enough that any noise might make him throw a vase off a ledge.

At the worst of his desire, he overturned tables and clawed at tapestries with the fierceness of a young wolf. He hurled candlesticks and saltcellars into paintings and cut glass into the hearth. The pieces sparkled like ice that would not give to the fire.

Each morning he was as much a gentleman as any prince. Each night he was wild as an unbroken colt.

His family asked if he might be ill. I told them I didn't know. My mother would have warned me against cursing my new husband. His family's name, along with the opal, would keep me from being outcast as a witch. But she knew how women in our family held grudges. My grandmother had once gone a year without speaking to my grandfather because he had forgotten to bring her wildflowers on her birthday. Caspian had held my hands, and then left me a maiden. For him, I dressed in his family's green and not the cream of my girlhood. For him, the weight of the opal made me sorer each night. I would not forgive easily.

At night I grew drowsy from the scent of wood and river stones that came off his skin, even as my shoulders and back cried out against the pull of my mother's opal. My body rebelled as the star's light built within my body. I fought to keep it inside, like biting my tongue against screaming.

Once Caspian had marred the inlaid wood of seven writing desks and armoires, once he had shattered half the crystal in his family's collection, once a dozen priests could not reason with him, the Luceros decided something must be done.

He could have his freedom from dawn to sundown, they decided, when he was reserved, cold as the winter sunlight that matched his hair. But at night he again became that untamed colt, thrashing and writhing against the desire I had wished on him. They feared he might steal horses from bordering lands, sparking feuds between families, or throw andirons through every stained-glass window in the nearby church, banning the Luceros from the parish.

They consulted those town priests, who decided a chair gilt

with pure silver should be forged, blessed and placed in the
darkest room of the estate. Engraved with ornate crosses and
celestial orbs, it would draw those strange stirrings out of him.
When his ravings began, he was to be bound to the chair until
morning.

At the first of his madness, several strong men brought him
to that dark room and fastened him to that great chair. The first
night, I heard his fury and the breaking of glass and saltcellars
as they worked to restrain him.

It would cure him, the priests insisted. Each night bound to
that blessed chair would ease his affliction. But he fought his
bonds. I knew by the thin cords of red encircling his wrists in
the morning. If he ever touched himself, I did not know. If he
even knew that it was desire that tormented him, he never let on.

We did not speak. We bristled at each other, him in his
defiance, me at the growing weight of the opal, which I never
removed, even to bathe.

A week after the chair was brought to the estate, a letter
from my mother arrived. *Estralita*, it said. *What have you done?*

I put it away. Her words still left me fevered with guilt.

Over the next few nights, the moon thinned to darkness in
the sky. The stars were bright as pearls, and they grasped at the
part of me that was theirs. I was water pulled into tides.

I woke to the sound of Caspian's cries, rooms away. The
opal's weight was breaking my body apart. It rested in my
collarbone, heavy as an orb of iron. If I let it, it would crush my
bones and turn my body to dust.

I screamed into the sound of Caspian's ravings. I fought the
burden of the opal. It would not let me sleep. It left me so sore
and bitter I barely stopped to notice the sunlight on garden
roses. If I lay on my back, I felt as though my ribs would snap
beneath the opal's heft. If I turned onto my stomach, I thought

of nothing but it dragging me through the bed and floor and into the earth with the heat of a falling star.

It had made me pink and beautiful, but for what?

I sat up in bed, still screaming, still hearing the cries of a man whose body would not let him rest.

I saw myself in a mirror near the bed. The features of my face were as they had always been, but the coloring was wrong, as if a painter had worked in poor light.

The mirrored woman looked less like a reflection and more like a strange twin. Her eyes were pale instead of dark, her hair flaxen instead of the color of river water at midnight. Pink and peach tinged her face, no gold or silver.

She was not me.

I tore the opal from my neck.

My wrists again glowed. My hair turned blue-black. My eyes darkened.

I ripped the green brocade of my nightgown and cast it off, leaving the white of my slip. It didn't hide the glow my star blood left me with. I did not care.

I threw the looking glass from the table. A few pieces skittered toward the fire. They settled into the flame like the crystal Caspian had broken in the hearth.

I carried the opal down the hall, clutching the cord like I had the thing by the neck. If my husband wanted to shun his wife, he could do it to the woman I was, not what this enchanted jewel had made me.

He was quiet now. No one guarded him. Each night they bound him fast and left him. I slipped into the dark room, once a wine cellar. That great chair's crosses and scrolled flourishes shone in the single candle's glow. At first all I saw of my husband was the dark shape of him. Strapped to the chair of silver, he looked as small as a boy.

His winced against the light from the cracked door. He moaned a little, his head lolling to his shoulder. I shut the door, and there was only the glow of that single candle.

He still cringed, more as I came closer. What was hurting him? I reached for that single candle to blow it out and caught a glimpse of my wrist. It glowed like snow under starlight. I was paining him. Even with my hair dark, the light of my body pierced him.

I came close enough to rest a hand over his eyes, surprised that I still had mercy left in me.

"They think I'm mad," he said.

"Do you?" I asked.

"I must be."

He spoke softly, even as his hands fought the ropes, his thighs restless as his erection strained against his trousers. I flinched between my legs, giving up the same wetness as on our wedding night.

I kept one hand shielding his eyes and slid the other along his inner thigh.

"Please," he said, his breath catching at the back of his throat.

I paused, my fingers inches from his hardness.

"Don't," he said.

I drew my hand back.

"I have a wife," he said.

"What?" I asked, my fingers wringing the opal's cord.

"The only good I've been to her is faithful," he said.

Had he been married already before we married? Was it loyalty that kept his hands from me?

"Who is she?" I asked.

He hung his head and answered with my name. "I've never been with her," he said.

He hadn't recognized me. Now that my body was free of the green dress, my hair again dark, my skin again luminous with my family's curse, he didn't know me.

"Why haven't you been with her?" I asked.

His shoulders tensed, the candle's light tracing the line of the muscle. "I knew I couldn't please her."

The guilt from my mother's letter stung. He had never been with a woman. So few boys grew into men without having a girl in some dew-wet field; it had never occurred to me that my husband might not know of such things.

"I miss the wind at night," he said. "I miss the sky. The stars."

The stars. If he missed them, he might not hate me.

I opened my fingers just enough to let him grow used to my light. When he did not wince, I let my hand fall from his eyes. He looked at me, no glint of recognition.

I loosened the ropes from his wrists and ankles.

"Don't," he said. "I must be kept this way."

I unknotted the rope around his chest. It fell away.

He would not rise from the chair of silver. He would not even take his wrists in his hands to ease the ruts left by his bonds.

"Caspian?" I said.

He bowed his head. "I am not cured of my sickness."

I had never felt guiltier for any wish.

"They told me that with patience I would be cured," he said.

I'd heard his family speaking in hushed tones outside the brick room. They were sure that the blessed chair would be his salvation, that enough nights bound would give him back the manner and grace he possessed in daylight.

They had told him the chair of silver would deliver him from his wildness, just as my mother had promised that the opal's enchantment would make me a wife free from the taint of feral stars. I had been told I possessed darkness and light in the

wrong places, the wrong proportions; now my body ached from
carrying the charmed necklace. Caspian had been punished for
desire as natural as the warmth of his hands. We had both been
promised that these things would save us: the corded opal and
the chair of silver. The jewel had only confined me as the chair
had imprisoned him.

The rage sparked from my heart to my fingers. I threw my
mother's opal at the chair's back. For a moment the great chair
glittered, as though inlaid with a hundred thousand opals. Then
the ornate silver gave like a bough cracking loose from a tree.

Caspian lunged from it and grabbed me, shielding me from
the spray of silver. He pulled me down so I knelt, guarding me
as the silver broke like ice and spider silk. It made the sound of
thousands of icicles shattering against winter trees.

Then there was quiet, nothing left of the silver chair but bent
and buckled metal.

Caspian lifted his chin from my hair. He squinted and
blinked, his eyes adjusting to the light.

He studied the shape of my eyes, the curves of my nose and
lips, all the things the charm had not altered. He took a lock of
my hair and considered the color. He turned over my hands and
examined the glow on my inner wrists.

He gently held his hand under my chin when I tried to look
away. "Estralita?" he said, and I knew that he understood. I
wasn't fair-haired, but dark. I wasn't the richness of green, but
instead white, gold, silver. The only pink I had to offer him was
the tint of my lips, and my blush when I couldn't hide how I
wanted him.

He understood that his bondage in the chair of silver had
been my doing as much as the town's priests.

"I'm sorry," I said, an apology for the wish that had punished
him, for my blood, for my name.

"You're different," he said.

So often we had been called demons or enchantresses. We had been driven from the towns of those who yelled "witch" at us as though it was our shared name. They were suspicious of us, sure we would kill their crops and lure their husbands to our beds or their deaths. They never believed us when we told them we had no such power.

We had only wishes and stars.

Caspian cleared a tear from my cheek with his thumb. "You're beautiful."

I lifted my gaze to his. "Your family," I said. If they knew, I feared they would imprison me in darkness worse than the old wine cellar. They would feel tricked and cheated that they had given their young son to a star-blooded girl.

Caspian looked where the chair had been. Nothing remained but a few twisted branches of silver.

"I'll tell them you were my cure," he said.

Maybe they'd believe it. He had calmed now that we were touching.

I could still feel his erection, and the flinch in his shoulder muscles that gave away his wanting. I kissed him quickly. His lips would not let mine go. I did not shy away as his hardness pressed into me. He freed one of my breasts from my chemise and saw that the tip was more gold and brown than pink. He kissed it, his mouth lingering on the underside where the softness met my rib cage.

There would be time for our bed. Now I wanted to show him the stars. I knew them better than anyone. Not their names or their place in the heavens like scholars did, but the dust of them, the shimmer and glint, the feel of their bodies.

I led him out into the night air, cool and clean with early fall, perfumed with autumn roses. I pulled him onto the grass beneath a flowering tree and kept him under me, so he could see the sprays of stars through the branches.

He kissed my other breast. I wasn't pink. He didn't seem to mind.

My tongue traced each of his scars, and his breath deepened to groaning. Even in the dark, my hand found his hardness easily. He bucked at the first touch, gripping my thighs beneath my petticoat.

"We don't have to," he said. "Not yet."

"I want to."

"We don't know each other," he said. He was right. I wouldn't have known his middle name if my mother hadn't told it to me. I knew nothing of what trees he preferred climbing as a child, his favorite season, if each of his scars was from defending our town as a young man, or if some came from his boyhood.

I would learn. He would learn me.

"Let me be your cure," I whispered, my words veiled from anyone but him by the wind through the flowering tree. He was still tormented by my wish. He would be until he knew pleasure.

He let me take hold of his erection, so taut I thought he might finish with the first brush of my fingers. I wouldn't have minded. But he lasted, holding my hips as I guided him into me. He broke me, and I felt the sting and rush of it. Even in his pleasure, he looked guilty. I kissed him, inviting his tongue between my lips, and we both forgot our shyness. He found the point between my legs where I was most sensitive and touched it as relentlessly as he had fought his bonds.

I bit the base of his neck to tell him to press into me harder. His body obeyed. He held a hand on the small of my back to stop me moving so he could keep me still and keep his fingers on me. My body filled with light and heat. I had never known this of the flicker of stars in my blood, that it held such heat.

I cried out at the surprise of it. He held me but would not stop. My body was releasing all the star's light I had held inside me under the opal's weight. Now it blazed like a moon stripped of clouds. It screamed from me, a thousand blades of light. I was sure the world would break like the silver chair. The stars would rain onto the earth around us, our bodies shivering with their tremulous light.

IN THE KINGDOM OF ROZ

Madeline Moore

I am the daughter of a king who has twelve daughters and twice as many sons, born to him by five wives. I am the only daughter of his fifth wife, Queen Shalilah. While I am not the most, oom, important daughter of a king, my mother tells me she is his favorite and certainly she is his youngest. She was married on her Woman-Day because the King of Roz wanted her. Today I am finally a woman, too, but no king has claimed me, so it is not my wedding day but the day when my husband will be chosen. My name is Asha.

In the Kingdom of Roz we do not have slaves; instead we have servants who stay with us forever, whether they wish to or not. When a child of nobility is born the baby is gifted with the babies of servants. I was gifted with six girl babies when I was born, but my favorite is Matinna. She is the one I like to night-play and sleep with. She is sleeping now, while I am awake, my dreams dismissed in favor of the deliciousness of real life. I pinch her plump cheeks until, with a groan, her lids flutter open to reveal bleary pale blue eyes. I giggle when her grumpy moan abruptly ends as she remembers the importance of the day. Her eyes goggle. She thrashes at the heavy coverlet to escape its confines and throw her arms around me.

"Happy Woman-Day, Princess Asha," she whispers.

Our lips meet in a gentle kiss that quickly becomes more amorous than playful. We have been girl-playing since puberty. That's the way things are done in the Kingdom of Roz.

"Draw my bath!" I toss my head imperiously. Honey-colored hair cascades down my back. By the time the doors to our walled kingdom are thrown wide and I ride through them, naked as a babe, only this hair (and the ornaments my servants weave into it) will afford me a minimal veil of modesty.

"Yes, Princess," she says. She curtseys, pretending to hold out the sides of an imaginary skirt. Like me, she sleeps naked. If she is sad that this is the end of our nights together, she shows no sign. She's a good servant as well as a marvelous playmate. Her role will be different after today, but she will still be mine until the day I die. Only then will Matinna be free.

Chaos! What a flurry of activity circles me after my bath. I am descended upon by a buzzing cloud of servants; like bees they hover and yes, occasionally, sting. I do nothing but sit or stand or turn this way or that as they polish every inch of me until I am iridescent and my hair gleams, sparkles and miraculously extends all the way to my knees.

We aren't early but we are not late, so when my mother arrives for a quick council before I am smuggled out of the palace so that I may reenter astride my mare, she is pleased. I know this because she allows the smallest of smiles to cross her lips while she shoos my girls away.

As she speaks she expertly weaves into my hair some of the long, strange feathers that began to arrive, one at a time, starting at the moment of my birth and continuing to do so on each of The Day of Festivities that celebrates that glorious moment. Every time, at the end of The Day, my mother shows me the new long, thin, vibrantly hued feather and then spirits it away, always with a finger to her lips to remind me that this is our secret.

"Keep your back straight. Do not appear coy or embarrassed. You must stay serene, no matter what. Do not respond to any calls from the crowd. Keep your eyes forward, focused only on the palace."

She pauses to present me with my newest secret gift. This time the feather is particularly exquisite. It is scarlet, darker in some spots than others. When I touch the feather the dark spots are wet. Wet like the eyes of the Queen when I look at her, the unspoken question hovering between us. When she takes the feather back, her hand trembles briefly, then she is all business again as she nimbly braids it in with the others.

"If a nipple should show, care not, but correct the situation as soon as possible. Watch for us. Your father and I will be seated on the dais before the palace doors. There will be an empty throne between us. When you arrive, allow a groomsman to offer his hand, if you need it, to help you dismount. Better if you don't require it, but much better to accept his assistance than to appear ungainly or, Gods-no-shadow-upon-us, fall.

"Approach the throne with deference. Your father will drape the white fur cloak around you and seat you between us. After that, you need only sit prettily while your suitors present themselves. There will be many in the first round, which will pass quickly. We, the three of us, shall choose six and from those six your prince shall be selected. By sunset, you will be engaged to be married. Married, Asha!"

At this, she opens her arms wide in a mock embrace. She

kisses the air around me but touches me not. I am exquisitely prepared for my entrance to the kingdom and even the Queen dares not chance marring my perfection with a caress.

It is a shock to see that she has begun to weep. I yearn to do the same, I know not why. But I cannot allow the tears that film my gray eyes to spill. Although my face appears unadorned I have been dusted and sparkled and delicately rouged and glossed. Tears, my tears, are not allowed.

My mother laughs and the weeping ceases.

"I fear I become a crone," she mutters as she dusts her cheeks with my powder. In a moment her face is once again the mask of perfection I am used to.

She leads me through the secret tunnel from my room to the back of the palace and out, ever so briefly, into the bright blue morning. There sits a carriage that will take me from the palace to the place where my mount, as polished and decorated as I, awaits. The ceremony begins at high sun.

I tremble as the carriage driver throws open the door to the plain carriage that is, according to ceremony, to spirit me undetected away from the castle. Normally he would help me, but today it is my mother who stands by in case I need assistance. If she sees the subtle shaking of my knees she doesn't comment. I enter the carriage gracefully without her help and am rewarded with an almost imperceptible nod of her head.

I'm thrilled to see it. I have always known my mother loves me but today I know Queen Shalilah is proud of Princess Asha. My heart hammers with joy.

From my velvet cushion I can peek out one corner of the curtained carriage window as we pass down the road that is already decorated for my arrival. The crowd will not be allowed to assemble until the great doors shut behind us. Until then, the kingdom must pretend there is nothing special about today and may not pay attention to the simple carriage that passes down the road on The Day of Festivities. Such a wonderful game we are playing! The people of the Kingdom of Roz know their duty and fulfill it admirably. Even the children, who will shortly be shrieking with delight, are hushed. I notice one little girl who must hide her rosy cheeks in her mother's skirts to keep her face from betraying delight. I feel love for her, love for the people, love for my soon-to-be-prince. I am full to overflowing with it, so much so that when we have passed through the heavy, open doors to the kingdom and arrive at the meeting spot outside the palace walls, my velvet cushion is damp.

Oh, I am so ready to be married!

I must wait inside the carriage, its door open, while the kingdom completes the preparation for my arrival. I can hear the cacophony as the crowd surges forward, jostling for position alongside the road. I wriggle on the velvet cushion, wetting it further. Carefully, I reach between my legs, lift my bum and flip the cushion over. None too soon, as a moment later the carriage driver appears, signaling that the time has come.

I alight, again unaided, and wait while my mare is brought to me. I almost gasp with delight at her silky white coat and gaily decorated mane and tail, but remember, just in time, that I am a woman princess now and not a girl who exposes every fleeting thought to those who serve her. Instead, the same almost imperceptible nod I have observed (and practiced) as my mother's lets them know I am pleased.

Gilded reins lay limp across my horse's back. There is a soft suede patch that is placed so that my private parts will be protected whilst it will appear that I ride entirely bareback. We are an athletic people and I will ride astride her, not sidesaddle, as some silly princesses in other kingdoms must. There will be no bloody sheets waved to the crowd the morning after my

wedding night either. Most of the princesses of the Kingdom
of Roz, though each must of course be a virgin on her wedding
day, do not bleed upon first penetration. There have been too
many hunts and games (to say nothing of the girl-play we are
encouraged to engage in) for such foolishness. A princess of
Roz is not required to prove anything. It is her prince who
must prove he is strong and healthy and rich and worthy of her
hand. Hah!

I place my foot in the palm of the groomsman and mount
my horse. She tosses her head. Bells tinkle. Oh, she is vain, my
pretty mare! It's a surprise to see that among her ornaments are
the rest of my strange, secret feathers. I stroke her mane gently,
careful not to dislodge any trinkets, hers or mine. I arrange my
hair so that my nipples are covered while my firm white mounds
remain visible. Great Gods of Roz, this is going to be fun! I
nod. The driver and groomsman jump up on the carriage. A
moment later, the heavy doors to the Kingdom of Roz, made of
whole trees and solid bolts of iron, begin to close behind them.
The roar of the crowd, all pretense at normalcy vanished as
the empty carriage bounces toward the palace, assaults my ears
before the great doors swing closed again and all sounds from
inside are muted.

Time passes. I cannot remember when I was last alone. It's
discomfiting. I remember my mother's words: back straight,
eyes forward, nipples covered. What if the one for me is not
among the princes already gathered at the palace? My mother
has been happy with her king. If it bothered her to be the last of
five wives she never said so. She has led the pampered, protected
life of a queen but—what if that isn't the life for me?

Goose bumps pimple my skin. No! I will *not* have my people
see me frightened or cold or whatever it is that has caused this
aberration of my flesh.

I prepare a regal expression with which to greet my people. This was all decided long before I was born or my mother was born or her mother and so on. Even the King, an old man now but still all powerful, could do nothing to change the course of events about to unfold, if he wanted to, which I have no reason to believe that he does. Yes, it is different for a prince or a king when the time comes to choose a wife, but that isn't my father's doing or his father's or even his father's...and so on.

This is the way things are done in the Kingdom of Roz.

My scream is stifled to a strangled "Oomph" as I am snatched from the back of my mare before my ears have even registered the noise of galloping hooves behind me. It cannot be.

I have been kidnapped!

It cannot be!

My obedient mare stays put. Likely, once the great doors open again, she will begin her practiced prance toward the palace, sans princess, because the princess is now thrown across the broad neck of a black stallion, in front of a saddle. A new scream attempts to follow the first but this one is spanked into another ineffectual sound. Spanked!

Three more blows strike my helpless bum. A leather glove provides extra strength, not that it is needed. The slaps hurt, each more than the last. And the indignity of it! I am actually more indignant than afraid, at this moment, but when one gloved finger carelessly penetrates me fear obliterates any other emotion.

I wriggle, which causes my captor to laugh.

"You like it deeper? Allow me to oblige." He pushes his thick, gloved finger all the way inside me so that the rest of his gloved hand is splayed across my rear. All the while, one-handed, he urges his great black steed deeper into the woods.

"Stop it!"

I dare not wriggle for that obviously encourages him to abuse me further. Perhaps it is possible to reason with him? I try to look to the side and get a mere glimpse of a muscled body dressed in black before a tree branch snatches at my hair.

"If you value your pretty face you'll keep it down," he growls.

There is truth to his words. With my face against the stallion's neck, my threats sound muffled and ineffectual, even to my ears.

"My father is the King of Roz! You will be hunted down and beheaded! Release me at once!"

At this he pulls tight on the reins. His steed rears, thrashing its front legs. My captor's invading finger slips free of me, but only so he may thrash me with the reins, first on my bum and then as I roll across the back of his horse, over the saddle and up against his crotch, across my naked thighs.

"Do not ever issue orders to me. Understand?"

My back is breaking. The sting of the reins is so deep I'm sure they are cutting my flesh. I burst into tears.

The madman allows the horse to touch down again just long enough to roll me over so I am facedown, my body still pressed against his crotch, then pulls hard on the reins and up the steed rears.

"Answer me!"

I wail with fear and pain.

Two gloved fingers penetrate my quim, stretching me wider than I have ever been stretched.

"I am Princess Asha!" I scream it as loud as I can.

This is not the answer he desires. His fingers plunge faster, harder, while his thumb finds my pleasure point and mashes it. Still he lays on what stripes he can while urging his steed to rear, drop and rear again.

To my utter amazement, I am filled with a rolling sensation, fast as a wind-driven thundercloud. My shrieks become moans. The cloud is dense, dark, centered in my loins for an intolerable moment before it releases a crack of jagged lightning that is the harshest, wildest climax of my life.

The horse ceases rearing. The reins stop thrashing. The punishing fingers slide free of me. My pleasure center clenches and releases a dozen times, each release accompanied by rain that wets me, the saddle, the heaving sides of the stallion.

I sob against the horse's shiny satin neck. The orgasm has utterly betrayed me. I finally understand what has happened. I am helpless.

"Answer me," he whispers.

"I understand," I reply. I close my eyes.

The forest is suddenly silent.

My captor dismounts. He cradles me in his arms and coos, "Brave little princess, pretty princess, so sweet, so fearless..."

My eyes remain closed and my body limp, but his words soothe. He cuddles me to his chest. I smell man-sweat and the deeper scent of musk, which must be man-lust. So he doesn't want to murder me, at least, not before he takes me. If his intention is only to rape me he might as well finish me off, for a sullied princess is of no use to anyone but the crones that tend to the temples.

Though we are deep in the forest we hear the sound of the great doors opening. Once my mare begins her solo journey past the shocked faces of the crowd, a rescue party, perhaps made up of princes, will soon set out.

"They won't find us," he says.

Chaos on this man. Is he a mind reader, too?

He props me up against a tree.

"Time to test the princess," he says. "Open your eyes."

I am wise enough not to disobey him. My raw, burning bum,

now pressed against rough bark, is an easy reminder of the
consequences of doing so. I open my eyes.

He is not what I expected from the brief glimpse I had of him
earlier. I'd imagined him in black leather but the hide he wears
is soft and there is not a lot of it. From hip to ankle he is covered
but where a gentleman's breeches should be there is nothing but
a pouch, a rather large pouch, and strings to keep his private
parts, oom, private.

"So far, so good?"

Mother Matron's Veils! A blush betrays me! My gaze travels
swiftly up, from his chest, almost as broad and muscled as his
steed's and covered only by a vest of the same dark material as
his leggings, to his face. Long black curls, slightly matted at
his temples, frame the handsomest features I have ever seen.
A thin, aesthetic pair of lips, a proud nose and eyes the color
of—oom—the color of nothing I have ever seen before. Pale as
river moss yet vibrant as new grass...impossible, but true. Green
shall have to do.

"Why—why do you say they will not find us?"

"We are in an enchanted glade."

My knees buckle. He catches me and props me up again.
Moving quickly he arranges me, legs spread, arms by my sides,
chin up. He circles me, winding strands of silvery thread around
me until I am bound like an insect in a web. Only my neck, face
and pubis are left free.

"You are a spider demon, then?"

He takes my right nipple in his teeth and nibbles it, gentle as
a girl for a flash, then sharp, like the sting of an insect. At the
same time his tongue soothes the pain with soft, wet circles.

'Tis similar to when one is unwell; I am feverish and chilly
at the same time. My nipple blushes and becomes hard enough
for him to grasp with his teeth while he winds his magic thread

around its base and knots it. His teeth move from my already aching pleasure peak to break the thread. He repeats this with my left breast. When he's done the nipples have begun to swell and throb, two pleasure peaks that send a message to my pleasure point. It blushes and swells, too. I ache in three spots though he's only torturing two.

"Yes." He admires his handiwork.

I'm dazed. My gray eyes goggle.

"I am a spider demon. Would you like to see my extra legs?"

Inwardly I am shaking but the webbing is so tight it doesn't show. When he is finished with me he shall chew chunks of flesh from my sides until I die or sprout the long, black, clickity-clacking legs of a spider demoness. I am doomed.

He closes his eyes, clenching and unclenching his fists.

I wait for the legs to burst from the sides of his rippled chest.

"Ah, well." His eyes open. He grins, which lights up his face and makes him more handsome than he was a moment ago. "Perhaps I am not a spider demon after all."

I try to stamp my foot but, of course, cannot. "Lying lecherous hodge. I shall see your head on a stick!"

My fury makes him laugh. It's a lovely sound.

I don't want his head on a stick; I want to laugh with him. I want to enjoy the joke but how can I, when it is on me?

He removes his gloves and shows me the pouches hidden inside each, from which still hang silvery strings of web. "It is useful in battle, or when I wish to frighten a pretty princess."

"And do you do so often?"

"Battle, yes. Princesses, no." He smiles again, beautiful teeth, sensuous mouth. "Not that often."

My training keeps me from smiling back. That and the pain in my backside and my throbbing pleasure peaks. He may not be a spider demon but he must be some sort of demon, for he has obviously cast a spell upon me.

"My queen," he says, "must be able to take this." He releases the strings binding the pouch to his privates and his male member, huge, with a great sack drooping below, are exposed.

My mouth gapes. I have glimpsed such things before, on my brothers and palace servants, but never one as magnificent as this.

"Good girl," he exclaims. With a nimble leap he grabs two strong branches above me and hangs there, his wagging member inches from my face. He nudges the head between my still-parted lips and, just like that, it is in my mouth.

Of course I've heard stories but this is not something girls at play can do. I'm startled but not frightened. My lips curl over my teeth so as not to harm the fat, firm, smooth tip of his manhood. There is no point in biting it as long as I am bound to this tree and anyway, I don't want to.

"Use your tongue," he commands. He swings closer, lodging his feet on lower branches to either side of my face.

Obediently I circle it with my tongue, lapping like a katarine preening.

He grunts.

The sound encourages me. I taste a wetness that is not of my mouth. It is thicker, like the cream that seeps from between my low lips when I am aroused—the cream that is seeping from me now.

Slowly, his column, hard as a bone covered in skin stretched thin, enters my mouth. I lap and suck it as if it is a sticky treat. Fear has abandoned me, as has fury, as has pain. I am neither princess nor woman, I am lips and tongue, I am mouth and, as he thrusts himself deeper, I am throat.

His pace quickens.

When he begins to groan I match his sound with a hum of

my own. His raggedy breath is echoed by my gasps as I grab what air I can while my tongue rolls round and round the rigid, living bone that swells as if it might burst and then, Mother's Veils, it does!

Cream fills my mouth and throat and now I *would* choke except as each burst of liquid spits from his manhood it begins to soften and shrink, until it slides free of me and I swallow and cough and drool without embarrassment. Whatever that was, I obviously did a very good job of it.

He drops to the ground and wraps himself around me and in that way I become woman again. It is his knees that shake, not mine, as he clings to the tree and me, and moans. "Asha, Asha…"

It's as if he is in need of my mouth to quiet his and I almost pity him, though my own need burns fierce in my loins. I lick his temple (another tempting taste) until he turns his face to me and I can press my mouth to his.

Matinna and I perfected the art of the kiss. I tease his tongue with mine, darting in and out of his mouth, pushing my soft lips against his thin ones until he nabs my tongue with his teeth and sucks it into his mouth. The tip of my wriggling tongue explores the cave it is held captive in; the backs of his teeth, the roof of his mouth. I tickle and lick until he sets my tongue free to lure his into my mouth. Our lips are slippery but we keep kissing until there is no more air to share and finally we pause, panting, pulling back to gasp for breath and stare at each other in mutual amazement.

His body is still locked against mine. I feel his naked manhood pressed against my belly. Once again it is a thick, hard column. He desires me.

"Queen, you say?" I can't stop the triumphant little smile that plays across my shining lips. "What land would be your kingdom, Sire?"

He glowers. "I should break you now and be done with it."
He cups my quim.

I am soaking wet down there; could not be wetter had I peed
in fear but I have not. It is all the wet cream of my desperate
desire for release: from the tree, from this place, from my body
and into him.

His free hand slides between the back of my head and the
tree. He grabs a fistful of my hair and twists it hard, this way
and that, my head forced to follow.

"I've got you now, don't I?"

I try to nod but cannot. "Yes."

He makes my head nod by twisting my hair.

"You have heard of the land where there be dragons?"

"Yes."

"That is my realm."

"You are the dragon slayer?"

"I am. I have killed a thousand of those fire-breathing winged
monsters and every year I have sent you a feather from the pret-
tiest one whose throat I slit."

"Why?"

"So you would come to understand your fate."

"Which is—"

"To be used by me, and when I am finished to be sent to my
stable to be used by all who dwell there, man and stallion alike,
and then, when they've no more need of you, to be used as bait
to lure the last of the dragons out of their caves so I may kill
every one."

"Why?"

"Because that is what I do. I kill the beautiful. And you are
the most beautiful woman I have ever seen." He lifts me to my
tiptoes with his palm. His mouth descends on mine, bruising
my lips.

My head is released so he can tug the silver thread from my pulsating, purple nipples.

The pain is excruciating. I scream.

Again, he presses his body hard against mine. His chest seems to absorb some of the hurt. I'm grateful, though he is the one who caused it in the first place.

"I want you," he whispers.

"Take me," I reply.

"No."

He nips each of my nipples before he drops to his knees and begins to slowly stroke the length of my slit with his tongue. Each languorous lap ends with his mouth sucking my pleasure point until it pulses as if it has a wee heartbeat of its own.

I am astonished by the gentleness of his touch.

One slim, long, gloveless finger slides between my low lips and curls upward in a gentle massage. Now his mouth concentrates on my pleasure point, sucking and licking until its tiny heart explodes.

When the climax hits I do not need his hand to lift me. I shudder and shriek and make wet and each magnificent spasm snaps the threads that bind. I rise from the ground that has held me down my entire life and fly through the blazing blue sky. I am the feathered beast that he is so keen to kill and I could not care less. Oh, but let him catch me first!

Which he does, when I pitch forward, free of the tree but no longer winged, not dragon or even bird but simply a broken woman.

"Hush now," he coos. "Brave Asha, lovely Asha, my princess, my queen."

There is the pounding of hooves as a lone rider approaches. Through bleary eyes I see my mare, now saddled and trinket-free. The rider is dressed for battle but at the sight of us, crouched at the base of a tree, the helmet is discarded.

"Mother!" I could not possibly be more shocked.

"Queen Shalilah," whispers the dragon slayer. He lays me gently on the ground so that he may kneel properly as she dismounts.

Once again I am wrong. His deference to her shocks me further.

"Oh, Rodarren, what have you done?" She pauses to allow him to kiss her hand, then with the same hand draws her sword. "Have you taken her against her will?"

"No!" I am the one who cries out. "I am still..." I would like to say "pure" but that doesn't seem quite right, although essentially—

"I would have her as my queen, if she will take me as her king."

"Yes, I'd heard you were King of the Dragon Realm, now. Congratulations."

"I'd not have wished my father's death to come sooner, Shalilah, but..."

"I had no choice, Rodarren. The King of Roz laid claim to me, a mere countess of the court. We have been happy."

My mother bends to take me in her arms. She holds a flask to my swollen lips and I slurp the water like a babe suckling.

"What a mess," she mutters. "Could you not have simply claimed her, as a king?"

"And see your husband put my head on a stick?"

"Mm." Her attention returns to me. "Would you have him?"

"Not if he loves another," I murmur. Things are beginning to make sense to me, and I don't like what I have deduced. "I am not a gift to console a man who cannot have the one he wants."

Deft fingers work the feathers from my hair. "Nonsense. It

was another time. I wasn't brave enough. And he was not even equal to me in years. A boy."

He frowns but doesn't disagree.

"And I don't want to be tossed to stable grooms or used as bait for dragons. I don't think dragons should be killed at all!" Rodarren's face reddens under my mother's cool gaze.

"Rodarren, is it possible you are still too young for marriage?"

"It was a test. That's the way we do things in *my* kingdom. She passed."

He looks at me now, his eyes glittering like green stones in a clear pond. His smile is true. "Princess Asha, if you will grant me the honor of becoming my queen there will be no other, for either of us, ever."

My mother helps me to my feet. She tucks the handfuls of feathers she has taken from my hair into one of my saddle bags and pulls my riding clothes from another. "Get dressed. Much of your dowry is here, Asha, should you choose to go. But... you must hurry. I knew where to find you but the others...your screams were heard by all. They will come."

Rodarren ducks his head and disappears.

It seems three ages have passed since I was last alone with my mother, although it was not even one darkness ago.

"Mother," I whisper, "he kills dragons."

"No, Asha. He is the Protector of the Dragons. You will see, if you go with him. You will ride over the mountains to the Enchanted Forest where the dragons live and make the rest of your journey on the back of a living, fire-breathing, winged dragon."

"Great Mother's Veils."

"Indeed. But you can never come back, my babe."

"Oom. I am mad for him."

"Then go. They shall find me here, woeing the loss of my

daughter to the Demon Spider." She grins.

Rodarren approaches, holding the reins of his horse. He wears his gloves and his groin pouch as well.

"I accept," I whisper. This is the first time I've been anything but nude before him, yet I am inexplicably shy.

"You will never regret this decision," he says. "I promise."

We mount our steeds.

"Queen Shalilah," he calls to my mother, "we shall send you a dragon feather for each babe that is born. Perhaps you will come?"

My mother's smile is brilliant, but her voice is small. "Perhaps. Go. Now!"

"Follow me, my love," he cries.

With a whoop we are off, galloping through the forest, low to the necks of our horses. Rodarren leads me away from the Kingdom of Roz, to the Dragon Realm where I will fly, sometimes on the back of a magical beast and sometimes, I know, at the brutal, adoring, magical hands of my king.

KEY TO THE QUEEN'S ELIXIR

Jo Wu

Your Majesty, here is an intruder we just found."

The Snow Queen's wolves dragged before her a disheveled man weighed down by his iron armor. Each of his biceps was clenched between the wolves' unyielding white fangs.

"You have done well, Bone and Marrow." The Snow Queen stood regal and proud from atop her dais of ice. She was as fair and flawless as the pure snow that blanketed the ground all around them, with white hair that hung behind her straight back in a silky curtain. Even her lips were bloodless. Only her eyes, a deep brown that shone like polished wood, contrasted with her skin. Her gown was sleeveless, baring her smooth arms and shoulders to the bitter eternal winter cold that she was immune to, her white dress like a lacework of snowflakes cupping the curves of her breasts, waist and legs into a white silhouette.

"He was at the borders of our land, too weak to even draw his sword. The scent of his meat promises a fine meal." Marrow was the wolf with an auburn tint to his fur. He licked his lips with a long, slick tongue.

"Hurry and butcher him, Your Majesty!" Bone's yellow eyes glowed against his silver fur like gold. "He's making me hungry."

The Snow Queen gave a small smirk as she slinked off the dais, a dagger of ice in her right hand. "You don't have to wait long, my darlings. You know I always interrogate your dinner before you eat them."

A soft groan emanated from the knight. His head hung like that of a lifeless mannequin.

"Can you hear me?" demanded the Snow Queen.

No response. The Snow Queen clutched a fistful of the knight's brown hair, forcing his face upward. He now awoke. He was about forty, with strong cheekbones and thorny stubble pricking his chiseled jaw. His eyes were as brown as his hair, flecked with shards of apple green. They rolled in a drained fashion in his sockets, trying to sink into sleep.

"Who are you?" hissed the Snow Queen. "Why have you come here?"

The knight was gulping the frigid air.

"Speak, or you will be dinner for my wolves sooner than you think!" She twisted his hair, nearly ripping it from his scalp.

"My name is Gerhard, a knight from the kingdom of Elswood." His weary voice was as rough as the bark of an evergreen tree. "I...I have come to seek help..."

"What sort of help?" snarled the Snow Queen, shaking his head as his voice began to falter. Bone and Marrow's saliva froze into small icicles along their grizzled muzzles.

"There's an epidemic...inflicting the children of Elswood." Gerhard was gasping, nearly choking. "Mothers and fathers are weeping over the children they have lost. Many more are fearing for their children's lives. I have been advised to seek the Kingdom of Ice, where it is always winter and time is frozen, and the queen who reigns is forever young and beautiful. I was told to find an elixir here."

"There is no such thing!"

The Snow Queen smashed Gerhard facedown into the thick snow. He only flopped upon the white surface, as if he welcomed a long-desired slumber.

The Snow Queen sneered. "An elixir... He is sorely mistaken. He cannot obtain an elixir from me."

Bone and Marrow turned Gerhard onto his back so that his exhausted face with its closed eyes and parted lips faced the pearl-gray sky. With her dagger clutched between her bloodless fingers, the Snow Queen brushed away the matted brown hair that congealed to Gerhard's neck. When she did so, a glimmering trinket slipped out from beneath his armor, dangling on a delicate silver chain around his tanned neck. A silver key lay upon his red skin like a pearl set against a brilliant rose.

An image flashed in the Snow Queen's head. A delicate hand with peachy skin and slender fingers, outstretched as if it were her own, stroked a very similar key as it dangled from a thin chain on a warm day, with sunlight that rendered a dazzling field orange and crimson-gold.

Then she was back in the present, on her knees by Gerhard's body, her dagger now lowered by her legs. She was stroking the key around his neck. Perhaps it was the exact one she had seen in her vision.

"Your Majesty, what are you waiting for?" Marrow was baring his fangs in hunger.

She stood up, gazing down at the knight who lay at her feet like a child sound asleep in a warm bed. "Take him to a bedchamber inside the castle," she ordered.

Bone and Marrow's eyes widened with dismay. "I beg your pardon, Your Majesty?"

She delivered them an unflinching gaze. "Take him to a bedchamber. He must be fed and well rested. I have more interrogations for him."

"Your Majesty, our apologies, but what of our dinner?"

"Remember the wild boar you hunted this morning for my dinner? It is now yours to devour."

The wolves now panted and hopped upon their feet in delight.

"But take this knight to a bedchamber first!"

The Snow Queen's castle was completely constructed from glimmering ice. While the other beds in the castle were also made of ice, Gerhard was put in one bed carved from pine and maple, with a soft mattress, pillows and heavy blankets. His armor and clothes were removed, so he lay only covered by the blankets that kept him warm. Sometimes the Snow Queen heard him pant heavily, caged in his feverish flesh. He would toss about in bed, roll onto his face, heave out great moans and even fall out of his bed so that the Snow Queen would have to pitch him back onto the mattress. Yet he continued to sleep. Two days passed with him in this state. Though the Snow Queen bristled at how childish he was in his slumber, she could not help but to feel a twinge of pity. Unlike everything else in the Kingdom of Ice, Gerhard emanated waves of scorching heat.

On the third day, the Snow Queen let her white robe fall in a creamy pool around her slim ankles. She peeled back the red blanket, exposing his smooth, muscled chest, which rose and fell with his labored breaths. His skin was tinted like sunwarmed peaches, and his fever threatened to melt the ice walls of the bedchamber. The Snow Queen frowned, mentally forbidding him to incinerate her property with his body heat. Perhaps if she could absorb some of it, he would stop squirming around in bed like a squelching mouse.

She slowly lowered herself onto him. It was a foreign sensation, having skin-to-skin contact with another person. Her breasts were like mounds of snow, her nipples like beads of hail, and her hands felt frostbitten against his smooth, scorching shoulders. She pressed against him. He smelled of forest soil and smoky fire and warm fleece, scents that she could only vaguely recall. The ridges of his collarbone cut into her cheek and as she lay there, she felt her nipples soften against his skin like ice melting into running water. With one hand, she fiddled with the key that hung from the chain around his neck and ran her fingertips over the smooth silver, warmed by his body. Why did he wear this key? It seemed to be a woman's trinket, ill suited for a man.

His chest fluttered beneath her.

"You're quite forward."

The Snow Queen lifted her face to see that Gerhard was looking at her. His brows were raised with a quizzical expression.

"You were burning with fever!" As the Snow Queen tried to leap off the bed, her legs became ensnared by the crimson sheets, causing her to gracelessly squirm off of Gerhard's body, off the side of the bed. Her bare back smacked against the floor of ice. Now that she had absorbed Gerhard's body heat, the floor felt bitterly frozen against her bottom. The pain bloomed out of her rear, exploding through her legs and back.

"Let me." Gerhard held out his hand to her.

"I don't need help!" The Snow Queen snatched her white robe and threw it over her shoulders, clutching the fabric in front of her chest. She glared at Gerhard. He was gazing back at her as he pulled his blanket back over himself, looking at her without a blink. She grimaced and turned her glare to her pale foot.

"I thought you were going to kill me," said Gerhard. "Or is this supposed to be my deathbed?"

The Snow Queen still stared at her foot, the blue veins visible through her translucent skin. "I have to know more about you."

"Why do you wish to converse with me? At least, from where I live, it is not customary to make pets out of creatures that will only be butchered."

The Snow Queen's face soured when she looked back at Gerhard. "Who are you?"

"I believe I already told you. My name is Gerhard and I am a knight seeking an elixir."

"Tell me more!" She eyed the key that now hung over his heart. "Why do you wear that necklace?"

Gerhard's hand rose to tuck the key into his gentle fist. "Why would a necklace interest you? It is a plain trinket, not meant for the likes of someone as beautiful as you."

"I have no intention of taking it! I just want to know who gave it to you!"

Gerhard's eyes lowered to his fist. His voice softened. "I have worn this necklace for a long time. Someone I knew during childhood gave it to me."

"Do you remember who?"

"She died."

"Your mother?"

Gerhard only continued to stare at his fist. The Snow Queen thought to press on with the identity of the gift-giver, but the question died on her tongue. She swallowed all shards of the question, letting it wash away in the back of her throat.

"How old are you now?"

"Thirty-eight." Gerhard slumped onto his side, his face

falling upon his arm. "Forgive me, but I am famished."

Extracting a silver bell from the pocket of her robe, the Snow Queen rang it, producing a light, tinkling ring. Bone and Marrow peered in through the doorway.

"Yes, Your Majesty?"

"Please bring the knight something to eat."

They gnashed their fangs, but obediently trotted away. In a few minutes, Bone balanced a plate of a roasted boar leg on his head, while Marrow held the handle of a water pitcher with his fangs.

"Thank you," said the Snow Queen after they set the nourishment upon a table by the bed. "You are both relieved of your duties for the rest of the day. I know that a moose is traveling toward the vicinity northwest of the castle. You should be able to hunt him down."

"You are most generous with your knowledge, Your Majesty." After the wolves sank in low bows before her, they scampered off through the doorway, baying with excitement. The Snow Queen swept out of the room to let Gerhard eat in privacy.

Gerhard fell into a deep slumber again for another two days. The Snow Queen felt her spine bristle with aggravation. What had crossed her mind to act as a hostess for this intruder, to let him deprive Bone and Marrow of their rightful meals, and to become enraptured by the heat of his skin? He was not as feverish as he used to be, and now that the Snow Queen had lain against his skin, she was not as immune to the impervious chill of her kingdom. Before, she could do with wearing nothing more than a silk gown that bared her shoulders and skimmed her smooth legs. Now she had to be bundled in a fur coat. The skin on her hands even turned a blotchy pink if she did not protect them in a muff.

She drew out her dagger again. Her breath grew shallow as she kept her eyes on Gerhard's face. Perhaps she could keep his necklace as a souvenir of her victim?

She took in a sharp breath when she saw Gerhard's brows quiver. He squirmed in bed, turning his head so that his cheek lay against the pillow, facing her.

"Eira," he breathed, half speaking mellifluously, half whispering hoarsely.

The Snow Queen froze. Eira? Who was Eira? Was Eira his mother, a sister, a lover, a daughter or a wife? Or the person from his childhood who had given him the key necklace? Suddenly she felt a momentary sensation of warm sunlight against her back and the tart taste of fresh apples upon her tongue.

When Gerhard awoke, she immediately barked, "Who is Eira?"

His eyes widened. "How do you know about her?"

"You were calling for her in your sleep."

Gerhard looked away from her, his fingers rising to touch his key.

"I'll make you a deal," stated the Snow Queen. "If you tell me your life story, tell me who gave you that key and tell me the significance of that person, I'll set you free. I promise you that my wolves won't eat you."

"My lady, I came here for an elixir." Gerhard looked at her with grave eyes. "If I cannot find it, then it would be more honorable of me to die seeking it than to return home empty handed." He paused. Their dark eyes met each other's. "An old hag I encountered many weeks ago informed me that the tears of the Snow Queen would cure the epidemic."

"Bah! Tears? I do not cry."

"And you are the only Snow Queen here?"

"Of course I am!"

"How long have you reigned?"

The Snow Queen faltered. Her brows furrowed as her lips fell open. "I have reigned for as long as I can remember."

"You have no family? No children?"

"You are in no position to question me!" The Snow Queen felt a rush of angry blood flood her face, an uncomfortable sensation that made her feel like an icicle that fell into the jaws of a roaring fire. "I'll revise my challenge. If you tell me everything I requested you to tell me and manage to move me to tears, I will fill a vial with my tears and set you free. If you cannot manage to make me weep, then each of your arms will be fed to my wolves."

"Actually, they can eat all of me."

"How generous," sneered the Snow Queen. She raised her chin as she looked down upon Gerhard. "Begin, then!"

Gerhard cleared his throat. Before the Snow Queen knew what she was doing, she sat at the foot of his bed, eyeing him like a child expecting to be engrossed by a bedtime story.

"I was born in a village about fifty miles away from the kingdom of Elswood and lived there all my life. All of the people in my village were peasants, growing crops and raising animals. I had a loving family, with a mother, a father, three sisters and a younger brother. A scout from the king's castle visited my home when I was five and predicted that, as the eldest sibling in my family, I would make a fine knight. I was convinced that it was my destiny to become a knight. But…I must admit, there are times when I wish it wasn't so."

"Why?" asked the Snow Queen.

Gerhard hesitated. "If I hadn't been a knight, then…then my wife would not have died." His Adam's apple bobbed, pulsing against the skin of his throat. "Eira was my wife's name. Before we married, she had been my childhood friend. We did have a happy marriage, but after I was called away to live at the castle, she...she died."

The Snow Queen's eyes widened as she was suddenly engulfed in a vision.

Sunlight poured upon the sheep and cows in the evergreen field. She wanted to pet a lamb, one no taller than she was, and feel its cloud-like fleece. It bleated and rushed away from her. Suddenly she heard a laugh and turned to see a young boy smiling at her. He was about three years older, aged eight, with floppy brown hair that glowed with a tint of autumn-orange in the sunlight.

"I'm Gerhard," he said. "What is your name?"

The girl shot him a gap-toothed grin. Her golden hair fluttered behind her like a wedding veil, and her cheeks were pink from the blazing sun.

"My name is Eira!"

Gerhard was swallowing. He looked as though he had difficulty breathing. "We were very close. As we grew up, there were days when we couldn't bear to be apart. We would tend the sheep, pick apples, gather firewood, cook dinner and watch after our mothers' babies. After I was knighted, I came back to the village and we married."

A beautiful bride was spun around on the dance floor by her groom, his arms wrapped around her waist. All around them, their families and friends danced to the music of a fiddler in the corner of the wooden room. There was a roaring fire in the hearth, and corn cakes and roasted beef lay on the table. It was not a spectacularly grand wedding, but the newlyweds were at least clean and healthy and brimming with joy to be together.

"There came a time when I was called to the castle. I was told that I couldn't live in the village anymore. I wasn't even allowed to bring Eira with me."

*Eira clasped a delicate silver chain around her husband's
neck. He touched the small key that hung from the chain,
glancing down at the charm before he raised his eyes to meet his
wife's eyes and lips. Eira's eyes were warm with molten tears.
Around her own neck hung a lock upon a chain identical to
Gerhard's.*

He swept her into his arms, kissing her tear-moistened lips.

"She was starting to carry our child after I left. But I was
at the castle for so long and so far away from home, that..."
Gerhard's voice quavered. He lowered his head to his bent
knees, cupping his face with his large, enveloping hands. His
fingers twitched as his shoulders shook. "I...I had an affair with
a maid at the castle." His voice ruptured and regret bled from
his tongue. "I only craved intimacy. I never cared for the maid
and I missed Eira so much, and I never intended to hurt her. I
don't know how she found out, but she did, and she was devas-
tated. After she knew of my affair, I found out that she had a
miscarriage."

*Eira was standing on the edge of a cliff. One hand was pressed
over her now-empty womb, the other clutching the lock on her
necklace with a punishing grip. Her head was lowered and her
disheveled hair whipped over her face. Tears slipped down and
off her chin, hurtling into the abyss far below, crashing into the
roaring river that convulsed and veered nearly a mile beneath
her bare feet. The wind mercilessly scratched at her white skirts,
threatening to tear them into shreds, to expose her hidden legs
and hips and shoulders, to blow her away down into the ravine
like a weightless paper doll.*

*She jumped. Her fluttering hair disappeared over the edge of
the cliff like torn sunlit strips of paper.*

"I could never be with another woman after she died."
Gerhard's breath quivered like a harp string that threatened to

snap apart. His eyes were glassy, but no tears spilled down his cheeks. "It's been nineteen years. I think of her and our dead child every day. I can never stop thinking of how our lives could have been if I was never a knight. Because of this, I can't bear the pain of the parents who watch over their dying children. So I came here. I'm willing to either die or to succeed in my quest."

The Snow Queen abruptly realized that her face was hot and wet. Her tears, like red-hot coals, dissolved the customary cool surface of her translucent skin. "I…I…" She stood up and turned so that her back faced Gerhard. "Please excuse me." Clutching her fur robe tightly around her, she started to rush out of the room.

"Don't forget our deal!" called Gerhard.

"I didn't!"

She wound her way up a spiral ice staircase, too hurried to realize that, as she rushed past the narrow windows on the rounded walls, bits of sunlight were sifting through the thinning gray clouds. She entered her own bedchamber, which was larger and grander than the bedchamber Gerhard was in. It consisted of a canopy bed made of ice, entwined with vines of holly around the posts, and a vanity that was also carved from ice. Upon the vanity in front of the tall oval mirror lay a velvet box as slender as a slim book and as richly colored as the hue of plums. She had forgotten about the box for about twenty years. After she grabbed a glass vial corked with a rose's thorn from her bedside table, her hand quivered as she reached out for the velvet box. She could not tell if it was from the fear that what she hoped would be inside would be gone, or if it was from the harshly cold air, or both.

A warm, smoky breath of relief escaped her like a cloud of fog that disappeared before her lips. Lying upon the dark velvet lining was the lock from her memory, the one she wore when she leapt to her demise. When the Snow Queen clasped the necklace around her neck, she saw that, in the mirror, she had lost some of her icy pallor. A tint of peach stained her skin, and her cheeks and nose were red from the cold. Her cheeks were not so hollow and her arms not as bony as they had been. Her long hair looked as though gold had been dusted through the white strands. She reached out a hand. When her touch met her reflection's fingers, she felt the glass sting her with its chill.

A drop of water fell from the ceiling. It burst upon the velvet lining of the box where the necklace had nestled. The Snow Queen looked up. The ceiling was beginning to thin.

She ran downstairs, back into Gerhard's bedchamber. When he sat up and looked at her, she stood frozen in her tracks, breathless from both her run and her revelation.

"I never knew your name," Gerhard stated.

"It's me!" The Snow Queen threw herself upon her knees by Gerhard's bed, her hands clutching the blanket over his lap. "Gerhard, it's me! Eira! Your wife!" She bit her lip with trepidation and lifted the chain around her neck to show him the lock she wore. Gerhard, barely breathing, fingered the charm.

"But…Eira…you couldn't have survived."

After she had thrown herself off the cliff, the young woman had expected to feel an explosion of blood and bones. But instead, when she opened her eyes, she found herself upon an expanse of snow. She only recalled falling, but she failed to recollect what had prompted her to do so.

In the distance, she spotted two wolves prancing toward her. One of them carried a robe of white silk on his back. The other clenched a golden crown between his fangs.

"Bone and Marrow made you their queen, and since then, you could never recall your past?"

Eira shook her head. The tears spilling from her eyes were

crippling her ability to speak. She thrust the glass vial that had been clutched in her fist at him. "I'm honoring our deal, Gerhard. Take my tears. Let them cure the children of Elswood."

After taking the vial in one hand, Gerhard pressed his other hand against her left cheek. He was so warm. She could see that he had more creases around his eyes and that he had more untamed stubble than before she had died. But he was so handsome, as handsome as she recalled, if not more so.

"You're just as beautiful as I remember you," he murmured. He gently pressed the vial beneath her right eye, letting her tears slip into the cold glass. After he corked the vial with the rose's thorn, his hands slipped around her waist and he yanked her closer to him, close enough for her to feel his burning breath on his lips, to see the kaleidoscope of rustic hues in his eyes, to feel his sudden hardness against the inside of her right thigh.

He crushed her into a kiss. He was not as feverish as he had been days before, but he still seared her with his hard, tangible heat, his tongue like a scorching serpent that ran over her own. She heard the discordant rips of her robe as he tore it off her, and she realized that the heat from his body was greater than the insulation her fur robe had provided. His skin was like the sun, which she had not felt since she died, and roughly chafed against her skin until her whole body was as warm as his. It was as though she had been made of ice, only to be melted away by a merciless sun.

She gasped. He entered her like a dagger that stabbed into her cove of secrets to where she had been numb since her death. He was so sharp, like a thorn or a sword, but at once she felt herself succumb to his arms. Her cheek fell against his chest and the wet sting between her legs melted into a heavy, hard pleasure that elevated within her. Suddenly, with a low growl, Gerhard flipped her onto her back so that she was now pinioned beneath him, his hardness still within her. She could barely breathe as he thrust into her, over and over, stabbing her, thirsting for the scarlet blood of passion of their union. His hands fondled and twisted her soft breasts and his tongue delved deep into her mouth. She sucked on his tongue, wanting to imbibe his seeping heat, to feel her body unite with his as if they were burning metal melding into each other. Her inner thighs became slick, and her hips were frantically grinding against his pelvis as he sank deeper into her, as though he was willing himself to drown in her. His hardness felt as wide as an evergreen trunk, propelling into her until she shrieked with honeyed pain and murderous pleasure.

"Your breasts, your skin..." Gerhard ran his hands over her. "You truly have not aged a day."

He shoved into her again. Eira screamed as she felt burning liquid implode from within her. Gerhard began to slide out of her, languidly dragging the length of his erection out from between her wetness, hesitant to leave her warmth. When only an inch of his sharp tip was left inside her, he froze, letting it rest at her opening. She moaned, lamenting at the current emptiness. But then, as slowly as he had exited her, he slid into her, inch by inch, her secret chamber easy and wet, until he filled her to the brim once again, the base of his member pressed between her legs. For a second and a third time he came out slowly, only to go back into her and then resume. When Eira was whimpering under his torture, he once again demonstrated frenzied bestiality, splitting her legs wide open until she thought she would tear apart as he stabbed into her with his full length again and again. His final thrust was like a murderous blow, a knife into her most secret parts, for Eira arched her back and screamed a scream that married deadly pain and tender love.

Gerhard collapsed atop her, both of them heavily panting,

their breaths shrouding their bodies in smoky, ethereal veils. When he tried to rise from her, Eira felt a pull on her neck. During their lovemaking, Gerhard's key had inserted into her lock and now refused to let go, for her lock rose off her chest, the key stuck inside it. Eira laughed at the sight of this.

The air was not as cold as it once was. Fat water droplets were dripping from the ceiling, one by one. Eventually two droplets fell at the same time, and then four. The ice walls were not as solid as they were supposed to be. They were slick with cold water. Golden sunlight poured through the windows, and the chirpings of robins and blue jays could be heard.

"Eira." Gerhard's whisper was like a velvet caress on Eira's breasts. "Come home with me."

Her smile faded. She turned her head so that one cheek was pressed against the pillow.

"Gerhard...I'm dead."

"What are you speaking of? I can feel and see you."

"This kingdom kept me alive. I'm not who I once was. Now that spring has arrived and destroyed my kingdom, I can't go back."

Gerhard got out of bed, not minding that he was treading over the thinning ice floor that was wet with the water droplets from above. He threw on his clothes, slipped into his armor and strapped on his sword. He turned to look at Eira. She was sitting up in bed, exposed from the waist up. She now looked like the Eira he once knew. Her hair was as golden as a field of wheat underneath an expanse of sunlight, her skin now as flushed as pink rose petals, her body more elegantly curved and rounded.

"You have to leave, Gerhard. Leave before the castle melts."

With Eira wrapped in the blanket, Gerhard scooped her out of bed as easily as if she was a fragile child. She stared up at him and felt as light as hollow bird bones in his muscled arms.

With Eira in his arms and the vial clutched in one fist, Gerhard ran out of the bedchamber. The grand staircases and halls were melting beneath the sun, succumbing to the warm weather that had been provoked by the lovers.

At the entrance of the castle, Eira could see that there was now green grass where there were once blankets of snow and flowers where there were once icicles. Gerhard set her to her feet.

"Come home with me, Eira." His plea was a pull on her heartstrings, and his hand grasped hers as though he wanted his flesh to melt into her skin. He stepped out of the castle. Now their hands were linked underneath the arching entrance. She was still inside, in the shadows of her deteriorating home. Her dark eyes met his, scintillating with sweet bitterness that ached with her heart.

She lunged out of the castle and threw herself down on her knees to kiss Gerhard's hand. Once the sunlight hit her, Gerhard felt the impact of her forceful lips soften. Eira was disintegrating into snowflakes. The blanket fell off her, exposing her white skin to the spring sun. Her hair fluttered as though it was blown back by a winter wind, the strands transforming into snow-flakes that floated all around her. Her skin chipped into count-less more snowflakes. Last of all, her face, so serene and smiling with peace, was the final fragment to go. When her lips became snowflakes, Gerhard watched them float up into the air toward the heavens like bubbles free to ascend into the blue expanse. He lifted his hand to see a snowflake clinging to the back of his palm, and on the ground by his feet lay Eira's lock, still threaded upon its silver chain.

HERE THERE
BE DRAGONS

Ashley Lister

D ragonmeister?"

Georgianna of Roxburghshire stopped moving. She snapped her head back toward the sound of the voice that had summoned her. Her heartbeat quickened. Above the stench of subterranean earth and dung, her nostrils caught the harsh stink of the burning-tar.

Mercifully, the burning-tar was unlit.

The night down here was as lightless as the tomb of a forgotten pilgrim. But the smell was assuredly the burning-tar, and that was a substance that had no place in the eastern catacombs.

"No," she whispered.

It was as much as she dared to say.

She was patrolling the catacombs, a thrice-daily chore for the dragonmeister of Gatekeeper Island, and inwardly cataloguing her stock. Here in the easternmost catacombs she kept a weyr of orientals that included three-toed Japanese dragons and five-clawed Chinese dragons.

The orientals were the most ferocious and dangerous members of the island's livestock. Maintaining their successful husbandry was an achievement that had won her shields of honor from Caleb the wolf slayer, laird of her fiefdom. But the husbandry of the orientals had never been a chore that George took lightly. It was a perilous job and she insisted there were rules that needed to be followed.

"Dragonmeister? Are you there Mistress Georgianna?"

After the question came the sound of flint striking stone.

George clenched her teeth and shook her head.

Her eyes grew wide in the darkness.

It was one of the apprentice hostlers. She recognized the adolescent squeak of his voice. He was one of a cadre that had arrived earlier that year at summer's end. In any of the other catacombs his ignorant mistake would merit little more than a stern reprimand.

But this was the easternmost catacombs.

This environment was not forgiving.

In the western catacombs, where she kept the European dragons, the apprentice hostlers were known to fly the beasts in tournaments and race them for pleasure or for daring or for gambling. The western catacombs were larger than their eastern counterparts and hosted a range of dragons that made her laird's fiefdom the envy of every baron beyond Gatekeeper Island. The western catacombs held Portuguese caco, Polish smok and Catalonian víbria.

And every one of those creatures was controllable and train-able.

The víbria were amongst her favorite beasts because they took pleasure and satisfaction from helping humans. The víbria lit fires for summer barbecues. The víbria gave gentle rides to small children. And a blazing torch of the burning-tar would not present a problem in the lair of the víbria.

Snakes of unease writhed in George's belly. She held her breath and silently prayed to the gods of the golden temples that they would not need the sacrifice of a death this night. Sensing the carnage that was about to take place, she strongly suspected that her prayers would pass unheeded.

Above the catacombs, guarding the golden temples of Gatekeeper Island, there was a family of wyverns: two-legged, long-tailed dragons. The wyverns were responsible for protecting the doorways from the temple to the catacombs. They were also guardians to the fiefdom's vault of treasure. George was slowly learning the language of the wyverns just as the creatures learned hers in an exchange of wisdoms and cultures. It was a fascinating area of study and she had already begun to fall in love with the rhythmic cadence of wyvern poetry.

And, as dragonmeister of Gatekeeper Island, George knew that the combined danger posed by every caco, smok, víbria and wyvern was not as menacing as the threat that came from a single oriental.

"Dragonmeister?"

There was another scratching crack as the flint struck stone. The stink of the burning-tar struck her nostrils with renewed force. George heard something growl with barely suppressed hunger. And she breathed a sigh of relief when the flint refused to spark for a second time. If the apprentice hostler survived this night she would flay him until sunrise so he could act as a warning to the rest of her subordinates.

"Are you there Mistress Georgianna?"

George insisted that there were three rules for working with the orientals. If she had maintained her needlework studies from when she was a strapling she would have stitched those rules onto a tapestry and hung the framed needlework in the golden temple on the doorway above the easternmost catacomb.

The dragonmeister always patrols the eastern catacombs alone.

The dragonmeister always patrols the eastern catacombs in silence.

The dragonmeister always patrols the eastern catacombs in absolute darkness.

She had thought those three rules were made known to everyone who lived on the island. But clearly this apprentice hostler wasn't aware of them. Or, if he was aware of them, he was too dunderheaded to heed rules.

Either way it was going to prove fatal.

There was another growl from the darkness. This one was heavier. And George did not need the gift of presentiment that came from working with dragons to know that it was now too late for the hostler.

"Dragonmeister?"

There was another scratching crack as the flint struck stone.

This time the spark erupted into flame. It caught the burning-tar. The catacomb was immediately flooded with liquid yellow light. George could see she had been right: it was one of the apprentice hostlers. She recognized him from the ginger hair on his head and the hessian tunic he wore. His name had been Bob, or Rob or something like that.

And he had entered the last minute of life.

"Dragonmeister?"

Bob or Rob peered toward her but he was clearly bright-blind from the flare of the torch he carried. If he had been able to see anything at all he would have noticed the dragons, three Japanese and two Chinese, circling around him.

"Are you there, Mistress Georgianna? The island has visitors.

We're called on by the esteemed Thane Vortigern of Merioneth who comes he—"

He didn't get to complete the sentence.

A Japanese exhaled. Its breath caught the flame from the torch and ignited. The fire seared the ginger hair from the hostler's head. Before he could properly start to scream a second Japanese dragon had acted quickly and ripped his tunic away.

The sound of aged and leathery wings flapped indolently in the shadows.

The dragons looked lemony-white in the glow of their own burning breath. The scene was ghoulishly played out for George as a brightly lit testimony to hostler stupidity.

Momentarily she stood riveted as the dragons snatched at him and nipped at him.

The Chinese clawed.

The Japanese snorted fire.

The hostler was naked and bleeding and weeping and screaming. His hands flailed in a pathetic attempt to keep the beasts away. His sobs were mercifully inarticulate. If he had called for her by name George would have felt guilty for abandoning him. A Chinese slashed at him with five-clawed talons. Black-red lines opened across his abdomen.

And then the hostler's screaming ended.

George turned away and fled.

The hostler had been beyond help before the dragons attacked. Going in to save him would only have ended her own life. Even if her work did not necessitate the gift of second sight, she would have known that much from having worked with orientals through her adult life.

As she burst through the temple doorway from the catacomb she was adamant that someone would tell her how a mistake like this had happened. And she was adamant that the person responsible would pay.

"Dragonmeister Georgianna of Roxburghshire?"

The man was tall and handsome. A pair of wyvern glowered down at him with characteristic suspicion.

George motioned for the dragons to stand at ease.

Obedient, the beasts relented from their stiff posture. They continued to strike a menacing pose but neither looked as likely to eviscerate the visitor.

The stranger was dressed in the polished silver armor of a lowland warrior. His shield was decorated with the emblem of a blood-red snake. Because he stood a head taller than her, George felt a little threatened and intimidated.

Defiantly, she threw back her shoulders. She met the challenge of his leering stare. Whether she was dealing with a truculent caco or a visiting warrior, she knew the secret to remaining in control was with a display of confidence.

Of course, it didn't help that she was near-naked.

Save for the leather thong she wore whilst working in the catacombs, George was unclothed. Any other type of garment could have likely given away her presence to the vicious oriental dragons. They would have heard the rustle of hessian skirts on her thighs. They would have smelled the feral memories of animal stink on full leathers or protective furs.

Hostlers were used to seeing George's bare-breasted presence on the island. When she was escaping the catacombs she looked no more undressed than the temple prostitutes. But she was aware that there were circumstances when her state of near-nudity could sometimes send out the wrong message to the island's occasional visitors.

And this was clearly one of those circumstances.

"How enchanting," the stranger breathed. He stepped closer

and cupped her right breast with his left hand. His fingers were warm against her cool flesh. His thumb absently stroked the nipple.

She was jolted by a sting of unwanted pleasure.

As the treacherous bead of flesh grew stiff she slapped his hand away.

He looked hurt. His eyes flared. There was a curl to his upper lip that turned his appearance from attractive to cruel. She noticed the narrowing of his brow.

"Vortigern?" she asked, raising an eyebrow. It was the name the hostler had used in the easternmost catacomb. "Is that who you are?"

He looked perplexed by the informality of her address.

If he was Thane Vortigern of Merioneth then the rules of cordiality dictated that she should address him with the full honorifics of his status. He was titled gentry and she was only a lowly dragonmeister. But George was still angry at having witnessed the unnecessary death of the apprentice hostler. And she strongly suspected that Vortigern was responsible for the tragedy.

"Thane Vortigern of Merioneth," he corrected.

"Are you the shit-for-brains that sent a hostler down to summon me from my duties in the catacombs?"

Vortigern's lips thinned. He looked as though he had been slapped.

"I am Thane Vortigern of Merioneth," he told her. "I sent your hostler down to summon you from your duties, dragonmeister. But you're being visited by a nobleman and his attendant retinue. I think that the civilities of ceremony and greeting are a little more important than counting livestock and sweeping dung."

She bit back the response she wanted to make. The apprentice hostler's life had been far more important than any demonstration of ceremony. But a gnawing sense of danger tingled at the back of her neck. Having worked with dragons long enough to have developed the gift of second sight, she trusted such instincts.

"What business do you have here, Vortigern?" she asked coldly.

He extended a hand.

It was the same hand that had stroked her breast.

"I have been sent by your laird, Caleb the wolf slayer. He has granted permission for me to visit here and oversee an exchange of treasures." Vortigern paused. His eyes sparkled. "Aboard my ship I hold *Y Ddraig Goch*, the red dragon."

George muttered a squeak of delight. She strained to look past Vortigern's shoulder in the hope she could see down to the harbor and catch a glimpse of his ship.

"The red dragon?" she breathed. "The Welsh dragon?"

Without thinking, she took hold of his hand.

The moment's prophecy flashed at the back of her eyes.

Vortigern had killed Caleb the wolf slayer. She could see the lowland warrior decapitating her laird with a single stroke from a steel broadsword. Vortigern's men had pillaged Roxburghshire. All that remained were smoldering huts and a handful of bewildered womenfolk and children. In her mind's eye she could see the charred buildings with smoke spiraling up from their remnants. And now Vortigern was here to inveigle his way past the wyvern and plunder the treasures from Caleb's fiefdom.

Her heartbeat quickened.

She could sense that Vortigern had said something but she had no idea what. It struck her that she needed to keep her newfound knowledge from the warrior. If Vortigern learned that she knew he had murdered Caleb and destroyed the fiefdom, he would not bother with the pretense of cordiality. And, George knew, it was only a pretense of cordiality that would allow her to survive this encounter.

"*Y Ddraig Goch*," she said carefully. She forced herself to smile for him. "That is the Welsh dragon, isn't it? The red dragon?"

"The very same," Vortigern smiled. "It's a gift from my people to Caleb. He said you would be able to make better use of it here."

"It's a very generous gift," George told him. "Thane Vortigern of Merioneth is clearly a man of immeasurable generosity."

For a moment she thought his frown was skeptical. She wondered if she had overdone the praise for his generosity and if he knew that she suspected his treachery. Then the expression of suspicion had disappeared. He was smiling at her bared breasts again with lecherous approval.

"I'm not a man of immeasurable generosity," he admitted. "In return for the gift of *Y Ddraig Goch*, your laird said I could expect two things."

"Two things?" George raised an eyebrow. She still held Vortigern's hand and noticed that it grew warm in hers. The sensation was pleasant. Disquietingly arousing. "What might those two things be?" she asked.

"Caleb said my men could retrieve gold to the weight of *Y Ddraig Goch* to fill my ship's hold."

George nodded.

There was no way the wyvern would allow Vortigern to plunder the vaults of the treasury and he clearly knew as much. But, if George granted him and his retinue permission to take gifts, the lowland warrior would be able to steal whatever he pleased. Knowing that she had to play this carefully if she wanted to survive the encounter, George asked, "What is the other thing that Caleb promised you?"

Vortigern stared poignantly at her bare breasts.

"He promised your hospitality."

The words hung between them like a challenge.

"The pleasure of bestowing that gift will be all mine," she told him.

Stepping closer to the thane, pressing her nearly naked body against him, she stood on toes to get her mouth close to his. The polished silver of his armor was cool against her bare body. Yet, when she shivered, she knew the response was coming from arousal rather than cold.

Being dragonmeister of Gatekeeper Island was a lonely existence. Aside from the annual visit from Caleb, there was no one with whom she could have a relationship. The apprentice hostlers were young boys—unable to satisfy the needs and demands of a woman's body. The temple prostitutes made for interesting distractions, but the experiences they provided were more spiritual than physical. And there were times when George yearned for something that was purely physical.

Vortigern, male, powerful and domineering, offered the prospect of something that was physically satisfying.

His hand had returned to her breast. As they kissed she felt his tongue slide serpent-like into her mouth. She raised one leg, smoothing her thigh against his hip and urging herself close to him as she savored his arousal.

The thrust of his manliness jutted from the crotch of his pants.

"Thane Vortigern," she murmured. Her voice had fallen to a husky whisper. "It feels like you're ready to welcome my hospitality."

"You're comfortable with us fucking in a temple?"

She stroked the bulge of his excitement through his pants,

enjoying the heat that radiated from him. He sounded doubtful about the prospect of sex in a temple but she supposed some of the lowland religions had strange attitudes about acceptable communion in plain view of the deities. She knew there were some churches that condemned sex as immoral, and others that deemed ecumenical orgies a necessity for proper worship.

Her personal belief was that sex was a gift from the gods. It didn't matter where it took place so long as the experience was enjoyed by everyone involved.

"Follow me to the altar," she insisted. She led him by the hand. "We'll be more comfortable there."

He unbuckled the harness that held his chest armor in place and then removed his hauberk. Beneath she saw his flesh was clean-shaven and glossy with manly perspiration. The sight made her inner muscles clench with greedy sexual hunger. When he removed his helmet and brushed a hand through his sweat-moistened curls, her need for him intensified.

He glanced up toward the golden architecture.

The walls were lined with stone dragons. The altar was guarded by two wyvern who stepped aside as George led Vortigern past them.

"I've never fucked in a temple before," he grunted.

She pushed him onto the altar and then tugged the pants from his legs. Exposed, his length was as formidable as she had hoped it would be. He possessed a broadsword of an erection that was long and thick and looked like it would be a fearsome weapon for the battle she intended.

Unable to resist the impulse, George leaned close to him and drew her tongue against his exposed skin. He tasted of salt and desire. The smell of him filled her nostrils with animal hunger.

"*Rhyfeddol*," he gasped.

She chuckled. She didn't know the word but she could guess

it was a term of approval. Placing her mouth around him she sucked on his swollen end for a moment until his eyes were wide and his grin was broad.

Then she climbed on top of him.

It was a slow journey. She made sure her bare breasts caressed his body as she moved. He had clearly been admiring them when she appeared from the catacombs. She suspected that he would enjoy having them stroke against his bare skin.

But she could see that he was also interested in her nether regions.

Tugging the crotch of her thong to one side she exposed the bare lips for him and moved closer to straddling his manliness.

"*Prydferth*," he said, reaching out to touch her.

His fingers fell into the crease of her need-oily skin. One broad digit disappeared into her warmth. Another slipped beside it, stretching her wide. A fat thumb stroked against the nub of flesh that she considered the root of all sensation.

Her breath quickened.

She regarded Vortigern with new esteem. The explosion of sensation he inspired was more profound than anything she had enjoyed with any man previously.

She reached for the base of his length and clutched him tight. His fingers sparked bolts of delicious magic from the lips of her sex. She had expected their union would be perfunctory—a civic formality of dominance and acquiescence. But it seemed that Vortigern was one of those rare men who believed in the benefits of shared pleasure. Unable to resist the unspoken invitation of his lips, she pressed her mouth over his and kissed.

Slowly, they worked their bodies together.

She held his length and guided it toward the sopping need of her sex.

His fingers stretched her lightly, preparing her for his broad

girth. And, when he finally entered her, they both sighed heavily
with the satisfaction of bliss. Vortigern allowed her to sit adrift
his length as he toyed with the swell of one breast. His finger
and thumb squeezed and rolled at an acutely responsive nipple.

"Dragonmeister," he sighed. "You should give up your position here. You should come and live with me in the lowlands.
You could care for my estates. I could re-home your livestock in
my catacombs. And we could play like this whenever it suited
your desires."

"Sex talk," she laughed softly. She knew a man would say
whatever he believed a woman wanted to hear whilst she was
straddling him.

Vortigern shook his head.

He continued to tease her nipple with one hand. His other
hand slipped to her rump. His fingers smoothed over her rear
and slipped saucily close to the union of their bodies. She could
feel the syrupy lips of her sex bristling to the light caress of his
touch.

"It's a serious invitation," he promised.

She was pleased to hear that his breath was ragged with
passion. Despite the import of his words, the pleasure she
inspired was having an obvious effect. It was a testament to her
skills in the womanly art of lovemaking that she was able to
distract a thane from his purpose.

"Rescind your loyalty to Caleb," he suggested. "Pledge fealty
to Merioneth and I'll install you as the fiefdom's dragonmeister."

George raised and lowered her hips. Sliding her sex along his
length took her close to the impending eruption. She caught a
breath and held it as the waves of excitement flooded through
her flesh.

And she tried not to be tempted by the offer he presented.

The gift of second-sight was showing her the future he

promised. If she did as Vortigern asked she would be installed in the scenic splendor of a lowland country estate. There would be catacombs for her to patrol and countless weyrs of wyvern, víbria and *Y Ddraig Goch*. She would spend her days with dragons and her nights with Vortigern. The sun's pleasures would only be outshone by the intensity of the night's passions.

All it would take was for her to renege on the loyalty she had once pledged to a man who had been her lover and was now dead.

A tear trailed down her cheek.

The ripple of pleasure flooded through her body. She bit back a scream, knowing the gods of the temple did not approve of such demonstrations of satisfaction. Vortigern's length erupted inside her. The copious rush of his molten seed flooded her womb.

Another surge of raw delight rushed through her flesh. This time, uncaring as to whether or not the gods approved, George screamed.

Trembling, she peeled herself away from Vortigern. She gave his spent length a kiss of gratitude. He tasted of their mingled pleasures. It was a flavor she savored as she licked her lips. And she knew she had already made her decision in response to his invitation.

It was an easy decision to make.

"There is the temple doorway to the fiefdom treasures of Caleb the wolf slayer," she said, pointing. "Take your retinue with you to collect your gold," she added quickly. "Carry as much as you can. Break your men's backs with the weight of the gold they carry because the wyvern will only allow safe passage the once."

Vortigern nodded as he dressed. First he donned his pants.

Then his boots. Then the hauberk and finally his armor.

"Your honesty is appreciated," he admitted. "And my offer to you is an honest one. If you pledge fealty to Merioneth, you can reside as dragonmeister in my fiefdom. Your skills would be appreciated and well-rewarded."

And I would be whoring my skills to the man who slew my lover and the laird who trusted me with the safekeeping of his dragons, she thought bitterly. Aloud, she asked, "May I consider the generosity of your offer whilst you're retrieving your gold?"

His retinue approached. They held torches dripping with the burning-tar.

"Consider the offer and know I'll stay true to my word." He strode to the doorway she had indicated. It was barred by a pair of wyvern.

George gestured for the wyvern to stand down.

Obedient, the beasts relented from their stiff posture.

His retinue started toward the doorway but Vortigern stopped them. He fixed her with a warning finger. "I get the impression you've lied to me."

She shook her head.

"We've lain together, Thane Vortigern of Merioneth. You'd know if I'd lied to you. I can place my hand on my heart and say I haven't lied to you once."

He considered this and then seemed appeased. Brushing her cheek with an apologetic kiss he motioned for his retinue to continue. A true leader, he snatched a torch of burning-tar and led the way.

George watched him hasten into the shadows.

A sad smile played on her lips. She hadn't lied to him once. She had lied to him at least three times.

She had lied when she said the wyverns would only allow safe passage once. That had simply been a ruse to ensure that

Vortigern and his entire retinue followed her instructions and went through the doorway.

She had lied when she said she would consider his offer. Her loyalty would always be to Caleb the wolf slayer, even though the laird was now dead and his fiefdom destroyed.

But, most importantly for Vortigern, she had lied by sending him to retrieve treasure through that particular doorway. There was no treasure in the easternmost catacombs where he was now headed. In the easternmost catacombs there was only the mortal danger of the orientals. It was a mortal danger that, she knew, neither Vortigern nor his retinue would survive.

FLESH AND STONE

Sacchi Green

A scarlet-crested helmet shadowed the face above me. I cast my eyes downward, willing my body to the stillness of any inanimate work of art.

"What price for this one?" The voice was low, husky—and female. Hope rippled across my skin. Even shackled in the slave market, I had heard of the woman champion. The capital hummed with tales of her that could not possibly be true.

The trader stumbled over his recitation of my virtues. "A...a rare pearl, Lady, from the house of the late epicure Mendelas. Young, beautiful, trained in all the arts of pleasure, skilled enough to satisfy any...any desires, adaptable to any taste."

I dared a quick glance and saw her amusement. His desperate attempt to avoid saying "any man's desires" had not been lost on her.

"Girl."

I raised my eyes again, looking into hers deeply enough to sense some hint of her mood.

"Can you cook?"

"Only simply, Lady."

"Can you mend cloth and leather?"

"I was taught as a child, Lady, before..." The slaver's grip tightened. I hoped he would recall that bruises lowered my value. "Yes, Lady. I was raised in the horse tribes."

"Then you know something of handling horses, as well."

The trader sidled in front of me. "If your eminence wishes a mere maidservant, I have others less costly."

"Than this 'rare pearl'?" Impatience edged her voice. "What price for her?"

Rattled, he named a sum scarcely larger than he expected. She disdained to haggle. I let myself breathe again. This was a mistress I would follow anywhere, do anything, be anything, she desired. I did not read in her eyes the sort of interest he assumed, but in time...who could tell? The trader had not over-stated my skills.

"Have you belongings?" A slave could not possess anything, but a craftsman's tools might be assumed to be included in the bargain. My "tools" were bits of exotic clothing and jars of herbs and unguents and, tucked beneath them, a few more arcane objects rolled in a length of embroidered silk.

I hid my joy and followed my new mistress meekly. The woman champion! A princess, some said, from a mountain kingdom to the north. A sorceress who could turn men to stone. I neither believed nor cared. All that mattered was that she was strong and skilled and brave, nothing like those coarse women brought into the Emperor's games as titillation for a jaded court.

She swung me up easily onto her horse and mounted behind me. I clutched my bag and concentrated on balancing, since my narrow skirt kept me from riding astride. I longed to lean against her bound breasts, to tune myself by touch to the resonance of her thoughts and desires, but tried instead to show that I had not lied about my ability to sit a horse.

"Have you a name, girl?" The cool voice made me tremble.

"My master called me Gazelle."

"What did your mother call you?"

"Shebbah, Mistress." Mistress. The word was full and sweet in my mouth.

"Well, Shebbah, I will be in disgrace when we get home. You are not quite what I had in mind, but no doubt something can be arranged."

I did lean against her then, searching through her body toward her emotions. Did she not intend to keep me? Why then purchase me? But her mind was bound as tightly as her breasts.

She swung me down before a modest house. An aging man-at-arms limped out to take the horse; he frowned, but the lady forestalled him. "I know, Rafen. Hecanthe will give me a tongue-flogging. The sooner you stable the horse, the less of it you'll miss."

The room seemed dim after bright daylight. A lamp beside a low couch lit the sharp features of the woman lying there. Another presence loomed in the shadows, and I would have turned that way if her snapping black eyes had not gripped me.

"What's this?" She knew already exactly what I was. "You go for a strong wench to cook and clean, and come back with this...this little yellow-haired 'bird of paradise'?"

It was clear enough who ruled this household. I knelt and looked full into her keen old eyes, hiding nothing of myself. "I am stronger than I look, Grandmother, and my skills are not only those of the harem."

"Indeed." She too could reach out with her mind, and recognized what she found. "You might do, after all." Then, more loudly and a bit harshly, "Did you think to distract the Emperor,

Domande, with this little sweetmeat?"

"If only it were that easy." My lady's voice was weary. "The Emperor desires my humiliation, not my flesh. Even *his* taste is more refined than that!" The note of buried pain spoke more than she herself knew. "Offering a more appealing bedmate would be pointless. He has ordered me to attend him tomorrow night. I will slay him if I go. Therefore, I must leave."

She had shed the cloak and the helmet with its champion's crest. Her tunic and clinging hose displayed the grace of a lioness; when she stretched and ran fingers through her short hair, I could not believe that anyone, of any sex, would fail to take pleasure in the touch of that smooth, taut body.

Bronze curls clung damply above amber-green eyes. Her finely sculpted face could have topped the statue of a young god or, softened by flowing hair, a seductive goddess.

"What then?" Hecanthe asked sharply. "A gift to placate *that* one, since you imagine you have wronged him?" Her eyes flicked toward the shadows. "If ever he returns to matters of the flesh!"

A presence seemed to advance, but there had been, could be, no movement. The man was made all of gray stone. No statue, no creation of any carver, but a naked, crouching figure of muscle and bone frozen in the moment of rising from a fall.

I looked wildly from Lady Domande to the old woman. Whose power had wrought this curse? Hecanthe smiled grimly, but her mistress forgot us both as she contemplated the stone face.

"It is the young man's own doing," the old woman assured me, "brought on by the Emperor's determination to humiliate Domande. She blames herself, out of mere foolishness."

"I could have let him win." My lady's gaze did not shift. "For Nyal the stake was freedom. For me the prize was only his servitude, which he might have known I would refuse. We had often talked, in the training fields, of our far-off homes; I knew how he burned for his liberty."

"You never in your life 'let' someone win," the old woman said caustically.

"He should have won! He is stronger, with skills close enough to my own; there was a moment when he had me, and loosed his grip for fear, I think, of hurting me, and I took advantage of the lapse. It was ill-done."

"It was ill-done to let the Emperor goad you into wrestling naked!"

Lady Domande shrugged dismissively. "If I claimed right to compete with men on equal terms I could not refuse the match. Such were known in ancient times. And I expected Nyal to win, to gain the freedom the Emperor dangled before him. I was prepared to be beaten—but when it came to the point I couldn't just *let* it happen!"

"Oh, gods forbid!" The old woman's voice was brittle with irony. "Girl! You, girl!"

I struggled to attend her, my mind still pulsing with images of those two magnificent bodies coupled in naked combat.

"Is it too much to hope that you might teach our lady something of a woman's proper weapons? And what may be won with them?"

"One may always hope," I answered meekly. Lady Domande swung around toward us.

"Shebbah will have little chance for such lessons. I leave before daybreak, and she stays to care for you, Hecanthe."

"No, my Lady, she goes with you. Leave Rafen to care for me until my hip mends. Surely you would not part us after all these years!" Mockery lit her eyes as the old man limped in from the stable yard. "Your delicate flower will, I think, do well enough for you. Girl!" Her hand flashed upward with a glint of steel.

I caught the spinning dagger in the air. So long ago... But the reflexes were still there. My fingers' dexterity and strength had only increased in six years of plucking harp strings and drawing melodies of sensuality from human flesh.

"What can you do with that toy, girl?"

"I can gut fish, fowl, or man; chop meat, bring down a hare, or carve secrets slowly out of an enemy." I fell to my knees before my lady. "I can serve and protect to the last flicker of my life, if you will accept my loyalty. Please, Mistress, take me with you!"

"Well." She was disconcerted at such a display of obeisance. "More to the point, perhaps, is whether you and I together can lift that stubborn lump of stone. I will not leave him here for the Emperor's mages to probe, however much he may deserve it."

She stood surveying the rigid figure. "I would not have kept him slave!" Her voice was low and rough with pain. "What did he think I would require, that being stone seemed less terrible?"

She put her hands on his broad shoulders and gestured with her head toward his loins. "You grasp him there below. A pretty little thing like you may lure him out of his sulking!" The joke was a bitter one.

As I touched the cool, hard curve of his buttocks I felt something more than stone. He was aware. Aware, at least, of my mistress; an unmistakable current flowed between them.

He was not truly as heavy as stone. We lifted him without much difficulty, though he was broader and slightly taller than she. I noted that before he had become stone one part of him had already hardened in the flesh, and most impressively.

Wrestling in the public glare of the arena with my gloriously naked mistress—could embarrassment transform a man into stone? I was tempted to try whether skillful stroking could turn that great stone cock back to flesh, but the undercurrents in my lady's emotions deterred me.

I sighed. My dreams of a mistress demanding the pleasures I could give, her strong body pressing mine into breathless submission, needed some adjustment. Matters promised to be more complex than that.

We departed, as she had said, before dawn, Nyal wrapped and bundled onto the packhorse. We bound other gear around him to obscure his form, an unwieldy arrangement at best.

"If there is pursuit, you must leave him behind. Shebbah, I charge you to be sure of that." Hecanthe transferred to me her scolding authority.

"If there is pursuit, it will be your fault for not persuading the Emperor's minions that I keep to my rooms with a fever."

"They will assume that your 'fever' is fueled by dalliance with your new little love slave," Hecanthe said wickedly. "The tale of your purchase will both infuriate and inflame the Emperor. Was that what you had in mind?"

A flush rose from my lady's smooth, strong throat to her face as she glanced not at me but at the laden packhorse. I sighed again.

"Go on now," the old woman said. "I know why Shebbah caught your eye. She looks very like the portrait of your mother."

"Yes…" My lady considered, as though she had not really seen me before. "You may be right. She is the beauty I should have been."

I stifled a moan of anguish. My fantasies retreated further. Her mother! My horse pranced nervously and I concentrated on keeping my seat.

We traveled for more than a week at a pace painful after six years of soft living. Even my mistress showed strain, more from weariness of thought than of body. She was wary of pursuit, and, after we had left the well-traveled highways, not always sure of our route.

"Have you been to this place we seek, Mistress?" She had come to treat me more as companion than slave, but her deeper emotions remained as closed to me as though she too had been stone.

"I was conceived there, if that counts." Her smile was wry. "Perhaps it does. I have a growing sense that this is the right valley at last, and the right river. Just around the bend where the forest comes close to the water we may find our refuge."

And so we did, though "refuge" was too grand a word. Even so long ago as my lady's conception this hunting lodge must have been a ruin.

The main hall had scarcely enough roof to shelter the horses. Only the kitchen offered any hope of habitability. I worked to clean and sweep and unpack our meager supplies while my mistress set off with bow and quiver.

There was, at least, a store of dry wood, and the chimney was not too plugged to draw. The place had once been well furnished; I scoured a huge kettle and a copper bathing tub and had water heating when my lady returned with a brace of hares.

The room had warmed by the time our meal was done, its unaccustomed comfort as mellowing as wine. "What do you think, Shebbah, should we unbind our companion?"

The question was rhetorical. She would not be distracted.

"Will we be here long, my Lady? You spoke of a messenger."

"It could be forever. I sent to discover whether...whether my father the King," she gave a grim half-smile, "would grant me asylum from the Emperor."

"Surely..."

"Nothing is sure, except that my father the General will try to persuade the King." Her greenish eyes glinted with bitter humor. "Besides devotion to the kingdom, they share a weakness for delicate blonde women. Like you. Like my mother. If I had grown to look like her... But she died while I was a babe, and even in his grief the King could not be blind to how little I resembled him. He did not cast me out, merely turned his back."

"And the General?"

"He took pity, when I grew tall and awkward, and trained me as he would a son. He is proud of me, I think, but he will be angered that I did not handle the Emperor more adroitly."

She was drooping now with weariness and painful memories. I could not bear to see that proud head bowed in sorrow.

"Come, Mistress, I will unbind your stone gladiator, and then you must let me unbind you, and bathe you, and ease you."

"You must be as tired as I, Shebbah."

"Please, Mistress, your ease will be my ease." This was truer than she knew. Longings suppressed by hard travel were rising in me now. If only she had inherited her sire's weakness for small blonde women!

I sensed tremors of longing in her, too, as I unwound Nyal's wrappings. The heat of her gaze brushed his cold form; I marveled that he did not melt under it.

She watched him broodingly while I filled the tub, sprinkled in some herbs from my precious silk-wrapped store, inhaled the sensuous musk, and felt that even stone might be stirred by such a mist.

"Come now, Lady, let me slip off your tunic." She raised unresisting arms. "And unbind your breasts... Ah, Mistress, how can you be cruel to such beautiful flesh?" I stroked the creases under her arms, then, very lightly, the silky curves of breasts freed at last from confinement. Her nipples tautened. So did mine.

"Legend says that women warriors once severed them, the

better to wield their weapons. At least I have stopped short of that."

"I am very glad," I murmured, drawing her toward the bath. I would make her very glad, as well.

She pulled off her hose before the fire. I ached to do it for her.

Her body, golden in the firelight, was so beautiful I could scarcely breathe. A pulsing emanated from the stone figure in the corner; he too was aware, and aroused. How long would he hold his rigid form, or was it even under his control?

"What herbs are these?" She bent over the tub, breathing in the vapors. The lines of smoothly muscled legs flared into taut, rounded buttocks, firm as any athlete's but just full enough to be unmistakably a woman's.

"A blend, my Lady, with special soothing powers." I slipped out of my own clothes.

"Soothing?" She sounded doubtful, but stepped in, and sat with bent knees as I poured more water and watched it sheet over her strong shoulders and swirl around the curves of her lovely breasts. The herbs were, in fact, more stimulant than relaxant, and I too felt their effect, but it hardly needed that to make my own breasts swell and a sweet ache build in my loins.

I closed my eyes and struggled to focus on my art and my role. To give pleasure, to seek out my mistress's longings and fulfill them, to show her unimagined joys; to be slave to her desires, even those she scarcely knew herself.

"Let me massage your neck, Mistress, and your back, to rub away the tension." She leaned forward compliantly. Short bronze curls wrapped about my fingers as I kneaded the stress out of nape and scalp. My hands moved over shoulders and upper back, and as my fingers dug into the firm muscles there I could feel the heavy pull of her breasts against the skin.

"Does that ease you, Mistress?"

"Mmm." But I knew already. At last she had opened to that sensual link that was my greatest skill, and I felt within her the stirrings of her pleasure.

I reached farther down, my breasts pressed against her wet flesh, and she arched under the pressure of my hands on her lower back. Then gently, slowly, I stroked around her sides to her belly and below until my fingers tangled gently in dark-honey curls.

"Do you call this easing?" Her voice vibrated through her body into mine, but there was no anger in it.

"The wilder the journey, the greater the ease at the end," I murmured. "If I may just show you the way, Mistress..."

She tensed, then grasped my arm and drew me around to face her. "Do you think me so untouched, Shebbah?"

I met her challenging gaze and said nothing. After a moment she looked away. "I was as curious as any other, but the 'journey' was always brief and disappointing. I found better use for my body in feats of arms."

"Let me show you, Mistress, how much more it can be."

She leaned back, and now her eyes were deep amber pools reflecting the fire. "Why not? Why should I not know what it is to be a woman?" She let one glance stray toward the stone figure. I could sense its mounting tension. Soon there would come a shattering, or eruption; but not, I hoped, too soon.

"Not just any woman." I slipped into the water and knelt astride her thighs. "A transcendently beautiful woman, indescribably desirable. Yes, it is true," as she started to shake her head, "and you must feel your own beauty to let your pleasure flow."

It was all I could do to keep from rubbing my throbbing ache against her wet thighs; only my training kept my focus on her sensations, not my own. I longed to kiss her full lips, but her head was tilted back; I knew she was open not to intimacy but to pure erotic stimulation. Even so, the mind is the body's most sensuous organ.

"Such beautiful breasts." I cupped and gently pressed them and flicked my thumbs across the nipples. "So swollen with pleasure, aching for more, and more."

She thrust against my hands, head still back, eyes closed, breath fast and uneven. I kept my touch light, tantalizing, making her reach for it.

"Watch, Mistress, see what your body does. See how full and round, how hard and pointed, how straining toward my touch. Feel the pull, feel what you need…" I licked with feather-light tongue one nipple and then the other, again and again, as her hands clenched on the copper rim and shuddering sighs tore from her throat. At last, when it could not be borne an instant longer, she grasped my head and forced my mouth hard onto her flesh. I sucked and bit at one nipple and then the other until her pleasure verged closely on pain.

I caught her hand and slid it down her belly and below, into the water, then gently pushed her fingers aside and stroked her myself, as lightly, or as firmly, as her mounting need demanded.

"And here, lower, deeper, so very deep, pulsing." My finger slid between her nether lips and gently into her clinging heat. I thought of raising her hips out of the water so that my tongue could probe her sweetness, but she was arching and thrusting against my hand with such hunger that I dared not withdraw it.

My mind melded into the pleasure-core of hers, touching her in the very ways and places that most filled and drove her need. I felt a flood of power greater than desire, as the strong body that could break me without effort writhed in unspoken pleading for what I could give. I pressed my thumb against her nub and slipped in another finger, and another, moving them in the slippery depths.

"So beautiful a body," I breathed against her mouth, leaning my breasts into hers. "Strong, and sweet, and surging with pleasure." So tuned was I now to her sensations that I too rode the wave, gripping her wet thighs with mine as she arched her hips out of the bath in her driving need to be probed ever deeper and harder. If hands were not enough there were other means in my silk-wrapped roll of "tools," but it seemed impossible to move away and reach for them.

Then her ragged moans resolved into a full-throated cry, and my own sobs of release began to rise, and the deeper roar that swept over us seemed only a part of the ecstatic whole—until our world crashed sideways, water swirled, metal clanged on wood, and we spilled out onto the floor.

Nyal loomed over us, all fury and solid flesh. Pain twisted his face even as lust engorged his loins.

"You!" he bellowed at Domande. "You..." Words were not enough to bear his rage. He dragged her upright. She was too dazed (I dared not hope too wise) to resist.

I was not so dazed as to forget my little dagger, but what surged between these two they must resolve alone. Even when he slammed her against the wall I made no move to stop him.

Nor did she. He bound her wrists above her head with her own belt, looping it tightly over an iron game hook so that her feet barely touched the floor. Still she hung unresisting. He shoved his body roughly against hers, and I began to throb anew at the thought of his hardness pressing into her belly, but she was silent and the only cry came from his own raw throat.

"You!" He gasped for words. "The ice princess, the unmoved, the untouchable. But not so untouchable after all!"

He wrenched away and turned his back to her. His gladiator's body shone with sweat and the swollen head of his shaft gleamed even slicker than the rest.

"Nyal!" At last she found a voice. "Now you are free! I am defeated, I do not hold you, you may do as you will!"

He should have turned to let her see in his face that he would never be free of her. But instead he lurched toward me and twisted his hand in my hair and forced me to my knees.

"Ease me, girl," he grated. He may have thought to punish me, but he had stabbed her deeper than he knew. I could not tell him what a fool he was; a slave's training runs too deeply. And what pressed against my face was too full and throbbing to refuse.

I took him into my mouth and teased his slippery tip with my tongue as I reached to stroke between his thighs, using all my skills at the game of stimulation and prolongation. He struck my hand away. "Just ease me, slut, quickly!"

He had been hard, after all, one way or another, for more than a fortnight. I brought him swiftly over the edge. His spending burst hot and metallic into my mouth and all the way down my throat.

The silence following his final gasp might have been seconds, or minutes, or hours. He slumped against the wall, head down. When finally I looked to my mistress she seemed at first immobile; but her long, smooth muscles were tensed, and I saw that she tested the strength of the wall-hook holding her.

I ran with my knife to cut her down, but her blazing eyes held me off. "Get away! And you," she spat at Nyal, "take your freedom while you may!" She began to arch her body in rhythmic convulsions. The wood around the hook started to splinter.

"Why so slow to run?" she taunted, panting from her exertion. "Hiding in stone again?" And indeed he seemed frozen, watching her strong, beautiful body strain at its bonds. "For her you are all eager flesh, but for me only stone! Such a Gorgon as I must be!"

"No!" He sounded strangled. "It is a curse in the blood! My grandsire had the skill to wield it as a defense, but I had not known it was in me until..."

"Until what?" she challenged. A final lurch brought the iron hook tearing from the wall, and Nyal ducked as it shot past just over his head. I darted forward to cut the belt still bound around my lady's wrists, but neither of them paid me any heed.

A slow smile lit Nyal's face. Only then, I think, did the last of the stone leave his system. "Until I was tormented past bearing by a rival and comrade who seemed untouched by the fire she lit in me."

"Did you think me so untouched?" Rage abruptly gone, she let the whisper of a smile curve her lips. "Try me."

Her wrestling stance would have horrified Hecanthe, who had wanted me to teach her "a woman's proper weapons," but the two gleaming bodies testing and striving against each other understood far better than I the erotic tension of strength on strength.

They began with classic wrestling moves, scarcely stirring for long moments as flesh strained against taut flesh. Nyal's shoulders were broader, but Domande's lithe dexterity countered his strength so that they were evenly matched.

He was instantly, magnificently aroused, despite his recent release. This might have given my lady the advantage, but her own tasting of her body's hungers had served only to increase them. She put her mouth to sweaty muscles straining to break her hold, brushed hard-swollen nipples against his heaving chest, then swiveled to clasp his probing shaft between tensed buttocks before a thrust of her hip sent him to his knees.

Any resemblance to formal wrestling crumbled. He grasped her hips and pressed his mouth into her belly, and she pushed his head downward toward the dark-honey curls between her thighs, and though my link to her was fading I knew by her gasps just where his tongue and hands caressed her.

When he pulled her off balance and pinned her shoulders to the floor she resisted only enough to savor the friction. His hardness stroked and probed her until she raised her hips for him to plunge in all the deeper, and gripped his thrusting buttocks with her long, strong legs.

Her moans grew rougher, more demanding. Suddenly, with a great heave, she flipped him to his back, covered his mouth with her own, then raised upright until she was riding him hard astride. His groans came between clenched teeth as he fought to hold on until at last her head went back and a cry of triumph tore from her throat.

My link was broken. The sight and sound of them made me wild with longing. I could not have told which of them I would rather hold, which I would rather be, but there was no one to ease me now. I did not know how to bear it. Slavery had never been such agony.

I retrieved my cloak and slipped out past the horses and into the night. With no clear goal I made my way along the overgrown road as quickly as moonlight would allow, mind and body in such turmoil that I nearly stumbled into a horse and rider coming toward me.

"Riette!" Eyes wide with shock stared down at me from a bearded face. I turned and ran. The deep voice rumbled again, cracking in pain, "Riette, come back!"

I burst into the lodge just ahead of him. "Mistress! Someone comes!"

Nyal leapt to his feet and grabbed my lady's sword, but she stayed him with a gesture. The giant figure looming in the doorway fixed his eyes on me as though I were a ghost, until the firelight revealed that mine was not quite the face in his dreams.

His great head bowed for a moment; then he shook off past sorrow and turned to my mistress.

"You are looking very fit, Domande." His tone was dry as he glanced from her naked flesh to Nyal's.

"Never better, Father." She grinned like an urchin, and his answering smile was a mirror of hers. His hair was a darker, grizzled version of her bronze curls, and his eyes beneath heavy brows glinted with the same green-amber flame.

He moved as though to embrace her but drew back and lowered himself to his knees. "Lady Domande." His tone was now measured and formal. "Your father the King is dead. The Council entreats you to return to lead your people."

Her face turned pale and set. "Do you think I would renounce my father the General?"

He rose wearily to his feet, leather armor creaking over massive shoulders. "No need of that. The people are not deceived, but they judge that your blood-claim through Queen Riette is sufficient. Your strength is needed to resist the encroachment of the Empire; backed, of course, by my strength and the loyalty of my troops."

"And mine." Nyal laid his arm across her shoulders; when she did not shake him off it tightened into an embrace. The General cocked an inquiring brow.

"Then so it shall be." Domande's face was serene with assurance and fulfillment. "Shebbah." She turned to me. I felt the General's weary eyes on me as well. "There are no slaves in my country, and there are none here. But it would be good of you to help the General to remove his armor and bathe away the dust of travel. Will you give him ease while Nyal and I go to view the river by moonlight?"

"I will, Lady." It was hard not to call her mistress.

As I took the older man's calloused hand it jerked, then tightened on mine, and the link took hold. I knew, now, who would give me ease, whose great strong body would press mine into submission, who would demand all I could give and fill me with all I desired.

Or almost all. I let one lingering glance caress Domande's smoothly muscled form as she went through the door, then turned my full heart and mind toward the master whose need was greatest.

SAINTS
AND HEROES

M. H. Crane

A genuine Singer-clan earthwitch!" Taking two steps for each of tall Borsa Eld's, the guide rubbed his hands together. "You could charge gold telling fortunes at the Sleeper's Temple tonight."

"I'm here to pray for guidance, not make money," said Borsa.

The guide looked at Borsa's worn clothing. "Consider it."

Borsa blinked at the noon sun pouring down into the narrow, banner-festooned street. He tugged the hood of his gray linen coat deeper over his face and tall, whisker-fringed ears. His pale gold beard, perfect for warmth in the cold south, felt sticky from the tropical heat.

A scream sounded from the maze of alleys.

"What was that?" Borsa couldn't track the sound through the hood.

"Someone celebrating early. The best courtesan houses are on this hill, and every wealthy merchant and noble is in Ajara City today."

"Market day?"

The guide laughed. "They await the Northwarden and his Lady Consort, the new Saint." He turned when he realized Borsa had stopped. "You didn't know about the Consorts' Progress?"

"Oh," said Borsa, feeling stupid. "I've been away in the glacier-lands. Consorts? I knew about the man, from twelve years ago."

"The Lord Consort never shows himself. Shy or not, he has to share now. The Northwarden's courted a Jade Coast princess for five years, and finally won her."

"What bargain did she drive, I wonder?"

"Whatever she wants. He's the Lord of Sorcery, awake and rutting again, after leaving us Sirrithani all alone for six thousand years. The richest man in the world, *and* immortal," said the guide. "And she's his latest ordained bride."

Borsa fought the urge to run for the nearest city gate. "So he'll visit the Sleeper's Temple. Lead me to Maker's fane, instead."

The guide edged away. "A place of ill repute."

"With so many crafters in Ajara, I thought she would be well loved."

"Ah," said the guide, visibly choosing words. "It's said that Maker abandoned her temple. Do you still wish to go?"

"More than ever," said Borsa, eyeing the banners and ribbons again. Red for weddings. Amber for the Sleeping Goddess who contained the world's inner fires. Green for the Northwarden, her emissary among mortals. And vivid night-sky blue for the lilies sacred to clever Biha-Arra, the Maker who crafted the Sirrithani race.

He saw one blue ribbon, fallen into an alley mouth, swirl in a fitful whirlwind. A stag-drawn wagon waited by a discreet trade entrance fifty paces down the alley. Three mercenaries stood guard. A fourth had opened the wagon's door and unfolded its wooden steps.

"What is down that way?"

"The Fountain of Roses," said the guide, urging Borsa out of sight. "I can show you cheaper courtesan houses."

Borsa looked back around the corner. Down the wagon stairs came a hard-faced woman in dark gray robes. She held a limp, barefoot child dressed in dark red and purple rags. Steel manacles glittered around the child's ankles.

"A youngling, sold to the flesh trade?"

"No child," said the guide, unable to pull Borsa back again. "A full-grown Dana. There's an Enclave of them in southern Ajara. They sell themselves sometimes to those craving, er, a little body." He trailed off as Borsa glared down at him.

"Doesn't look like a willing sale to me." Borsa knew of the Smallfolk, but he'd never seen one. He thought of why a Sirr man or woman would crave a short, fine-boned whore, and swallowed sour bile.

The victim's head lifted. Borsa saw a young man with honey-gold skin and a long brown braid. Seeing Borsa, the Dana-man shrieked: "Help me, by any gods you honor! I'm a traveler with Enclave safe passage papers! Help! Mmmph!" The duenna laid her hand over his nose and mouth, and he sagged witless.

The guide cursed as he ran, "You're on your own, Maker's witch!"

Borsa ducked back, praying silently: *Biha-Arra, since you brought me to this, a little help?*

The whirlwind kicked up thick dust at the alley mouth. Borsa lost the sound of coughing soldiers two streets away.

Half an hour and some wrong turns later, he rang a gold-washed bell hanging by a wrought-iron gate. Inside the court-yard, vivid green rosebushes and their scarlet flowers contrasted with the native teal and blue trees shading them. A fountain gurgled in a shallow red marble basin.

A Round-Ear girl swayed into view beyond the bars. Used to Sirrithani spans, Borsa thought her barely a century old. He remembered her folk died of old age before a hundred, and lowered his estimate to twenty. A shapely child in a tight, red silk dress. Gold-netted rubies lay at her throat, wrists and ankles. Her ears glimmered like pale pink shells under her dark braids. Her fingers and toes were tipped with small pink-white scales, not semi-retractable Sirrithani claws. To downplay her small irises and shock-pale sclera, the girl looked at Borsa through lowered eyelashes.

She tallied his worn clothing, boots and unkempt beard. "I'm sorry, my lord earthwitch. We're closed." She had no fangs, only squarish little white teeth.

"I am expected," Borsa said, not knowing what urge of his goddess's left his lips. "From Maker's fane."

"Ah," said the girl, opening the gate. "Welcome to the Fountain of Roses, my lord—"

"On Maker's errands, I have no name."

"A pity," the girl purred, but led him to a door hidden behind turquoise vines. Once out of the light, Borsa pushed up his hood. The girl's eyes widened at the sight of his: large-irised, blue as the Maker's lilies. "You have Singer-clan eyes, my lord earthwitch! How fair."

"On my grandmother's side." Borsa kept his voice low to match her hushed tone as they walked down a dimly lit spiral staircase. The red gems in her necklace pulsed with tiny fires at his every word.

"Are you here for the Progress?"

He weighed lies and chose a kind of truth. "My husband and wife are."

"Turn here. You married, and remained in your Order?"

"I had Maker's dispensation," said Borsa, playing along. "But my wife is more my husband's wife than mine. Oh, she would be the splendor of any family. Her gift with numbers and letters will put my husband's business to rights. She will give us strong and brilliant heirs."

"Yet you miss how it was." The stair ended in a door of silvery-blue gir-wood, expensive and strong. "I return to my post," she whispered close by his ear, her lithe tongue caressing his sensitive fringe. "Knock thrice, then once, and say you're from the fane."

Borsa wondered how deep his goddess would keep him mired in her new plots. He took a step backward and felt pain lash along his nerves. *That far*, he thought. Five years ago, he'd run from destiny and begged Biha to hide him. Of course, she'd ask a price.

When he knocked and repeated his errand through a tiny slot, he heard several bolts withdrawn from the other side.

"You took your time," said the tall, voluptuous Sirrithani woman dressed in the establishment's scarlet silks. She pulled him into a dry cellar smelling faintly of sex and incense. On the floor newly packed traveling gear and saddles hinted at a future journey. Getting a better look, she said, "You're not Aduano."

"I'm one of the Nameless." Borsa hoped he remembered his Order's signs and countersigns.

She didn't demand them. "I see no weapon but a staff."

"My will is my weapon," said Borsa. "Maker listens to me. Through her I can speak into the world's hot black heart where the Sleeper dreams. What is my task?"

She urged him toward another gir-wood door set in the other wall. "Our training in runecraft is limited. We needed an ally from Maker's Order as appalled at her Temple's decay as we are."

She turned the handle. Borsa heard a muffled scream.

There were a thousand poisons in the world. It was said Biha-Arra had invented most of them. Out of habit, Borsa still carried several of the less deadly in quartz vials and rubber spray bulbs inside his coat pockets. He uncapped one bulb as he followed the housemistress.

His Singer-clan nose smelled ink, herbs, grain vinegar, water spilled on dusty clay, a man's spent pleasure and a woman's honey-salt arousal.

The Dana-man, stripped and gagged, hung with his chest supported by an openwork gir-wood frame angled against a wall. His thighs were strapped to the frame, immobilizing his hips. His short, pointed ears, bare of Sirr whiskers, lifted through his loose brown hair. Cream-white semen dotted a shallow red stoneware basin in front of the prisoner. Herbed vinegar water waited in another basin on the floor between his legs. An older Sirrithani man in faded lily-blue robes held aside the Dana's hair. He painted runes on the Dana's back and legs with dark blue ink.

Borsa sprayed the housemistress full in the face. She slumped to the floor. The man looked up, eyes widening, his cry stopped unvoiced by the rest of the bulb. Both still breathed. Borsa barred the door again. He tied and gagged the two Sirr with the silken red ropes he found on the floor.

Easing the leather gag from the Dana-man's mouth, he said: "I heard you in the alley. I am Borsa Eld, a priest of Biha-Arra, among other things. I've come to free you. Thirsty? Here is clean water." He tipped his blue porcelain traveling flask to the Dana's chapped lips.

"I thought you a drug dream," whispered the Dana-man.

"Thank Kemurra's Ghost you aren't. I am Lai Kendoshil."

"Do you know what they were doing?"

"Preparing me for that perverted old man up at the Blue Temple," said Lai. "He hungers for children. He can't have them. So he buys Dana slaves."

Borsa looked over the runes. The rebel priest had copied from a gir-paper grimoire bound in indigo blue leather. The spell on the page nauseated him. "Did they say what they were painting on you?"

"Lust-spells, to make me pliant," hissed the Dana.

"They lied. We caught them before they finished the spell, but I can't wash it off."

"What does it really do?"

Borsa's fingers trailed along Lai's narrow spine, following the spell. "You're sealed as a sacrifice to one of the worst aspects of the Sleeping Goddess: Deathgold, who sleeps and wakes within volcanoes. This could destroy Ajara City." And though not the Northwarden, Borsa thought, certainly his new wife and countless other mortals!

"Good," said Lai. "I curse this country, its Queen and its priests. I curse the Northwarden for shunning my people as criminals. I may be the priest of a dead goddess, but in her name I curse this whole brutal *world*."

"I'd drink to that, some days," said Borsa. "But there are innocents among every race. Your folk are so rare that only a few Sirr have ever seen you. You should be as protected as the Round-Ears." When he said it, he felt Biha-Arra's attention sharpen within his mind. Her goal?

"As whores? Toys? Pets?" snarled Lai, his slim body wrenching at his bonds. "Twelve thousand years past, my people came here in ships faring between the stars. Look at us now."

"The ink won't vanish until the spell is set," said Borsa. "If

I freed you now, you'd spend the rest of your life with a half-finished prayer to Deathgold written on your back. If anyone touched you in love or lust, the ground under your feet would become a volcanic pit."

"Then kill me! If you free me to die later, Borsa Eld, I'll pick the biggest Sirrithani city I can find, and sell myself to some fool at its very center—"

"I can change the spell." Borsa tapped the partial runes at the small of Lai's back. "Here. Seal you to Biha-Arra, not Deathgold. Maker is a gentler mistress. You'd be alive."

"Perhaps I want to die," said the Dana-man fiercely.

Borsa wrapped his big hand over the back of Lai's neck. "I cannot leave you thus. You will be dead, or Biha's. Choose."

He knew Lai's choice when the Dana's body relaxed. "Change the spell. I will live. Whatever life an exiled exile can have."

Borsa traced the remaining runes of the spell. When he was silent too long, Lai asked, "What now?"

"It's set and triggered by rape. They meant to take away your memory so you couldn't warn the High Priest. When he claimed you, the spell would wake."

Lai laughed bitterly. "Finish the spell and do what you must. My purity was sworn to Kemurra's Ghost. They've robbed me of what little worth I had." His narrow buttocks wriggled, his thigh-length hair twitching aside to reveal the red glazed porcelain plug filling his channel. "They—opened me with some drugged oil. I fought, but the woman was very skilled."

"So? That was rape, not love. You are not to blame. Now don't move."

The blue-black ink was mixed, the Singers' fur brush waiting for another dip in the ink pot. Borsa finished the new invocation in three passes of flowing calligraphy. Softened, the spell no longer triggered from pain and domination, but only through willing pleasure. Even years away from his Order, Borsa's letters were finer than the rebel's. The ink dried almost instantly, sinking into Lai's golden skin.

"Finished," said Borsa, unlatching restraints and helping the Dana off the frame.

Gritting his flat little teeth, Lai said, "It's not finished. I don't know how you're getting us away, but I can't go outside in skin and blue scribbles." He looked up at Borsa clearly for the first time, gray eyes widening in real fear. Borsa stood nearly three feet taller than the Dana-man. Lai stumbled over to another pile of pillows in the corner and got down on his hands and knees. "I won't fight you," he snarled.

"Only your pleasure will set it now."

Lai dropped his forehead on the pillows. "That's a problem."

"You've never enjoyed yourself before?" Borsa asked, sitting beside him. He knotted Lai's silky hair up, twisting it out of the way.

"I was one of Kemurra's priests. We used drugs to keep such urges away unless the elders' councils chose us to breed. And I'm sterile," Lai admitted. "Will you, ah, find more of that oil? Your sex must be very large," he finished in a lost tone.

Borsa found the drugged lubricant. As befitting a quality brothel, it was fresh and potent. No wonder the Dana-man had succumbed! The oil tingled on Borsa's fingers. He kept his voice low and calm as he poured the oil along Lai's back and cleft. "Never that! Lai, I'm a married man, a moral one, and you're far too small. But I can pleasure you better than the housemistress in ways that won't hurt you. Just relax. Push outward against the plug."

Lai whimpered as the ridged plug came out and gasped when Borsa immediately replaced it with an oiled index finger. Borsa reached under Lai's belly, loosely grasping the Dana-man's phallus and testicles. As small as the rest of Lai, but as emphatically male. Mindful of his claw, Borsa curled his finger inside Lai's still-tight channel, finding the nub that should—

"Oh!" Lai moaned, hips rocking to Borsa's cadence. His phallus firmed, barely thicker than Borsa's thumb.

"Only this," Borsa coaxed. "Let the pleasure lift you. It's nothing bad of itself." The sight and scent of Lai's arousal nearly intoxicated Borsa, though most of it was the oil's fault. He felt himself swell to aching fullness. He wanted hours to relax and enflame the slender Dana, drive him to the brink again and again until that exquisite channel might accept more than a finger. Never Borsa's erection. The tip alone would split him. Borsa comforted himself with memories of his husband's pleasure: writhing, impaled, urging a pace so rough it would have damaged most men. He hoped his husband's wife had an adventurous soul. She'd find the marriage bed a wilder place than she'd bargained for!

Muffled noises made him look up from Lai's flexing hips. Two pairs of dazed eyes watched as well. Their owners reeked of fear and desperate arousal. Borsa grinned and lifted Lai to face his tormentors. "Look what you've done to them," he whispered.

Lai was far gone or had an exhibitionist bent. He screamed, hips hammering into and away from Borsa's hands. The runes on his back flared blue as night then vanished into his skin. Borsa felt Lai's passage clench. Lai's seed splattered along the pillows and tiled floor. He wondered about its taste and set the thought aside. He heard shouts and heavy objects banging on gir-wood.

He withdrew from Lai, cleansed his hands and the Dana's nethers with some of the mild vinegar water. Lai flinched when the door boomed again. Borsa stood, shrugging out of the bright blue coat.

To the conspirators, he growled, "Be thankful I stopped you or you might not have a city by tomorrow's dawn!" He thrust the grimoire into the pack slung over one shoulder, slipped his staff into his back-harness, and wrapped his coat around the trembling Dana. He lifted Lai in his arms. The weight of a ten-summer child, no more. No wonder Biha had abandoned her temple!

That thought withered his own lust and steadied his resolve. Time to stop running. Borsa whispered, "Think of your Enclave, Lai. Some place apart from it but easily reached, where folk might not gather today."

"Why?"

"I must make a door," said Borsa. He bent his forehead to Lai's.

His goddess's subtle guidance was still within him, but Borsa opened his mind to a name he hadn't dared think in five years. He was answered in the same heartbeat by a magic already seeking him, worried and infuriated by years of Biha's whimsical misdirection. A spot of darkness grew in the air in front of him, swelling to an eight-foot-high black oval bordered by brilliant green light.

For five years he'd used only an earthwitch's powers, pulled up from the Sleeper's domain. Once he stepped through this door, that magic and its two patron goddesses must abandon him forever.

"Earthwitches cannot gate, fly, cross deep water or even climb more than twenty feet from the ground," the Dana whispered. "Or they die screaming, or at least lose their magic. What *are* you?"

Borsa gritted his teeth and stepped through.

The portal opened on a rust-red sandstone scarp above a valley glittering with waterways. Neat fields made patchworks of alien scarlet, red-brown and purple vegetation. Small mud-brick buildings clustered against the lower cliffs. The lavender-blue sky was clean of city dust and smoke, streaked with thin cirrus. Beyond rose the distant mountains of the Ajara Vang and the end of the civilized world. Borsa almost longed for the wilderness south of the range. He'd been born out there, reared among isolated Sirrithani villages, bandit camps and Singer-clan caves. Offered his first prayers to Biha, joined her Order and gave up his birth name, expecting to live out his five hundred years in her service.

Until one day she'd returned his name and shattered his world.

"The Enclave!" Lai shivered inside the overlarge coat. "They won't welcome me back. Do you—would you suffer a companion on the road?"

"Lai, my wandering days are done," said Borsa. The black gate did not close. Borsa had been awaiting the two other footsteps and turned when he heard them.

A brown-skinned woman with tumbling black curls stared at up him, drawing her dark-green mantle closer around her. Her full, perfect lips silently shaped his name.

"Hello, Tari," Borsa said, unsure of his welcome.

She grinned.

"Where have you *been*?" asked the hooded man standing beside her. The sword-hilt at his back flashed with a poisonous green light, the same fire filling the eye sockets of his shadowed face. "And with what, a Dana whore?"

Borsa bowed to the Lady Consort. "Tari, will you hold Lai for me? This won't take long." She ignored her husband's offended snort and hurried to Borsa with outstretched arms. Lai, still not quite grasping reality, whimpered and clung to her. She set her hips to take his slight weight and smiled down at him, her arms curled around Lai's shoulders and knees.

"Borsa," began the Northwarden, his voice gone deep and dangerously vibrant. "When you ran, I thought you hated me—"

"Not you. I hated what I became to slake your needs," said Borsa, cupping that hidden face in his big hands. What would be killing cold to a normal mortal felt merely cool.

Against Borsa's fingertips, the Northwarden's lips moved. "You feared being my anchor, my companion, my conscience?"

"Your master. I was afraid I'd push you too far, and you'd kill me for it."

"Borsa, you great idiot. I was only greedy. My first two Lord Consorts were gentler souls. With you, I thought—"

"Ssh. When you found her, our Lady Consort, I thought you'd forget me while you courted her."

Tari laughed. "I only said 'yes' when he said he'd beg you to come home."

"Oh," said Borsa.

The Northwarden shook back his hood. Borsa stared at a mirror image wrought of black silk hair and pale opal skin, the misty green eyes paling to rainbow-flickering silver.

Biha bless, that's not me, surely? Borsa wondered. This hard-muscled giant with a straight nose and trimmed beard, his strong jaw unmarred by old fighting scars? In another ten thousand years would Sirrithani say, "Oh, look, now the North-warden wears the shape of the third Hero, the Lord Consort Borsa Eld"?

"My hunger drove you away. Why did you summon me with a sorcerer's gate?" asked his lover, his hands sliding up Borsa's arms.

Something Borsa hadn't planned in five years of wandering, or half a day in Ajara. "The Sleeper chose us for you. I should trust her and Biha. And I'd rather die with you than without you," he said, lightly pushing the other man backward against the cliff wall. Their mouths met in a soft click of fangs, a sinuous cool tongue warming to match Borsa's heat. Hands unclenched to caress and cling. A moan nearly below hearing rumbled in the broad chest pressed to Borsa's. "*Olan*," Borsa whispered the private name he'd given the nameless immortal on their wedding night. "There's been no one else." The moan became a low sob.

Then the white hands clenched again on his shoulders. "What about that?" the demon nodded toward Tari and Lai. "Why do you stink of its issue?"

"Lai Kendoshil is a traveler from the Enclave below," said Borsa. "As for why—Lai, show him your back."

Tari looked down into the Dana's face with a solemn nod. She let his feet slip to the floor, but kept the coat from falling below his hips. The Northwarden hissed, stalking closer, white fingers raised. The runes darkened into visibility. Tari took a step back, dragging Lai out of reach, and showed her fangs in a protective half-snarl. Borsa noted how his husband withdrew immediately.

"The last of it is in your script," the Northwarden growled.

"He was meant as a rape-sacrifice to Deathgold in a spell triggered by a false priest's twisted lust. I could only change it and give Lai to Maker. There are at least two traitors in the Fountain of Roses brothel in Ajara City, but I think they were misled by an enemy of Ajara itself. I have their grimoire. They didn't know what would happen. Look for their master among the Nameless, calling himself Aduano."

"Dana-man, why did you leave your Enclave?" the Northwarden asked.

Lai turned, still holding the coat to his chest. He did not kneel. "We heard you and the Lady Consort came to Ajara on Progress. We've begged aid from the Queen of Ajara before, more water rights and more honest merchants' fees. We get nothing. We cannot emigrate to another Enclave without her leave. And when we set foot beyond this valley—sometimes we vanish. We sought to plead to you directly, Steward of the Sleeping Goddess. Even though you shun us for what a few Dana did thousands of years ago."

"South of the Ajara Vang, two craters gape where the first Sirr cities stood," said the Northwarden. "Blasted by your folk."

"Dana peace emissaries died there, too. You destroyed our ships and our greatest city in return, Lord Steward. Have we not paid enough? As a pure race, we're dying. Should we pass in despair or dignity?"

"My Consorts?" asked the Northwarden after failing to stare down Lai.

"For the love of mercy, set them free," said Borsa.

"Give them honor, freeholds in lands that welcome them, and a voice in the Great House councils," said Tari, her hand still laid over Lai's bare shoulder. "Not here in Ajara, I think."

"My Saint and my Hero have spoken," said the Northwarden with a wry grin. The sword slashed down, dragging a black, rainbow-edged wind in its wake. "A hundred sorcerer Adepts walk in Ajara City right now. They'll soon unravel the plot. We are done here."

Lai looked up at Borsa. "What about the rest of the spell? Summoning that goddess, Maker?"

"That is by your will alone, Lai," said Borsa. "Turn around."

Lai did, and gasped. Where the trail snaked down the cliff a tall white shape awaited him.

Biha-Arra appeared as a purebred woman of the Singer-clan, wedge-shaped head tipped with a short sharp horn above her muzzle, large black eyes set in a wide forehead. Her thick mane fluffed around neck and shoulders. She crouched on strong hindquarters, forelimbs and clever paws held close to her chest, her long tail swept back in a graceful arch. Borsa, reared among Singers, thought her lovely. She cocked her head at him and Lai, murmuring a greeting-song in her four chorded voices.

I would have known sooner about the plot among the Name-less, she said into Borsa's thoughts. *If I hadn't been shielding you all these years.*

He cringed from that gentle reproof.

"Biha-Arra," said the Northwarden. "Will you stop hiding my husband from me?"

She snorted, becoming a naked Sirr-woman with cloud-white hair and skin as dark as Tari's. "Now that he wants you again and knows his duty to the world," she said in a single husky voice. She knelt before Lai. "Since my sister forced me to give up my favorite priest, I've looked for a new one. Would your kin follow a living goddess instead of a dead one's ghost?" She held out her hand.

Lai took it, brought it up to his heart. "They're very stubborn, my Lady. But I'll try." He released her, looking back with the first real smile Borsa had seen from him. "I owe you my life, my honor and my sanity. Thank you for seeing a person and not a toy. And for being kind."

"It's my job," said Borsa, grinning back. "I'm the Hero."

ESCAPE

Mitzi Szereto

Night after night, day after day I wait. I wait for what I cannot avoid: *the inevitable.*

I do not wish to marry him. He is old, and he is ugly. The flesh hangs from his neck and upper arms in mottled rolls; I dare not think of the rest of him! His teeth are the shade of rotting timber with holes riddled through by worms. His eyes rake over me with a familiarity that causes my body to flush with shame. It's as if he has already tasted my flesh, smelled my scent. When I see him I want to curl up into a tight ball and hide. But hide I cannot. For Father has other plans.

It is considered acceptable for pretty young women whose bodies retain the flush of youth to marry ancient trolls, but this is a fate I'm unwilling to bear. Of course, I realize I am not as young as most of the others; my choices are not those that can be made with any great degree of pickiness. Were it not for the circumstances, it should be unlikely I'd secure a husband at all, since the men of my land seek out those that are as fruit on the bough rather than those ready to drop to the ground. Indeed, some of us are old enough to remember such rarities as fruit before the evil of our leaders caused the gods to forsake us.

Having managed to avoid my fate for this many changes of seasons is a miracle in itself. Yet even with my seniority of years, I have something that allows me to be worthy of consideration: I bleed every month. Well, that and the fact that I'm still comely in appearance. A bleeding womb, prized though it may be, is increased in value by the package in which it's contained. I wonder if it is the same in other lands? Though I have never been to other lands. I have only been *here*.

Many years ago a terrible disease ravaged our already barren landscape, taking with it the majority of female children and girls and leaving yet more barrenness behind. Perhaps it was further punishment for the greed and wickedness of our rulers as they sought to acquire more and more of the territory surrounding us, annexing anything and everyone in their wake. The blood that has been spilled could fill rivers and probably has.

The lesson has not been learned, however, and the greed and wickedness continue to flourish. Our men grow worse with each passing day, becoming as cruel and ugly as the land upon which we live. The young ones learn from the old, since it is the old that seek out new wives after their current ones are no longer of use as bed or breeding partners. The discarded wives are either buried beneath stones in the town center or cast out of the kingdom, where they're left to wander toward the horizon until the elements accomplish the same thing as the stones. Our arid land is littered with the corpses of these women whose bodies could no longer provide their husbands with fruit.

There are no young men in our kingdom in possession of a wife. Rather they are forced to wait until the old have taken their pick of what little remains to be taken—and by then the young too, have grown old. And so the cycle begins anew when the female results of these unions attain womanhood and can produce future brood mares. I think it should be better if our race died out than to continue a life in this wretched place. But my opinion matters not.

Our women are kept imprisoned under lock and key from the onset of their menses until marriage; it's the only way to guarantee they remain pure for the men to whom they've been promised. The pedigree of the children they bear their husbands must not be in any way suspect. Even servants attending to the needs of these prisoners—for we are, indeed, *prisoners*—are female. It is not unusual for couplings to take place between prisoner and servant, and a blind eye is turned to such transgressions. The men do not care what transpires in the stone cells of our bedchambers as long as no seed has reached our fertile wombs. The touch of another can be as valuable as gold to a body hungering for it. Women locked away until such time as they are to be married off to husbands that will only maul and misuse them are starved for tenderness and affection. Me? Hah! I am no different from my sisters-in-misery.

It is past nightfall when my servant comes to me. The sky turns black the tiny window of the cell that constitutes my bedchamber. Even the stars refuse to twinkle over our land, choosing instead to shine on the verdant horizon most of us covet and dream of. A shaft of light from a lantern cuts a wedge in the floor as the door opens carefully; despite our nocturnal activities being common knowledge, the women and their servants are discreet. I lie in my small bed, my heart pounding in expectation of the pleasure I know I'm to be given on this night—the pleasure that assures me I'm still alive. At first I feel a caress of lips against my cheek so light it's barely discernible. A whisper of sweet breath against my ear follows, and it holds my name: Gwendolen.

Hearing my name spoken by my caller summons the moisture from my loins and my pelvis rises in answer. The voice is nearly enough to send me over into the oblivion of bliss. My limbs pull taut as the strings on a lyre when plucked by the miniature hands of the King's musicians when they perform in the public square. Like the women of childbearing age, the Small Ones are also imprisoned by their designated roles in society, their only function being to entertain just as ours is to procreate.

Gwendolen.

A hand reaches beneath my sleeping-dress and locates the core of moisture. A subtle shift of movement and I feel something sliding gently into me as warm lips close over mine. My thighs fall open as I sigh a name that I'd never dare to speak aloud. Despite the common bonds we share, even secrets cannot be shared in this place of women. The weight of another body is full upon me now, pressing me down into the straw mattress. The sound of my wetness fills the room as I'm penetrated with greater speed. A finger lays claim to that most responsive part of me, manipulating it with less gentleness than might be required. As my breath quickens, along with the beating of my heart, I find I don't mind the roughness. The swiftness with which events take place below my waist is dizzying, and suddenly my body bucks and writhes against that of my pleasure-giver's, my cry of delight hushed by a tongue as its muted response joins mine.

And so we spend our nights, taking what joys there are to be found in the arms of a servant before being dispatched to the arms of an aged brute. Such is the destiny of women.

The man I'm to marry is rich and powerful. He is a man who, with a casual flip of his hand, can have heads lopped off—and *has*. One of these heads shall be Father's should our union not take place. I would not shed a tear if this came to pass. Indeed, I would cheer the loudest, for Father is no better than the filthy troll who seeks to penetrate and impregnate me. Yet I cannot curse my betrothed and wish he'd never lived, because without his life, my heart would be as barren as this land.

For it is his son I desire.

It is Evrain whom I love.

It is his name I sigh when I am given pleasure.

He is young and beautiful, his flesh smooth and unmarred by battle or the relentless sun that bakes dry everything beneath our feet. His eyes are as brilliant and multifaceted as the jewels in the King's crown, and each time he looks at me, I experience a melting in the place where my thighs meet and a corresponding ache in my womb that I desire only to have filled by his sweet seed. How he can be the progeny of his father I cannot imagine, and I often wonder if his mother had secretly managed to offer a home inside her to the seed of another, rejecting the foul offering dispatched by her husband, Houdain. Oh, I can only wish it were so! For I could not love anything that originated from so repellent a creature as Houdain.

Evrain is being groomed for battle and, despite his youth, has already proved a formidable swordsman. Soon it will be time for him to be sent into the hinterland, where he will be successful and acquire more land for our miserable kingdom, or be killed by foreign soldiers. Alas, his taste for blood is not as highly developed as those of his peers; he has no appetite for battle and death; to kill or be killed are not fates he seeks. But time is running out for him.

And for me.

To flee is what the women of our kingdom seek, though there are few among us who would survive the journey across the dead landscape to the rich green mists beyond—mists that hold the promise of a better life for those cursed to have been born female. It's impossible to know if any of us has been successful;

a woman's disappearance can either signify that she's gone to her death or, if she's extremely fortunate, escaped from the land that dooms her. Not surprisingly, the men take every opportunity to regale us with tales of horror featuring great scaly creatures that exhale fire through their mouths and nostrils, turning everything in their path to cinders, especially foolish young women who think they can escape their destiny. And if one is so fortunate as to sneak past them, packs of red-eyed beasts with fangs sharper than the King's finest sword lie in wait to make of her a meal. Whether these creatures exist I do not know, but they reportedly guard the borders of our land (as if anyone should wish to come here!), also making certain that no one passes through to the green sanctuary that lies beyond.

As for whether I choose to believe in their existence, well...I am not as ignorant and silly as most of my fellow females; however, I'm also not willing to risk finding out for myself. Life is not easy for a woman without the guardianship of a man. Had I the protection and love of the one to whom I've given my heart, I might risk having my flesh scorched by these fire-breathing creatures or torn to shreds by their comrades if it meant I could be free. In fact, I might risk anything!

And so we plot our escape, for Evrain does not desire to remain here any more than I do.

My caller comes to me again in the night, full of quiet whispers and soft touches. But this time it's different. The day of my wedding draws near and with each tender kiss upon my breast and each impassioned lick of my sex, we know that our stolen moments will soon be at an end. This bedchamber that is naught more than a prison cell may seem like a lovers' paradise when compared with what awaits should my beloved Evrain and I fail in our escape. Yet as the heat of luxurious sensation builds in my loins, I muse upon a life far away from here—a simple and pure life with Evrain and myself living off the treasures the rich earth will offer us. We will build our home from the scented boughs of trees and walk barefoot on a blanket of cool green rather than being showered with gray dust, the smell of death perpetually in our nostrils. We will eat what is fresh and new and succulent rather than gnawing on what is gristly and old and dry.

The tongue between my thighs continues to lave and probe and circle, and my body tenses. The wave is near and as I feel it rising, I keep my breath deep in my chest, knowing that tonight this wave will crash down upon me with greater force than ever. I feel something slipping inside me, though I'm so wet it barely registers. Only when it moves around to make love to my other opening do I finally realize it's a finger—and that is when I lose myself. My pelvis hoists itself up in a maddened thrust, my hands clawing at the hair on the head moving between my thighs. "Evrain!" I sob into the night.

Evrain and I conspire in the darkness. We cannot let many more days go past, as Houdain awaits me in his bed and has made it clear to Father that his patience has its limits. It matters not that our wedding day has already been set; Houdain has indicated that he wishes to consummate the marriage before it has even taken place!

And there are few in our kingdom that would deny him what he wants, least of all Father, who shits himself at the mere sound of the man's voice.

Though my beloved does not share the bloodlust of others of his sex, Evrain is primed for the task at hand. We have discussed it in depth, and I believe in my heart that he'll not suffer a moment's guilt. Not only will it eliminate one problem, but it

will serve as a cloak for our escape, a way of directing attention elsewhere. This is what we require for our plan to succeed.
The fact that it involves murder does negligible damage to our
consciences. Evrain would not mourn the loss of his father any
more than I would the loss of mine. One is evil, the other a
coward. Both are equal in deserving our hatred.

It's arranged for me to be ready when the moon is at its
smallest in the night sky. There will be no time for lovemaking,
yet nevertheless we do so, for we are unable to be in each other's
presence without the need to touch. The fact that Evrain has
come to me with blood on his hands matters not. As always,
he slips into my room in the guise of the female servant who
has been slipping in all these many nights, the darkness and
servant's garb sufficient to avoid raising suspicion. I wonder if
any of the others are clever enough to have conceived of such a
ploy. Surely there must be more than one inside this stone prison
that has loved.

Evrain shucks off his servant's garments, allowing them to
fall to the floor, and climbs into my bed. I can feel his desire
for me pressing against my mound before our lips even meet.
The wet tip of him nuzzles me as he rubs it against my sensitive
place, each movement as maddening as it is exhilarating. I want
to shout out my joy, but we are so close to realizing our plan
that I dare not. Instead I bite back all sound as he continues his
movements, urging me toward release. His breath grows quicker
and I wonder if he's going to spill his seed before he manages to
slide inside me. I feel he is close, as am I. And then it happens,
and I'm soaring up toward the stone ceiling, his name catching
like a hook in my throat. The pleasure is sweeter for knowing it
may be the last.

Evrain shifts position, yet before he can enter me, I too shift
position and bend low to take him into my mouth. His shocked

intake of breath is loud and reverberates off the walls. I have never tasted him or thought to do so, but this night has made me daring—the danger of death has made me daring. He is tangy sweet and musky all at the same time and my tongue licks hungrily of the moisture he gives me. "Gwendolen!" My name joins the echoes of his sighs and my heart swells with love as he swells in my mouth. I feel him pulse against my tongue and he pulls out quickly, placing himself between my thighs and entering me with one hard thrust.

Our moment is short, for Evrain cannot hold back from his finish. His limbs tense and he collapses onto me with his full weight, his cry of pleasure smothering itself against my lips. It is at this moment that I know he has planted a child inside me. Now we have still more to lose if our plan does not succeed.

We are as two shadows as we make our way out of the town. I'm wearing the coarse dark cloak Evrain brought for me, and it covers me from head to toe. There are still a few hours remaining before daylight and the discovery of Houdain, who was driven to take his own life for reasons known only to him. Though he did not leave behind a letter explaining his motives or instructing his family of his final wishes, his death was neat and quick and dispatched by his own hand and his favorite jeweled dagger. The fact that his hand received some assistance from the hand of his youngest son is unlikely to become known. Nor is it likely that anyone in the family should seek to question his end. Houdain was despised in equal measure by all, particularly Evrain's eldest brother, who will now take control of the family's fortune.

Evrain holds tight to my hand, leading me farther and farther away from the town center and everything I've ever known since I first arrived screaming into this world. I've never ventured beyond these confines, and it's exciting, yet terrifying as well. But with Evrain I am safe; he won't let anything happen to me. Although it's too dark to see each other, I know we're both covered in a coating of gray dust. It's impossible to step outside into the open without the dead soil of our land covering our skin and garments and getting into our eyes and nostrils. I wonder how many corpses I've inhaled in my lifetime, for our land is littered with their dust.

Our last stolen moments of love return to me in a flash and suddenly I fear I'm experiencing the end of my life. They say you can see images pass through your mind when you're near to death. If it is to be so, then I'm grateful I'll die with Evrain's seed inside me.

I stumble over some rubble and cry out. Evrain's hand moves quickly to close over my lips, though it's already too late—the sound has been heard.

"Who goes there?" comes the gruff shout of a man from somewhere in the blackness behind us.

Evrain and I stop, our chests heaving with fear. We're so close to the edge of the town that we can almost touch the hinterland. To be found out now would be cruel irony, indeed. We remain still, waiting for a second shout. When it doesn't come, we continue on our way, our bodies stiff with unease.

We know we have left the town behind us when we feel the cold biting through our garments like sharp teeth. There are no stone walls here to protect us, nothing to hide behind. We're out in the open now and the dusty wind hits us at full force, the grit catching in our teeth so that we don't dare try to speak for fear of it choking us. Evrain draws my hood down farther over my face in an attempt to shield my eyes; I can barely see now and I must cling to his arm like the unsighted beggars that take up residence in the town square whenever there's a burial beneath stones, as if a discarded wife being put to her death is a festive occasion and worthy of inspiring the locals to be charitable toward the unfortunate.

It feels as if we've walked for hours, though it's possibly only minutes. The wind lashes at us and pushes us back toward where we came from, but we forge forward to the border. We will either leave this place forever or die; there's no other option. I'm sick with fright as I recall the tales of fire-spitting creatures and beasts with fangs that can rip the flesh from my bones, and with every step we take I await their appearance, certain not even Evrain can save us from them.

Yet as the night begins to give way to day, they do not come. And when at last we step away from the dead gray earth and into the misty green land beyond, I know they never will.

I wake to music, the melody sweet and cheerful in my ears. Suddenly I fear I'm back in the town and it is the Small Ones playing their instruments in the square that I'm hearing. I nearly shriek in horror until I see the brilliant blue of the wide-open sky and the jewel-dappled green of the leaves that partially shade me from the sun. My breath flies out of me in a cloud of relief when I realize that I'm lying on a soft bed of green with my beloved by my side. The music is coming from the tiny feathered and winged creatures that roost on the boughs of the trees surrounding us. It's birdsong. We didn't have birdsong in our town. We didn't have birds.

Evrain takes me into his arms. I am home.

EYEKEEPER

Aurelia T. Evans

Lydia stood in the middle of the cell. The floor under her bare feet was nothing but dirt and hay and dust mixed with disintegrated rat droppings. She had long since removed the cloth belt from between her legs where it held her skirt up away from her feet like pants. It was easier to creep around when skirts could not snag on corners, but she was not creeping now. She had been caught, betrayed by a man who should know better, sentenced to burn by the king whose coffers she pilfered, and shut away in the castle dungeon to await her execution at dawn.

The sky through the window slit revealed stars. She could not yet smell the morning fog, and she still smelled ale and sweat on the breeze, which told her evening was still upon the city.

There was a moldy pallet in the corner, next to a bucket. Lydia used neither, simply stood. Her clothing was ordinary and her face was smudged with dust. But something was different; something was wrong. It was a feeling in the gut, like looking into a forest and knowing there was a creature staring back, something silent and unseen. She smiled, the curve of her lips almost imperceptible.

The woman whom the king called Witchthief waited.

After the bell tower chimed ten, the warden entered. He could not look her in the eye, but his strong, narrow jaw was set, his fists inadvertently tight. He bore marks of distress and distraction—there were deep circles under his eyes and his stubble smudged his cheek like charcoal.

"Good evening, Hann," she said.

He bowed slightly. The gesture was automatic and somewhat mocking. "Lydia."

"You have had a good evening, have you not?" Lydia asked. "Very lucrative."

He shut the door behind him. His keys clinked in the lock. "Where is the rest?"

"You 'rescued' the bag when Micah alerted the king I was digging through his treasure room." Lydia stepped forward. Her left ankle dragged behind a bit, laden as it was with an iron shackle that attached her to the wall. "You failed to inform me that Micah kept a Scrying Glass in there."

"I have been told that an artifact was also removed," Hann interrupted. The timbre of his voice was official now. Cloaked in his profession, he found the fortitude to meet her eyes.

"Is that what Micah told you?" Lydia's expression remained placid and slightly bemused.

"The king ordered me to search you for any additional items stolen."

"I am sure it will be such a chore." Her smile became perceptible.

"Damn it, Lydia, where is the Oculum?" Hann shouted, grabbing her by her arms. When he shook her, he made her chains rattle. She just laughed, the low, husky sound vibrating over his flesh.

"Search me." She peered up at him through her dark eyelashes.

"Words cannot describe how glad I am you will burn on the morrow," Hann said. He pulled at the ties of her bodice, spreading it open before him with nothing but her light chemise underneath. As her skirts moved and brushed against her legs, the clink of metal on metal was more apparent. She could no longer cover it with the sound of her shackle. When Hann heard it, he raised an eyebrow.

"Really, Lydia. What did you think you were going to do with the treasure? Bribe the ferryman to take you the other direction?" Hann asked. Slowly, he slid the bodice down and loosened the final ties so that the material of her dress slid down her legs. There was a heavy clink as the full pocket-lined skirts fell to the stone floor.

Lydia said nothing, nor did her smile falter. She could see sweat forming above his lip as his gaze traveled from the ridge of her collarbone down to the shapes of her breasts under the thin chemise. Her remaining clothing was silent as he moved his hands over the full arms, down the back, against the skirts, now pressing against her firm thighs.

"I have to be sure you have not hidden it anywhere else. I know better than to think you would be too demure," Hann said. His Adam's apple bobbed as he deliberately pulled her chemise up. The hem tickled against the backs of her legs until it was all bunched in his hands. Her buttocks and cunt felt the coolness of each night draft, and still she was not fazed.

His breathing grew labored and he pulled her chemise over her head, revealing her completely nude body to his remembering eyes. He knew her, knew every inch of her body ever since she had captivated him three months ago, back when he had mused aloud on the contents of the king's coffers while draining a pint at the alehouse. She had told him that she knew how to get in without the king's sorcerer knowing—she had raised the dragon keepers and knew their favorite foods, and she was deceptively light on her feet to avoid the detection of any guards. They agreed to split the earnings before escaping to another land. Lydia should have known that their meeting was more than just fortuitous.

His long-fingered hands cupped her breasts, pressing them up and squeezing none too gently. His fingertips grazed the undersides, as though to make sure she hid nothing beneath them. Her tongue touched her lower lip as they drifted down her stomach to slide between her legs, searching between her folds. Her teeth caught her shining lip when those fingers entered into her, feeling for any sign of the Oculum in any place she might have hidden it. Her eyelids fluttered, but she made no sound.

"One more place to check," he said breathlessly. His cock was a long, hard branch in his pants. The head pushed against her stomach. Her glistening eyes were even more effective than her hand on him, making him tingle like a thousand feathers were stroking his body. His fingers that were not otherwise occupied touched her lower lip and felt the moisture there. As he continued to fill her with his other fingers, he entered her mouth, probing her cheeks and stroking her tongue and hard palate. Empty.

She sucked those fingers as he pulled out of both ends. A grunt and a brief closing of his eyes was the only sign he had come. In better light, she would be able to see the stain.

"Where is it, Lydia?" he asked when he had composed himself. The warden's voice had returned.

Lydia stood still and shackled and naked, but she was not

ashamed, nor was she humiliated by his actions against her. "You can tell Micah he will never see the Oculum again." Her voice was soft yet somehow filled the room. "And after tonight, you will never again know the touch of another woman."

He took one step back in surprise, then stumbled against the cell door, pointing at her. "You cannot curse me. You do not have that kind of power, witch!"

She did not blink. Not one time since Hann entered had she blinked. "Call it a broadening of your horizons. I *should* curse you for betraying me."

Hann snatched her dress and chemise from the ground, then fumbled with the keys in the lock. "You will burn," he snarled. "And whatever power you have will burn with you."

He opened the door and slammed it shut. Through the small window, he peered in at her with hardened eyes. "I will return your clothes to you when they have been searched."

After even the most devoted drunk had fallen against an alley wall to sleep in his own vomit, Lydia pressed her hand to her sternum, then slid it up her neck. Inside her mouth, she curled her tongue to draw the chain from her throat. When she tasted gold, she let her lips fall open. A necklace floated over her tongue and into the air before her. The fire opal, set within intricate golden filigree, glinted with rainbow flaws in the moonlight. She stared at each flash of light, and her slight grin deepened with satisfaction. Content with the success of her mission and flush with secret knowledge, she swallowed the Oculum once again.

The next morning, the executioner—arms thick and rippling from the regular use of his ax—looked out of place with a torch in his hand, waiting to the side while the crowd stared and shouted up at Lydia's pyre. She was strapped against the stake, kindling piled at her feet. Her hair swept over her face from the force of the wind, and because her arms were bound behind her, she could not brush it away. She was wearing the same clothes Hann had stripped from her. The skirts were ripped from the removal of all the pockets and jewelry she had fastened into her clothing, and they had been hastily repaired enough for modesty with thick, mismatching thread.

The crowd was in a celebratory mood; the air smelled of bread and smoked meat. An execution was always a spectacle; while a burning lacked the bloody excitement of a beheading, it did last a lot longer. Decapitation was over in a matter of moments, but there was never a guarantee that a real witch would be truly rid of her demonic spirit. With a burning, the fire purified the corpse, ensured that the demon within burned along with the person it inhabited. With a burning, they could watch the witch scream.

Lydia's demeanor was unchanged from the night before. Although she had an itch on her arm and cheek that she could not scratch, she was disturbingly calm.

There was a flourish of trumpets, and the king stepped out on the balcony overlooking the courtyard. Micah came out behind him, his eyes smoldering down at her in exultation, holding his staff tipped with a sphere of silver. After him came the queen, a third the king's age and pale as a moth.

The king held up his hand.

"King Eberhard calls royal advisor and sorcerer Micah to present the charge."

Micah unrolled a scroll, but he barely looked at it. Instead, he kept his gaze on Lydia, who stared back with cold lightning snapping in the night pools of her pupils. She knew that only he could see them; they were meant for no other body to see.

"The kingdom of Adal finds Lydia Witchthief guilty of trespassing in the royal treasury, thievery of the king's possessions, and enchantments of a malicious nature against this kingdom and its inhabitants. For this latter offense, she has been sentenced to burn in fire. At this time, we ask her if she wishes to repent of her heinousness and return the Oculum, which has yet to be recovered from her thievery." Micah lowered the scroll and raised one curled eyebrow with an affectation of inquiry. But they both knew Lydia would never do so.

"You will be cast from the castle's tallest tower before I ever expose the Oculum to the light of the sun again," Lydia said. Her honey voice carried effortlessly from the pyre to the balcony. "You are a coward, Micah Silvertongue."

Micah's face, embellished by curlicues and whorls of facial hair, contorted in almost comical anger. If her words were untrue, though, he would not be so furious. With a violent slash of his staff in the air, he commanded the executioner to set the pyre ablaze.

As the executioner lumbered to the base of the kindling, his feet quiet thunder, Lydia met those dark beetle-black eyes behind his hood.

"Mine is not the fire you wish to ignite," Lydia murmured. Now her words were for him alone. "As my executioner, you will have a portion of what I leave behind. Do whatever you wish with it, with my generous blessing. Use it, abuse it, discard it if that is your desire."

The fire quivered and snapped in his hand, but the rest of him showed no sign that she spoke to him at all. "God have mercy," he muttered, not in awe or fear, simply his grunted prayer for her.

"I have no need of it," Lydia said. She closed her eyes when the torch touched the kindling. If the crowd hoped for a show, they received none. Lydia was perfectly silent, even as her skin blistered and blackened and her clothing fell away from her cooking body. Ash and smoke rose in the air, and although Micah had not reclaimed the Oculum, he nonetheless smiled his spider's smile. He set a hand on King Eberhard's shoulder.

"The threat to Adal is vanquished, Your Majesty," Micah said. "The enchantress is no more."

"It is thanks to you that we have eliminated the evil of those enchantresses," King Eberhard replied, and the royal party reentered their castle. "Without you, I would have never known the depth of their danger to this kingdom."

"It is necessary that an enchantress's devil-twisted tongue be silenced before it reaches men's ears. I seek only to protect you," Micah said.

The lovely Queen Lilac cast her eyes down and kept silent. Neither man noticed her, as they rarely needed to. She was meant only to do their bidding, and so she followed them.

At the time of the burning, the days were warm, with the sun drawing sweat from men's brows in their labors. Months passed until the warmth of the days was interrupted by cold breezes from the west. The air was dry and smelled of ozone as a crackling, sparkling wall of clouds came forth in the twilight.

The inhabitants of the cottage at the edge of town were unaware of the coming storm. From the window came the glow of the fire, and if anyone ventured that far out of the township— rare, since executioners were thought to be a tainted lot—they might have seen shadows on the wooden window shutters undulating. Approaching closer, they would have seen the silhouettes of two men moving together, one under the other. The two of them would not be so bold to do so with the window open if Bruin thought any townsfolk would see them, neither would the man beneath him moan so loudly. His cry carried on the wind and mingled with its whistling.

Her bare feet moved silently on the dirt path as she approached the executioner's house. Her hair was loose and whipping in the wind against her face as it once had; her gown was different, a thick, jet-beaded black that trailed in the dirt behind her and yet remained as spotless as it began. Around her neck glinted a chain of gold carrying a flawed fire opal pendant set in golden filigree. Even in the darkness, it glittered with whatever light it could capture, which was now the light of the fire burning within the cottage.

The door swung open as though blasted by a violent gust. The man beneath Bruin started violently. He clutched for a blanket to cover himself, and the flush on his face drained away for a sickly pallor—and that was before he even saw the traveler at their door.

"You needn't hide yourself from me," Lydia said. The firelight made the cottage room too bright to see beyond the doorway, but then she stepped into the house. The door closed behind her. "I have already known you."

Hann stopped scrambling to cover himself; he stared at her as if she were an apparition. Bruin's face was mostly impassive, even though he had been caught completely naked and embracing another man by a woman who should be dead. Only his brows registered puzzlement.

"That is—th-that is impossible," Hann stammered. "Impossible."

"The amusing thing about burning a witch or an enchantress: a real one knows how to escape the fire unscathed," Lydia said by way of explanation.

"The other witches I executed are alive as well?" Bruin asked.

Lydia smiled tightly and came closer, toward the fire and around the bed. "They are worm food. Micah eliminates the complication of his fornications by accusing his women of

witchcraft. He underestimated me." She stoked the fire. A spark
rose up and settled on her skirt, but it went out without leaving
a mark. Hann tried to pull on his pants, but they slid off him
again, flung across the room by an unseen hand. Hann grasped
at air. He whipped around to glare at Lydia.

She wagged a finger at him and clicked her tongue. "We have
not discussed the subject of revenge, my dear, for betraying me."

"You have already had your revenge!" Hann yelled, standing
abruptly. "You cursed me that night when you told me I would
never touch another woman. You made me into this obscene
thing. You cursed me!"

Lydia floated to him and touched his cheek lightly. Her
laughter was soft but not gentle. "I told you then that it was not
a curse. I did not make you what you are." Her fingers trailed
down his chest and stroked the firm, lean lines of his abdomen.
He was tall and lithe, but he was not weak, and she could feel
his muscles twitch under her fingertips. He shut his eyes against
her touch. "You have always been this way."

"Not with you," Hann protested. "At least not before. What
did you do to me?" He reached to shake the answer from her,
but she would not allow him to grab her. His hands met invisible walls. Instead, she slipped her hand under his scrotum and
held him, stroked the fold of skin behind it. His cock showed a
little interest, but she knew it was not for her.

"You think that I made you desire the forbidden taste of
man's flesh in your mouth. You think I attracted your eyes to the
thick muscles of your lover." Her nails threatened the sensitive
skin of his perineum for a moment before she withdrew.

"Do you know what Micah and other small-minded sorcerers
say of enchantresses? That they are so much more dangerous
than sorcerers or witches because they have the power to
manipulate men's desires. That is why the laws of Adal forbid

enchantments, while they do allow some witchery—the witch-craft of herbs and poultices and harmless potions. But if the woman has true power...well, then she is an enchantress and must be eliminated." Lydia's expression darkened and the Oculum glowed in her pupils. "But then, Micah is right. I have far more power over desire than his silver tongue or his silver staff has over the minds of men and the hearts of women.

"I could have entered the King's treasury alone, but it was easier with a partner who had been inside, and I knew you would jump on the sheerest possibility that your lusts for squires and knights were simply an aberration of youth. I gave you my pleasures because it pleased me to do so. I had not expected you were deceitful from the start, under Micah's silver-tongued guidance. I could not See that then. Then I released you from your enchantment upon your betrayal and my imminent death, as it were." Lydia stroked the Oculum idly.

Hann stumbled back. His thighs hit the bed; Bruin steadied him before he could fall. Hann jerked away. Lydia saw the brief flash of hurt in Bruin's eyes. Hann strode to the other side of the room, looking away from both of them, his tormentors. He rubbed his hands over his face and through his light brown hair.

"I needed to retrieve what Micah stole and what was right-fully mine and made for me," Lydia continued. "I have always been able to See, just as Micah has always been able to talk his way into and out of anything, but his staff was made to augment his power, and my Oculum was made to augment mine. Our talismans. His manipulations divested me of it for a mere moment—that was my error. Once I had the Oculum in my possession again, though, my ability to See into the truth of things clarified once more. And I saw your future, your love for this forsaken man, your self-loathing for it. It is not my curse upon you. If I wanted to curse you, I would make you impotent entirely, never again to know the pleasure even of your own hand."

Hann turned around and looked at her with wide eyes. There was conflict in his expression, as though part of him believed that no desire would be better than the desires in which he now indulged.

"But then you would be of no use to me," Lydia said, crossing her arms over her chest and smiling with grim calculation. "The rule of Adal will soon be overturned, and I will need a warden and an executioner under my control. Your secret will remain safe with me…if you obey me when I sit at the right hand of the future leader of Adal."

Bruin sat back, widening his stance with no concern for his nudity, and considered her. But Hann strode back over to her, gesticulating wildly.

"So this is your revenge, to have me—us—under your thumb for the rest of our days lest you tell everyone of this…this…" He struggled to even say what he did with his lover, although Lydia saw as plain as his Roman nose that Bruin gave him true joy in their solitude.

"No," Lydia said, pushing him toward the bed. "That is merely politics. As though you did not have a similar arrangement with Micah. No, my revenge is to watch."

"Watch." Hann's calves hit the bed again, and this time he tumbled back onto it without Bruin to help him. Bruin still had that thoughtful look on his face.

"I want to watch what makes you ashamed, so that you will know that I have seen it," Lydia hissed. "I want to see what the executioner does to you. I want to see you delight in the flesh of a man, and I want to be a part of laying you low. Then you will know what it is that you did to me when you betrayed me, what it felt like to be caught by Micah, to be stripped naked by you, to suffer the indignity of a burning before the townspeople, to be condemned before all of witchcraft, even though I once preferred to keep my powers close and secret."

She straddled his pale, long body, nails digging into his chest. "I want him to fuck you. And I want to take pleasure in it."

"May dogs mate with you in Micah's bedchambers," Hann spat. "Even if I could want you, I would not want to touch your wicked-ridden flesh. Rot in hell and let demons consume those all-seeing eyes of yours."

"Oh, now, now, Hann," she murmured, pressing her lips to his forehead and leaving a wet, red mark even though her lips were unpainted. "Do you not remember the good times we had?"

"I care nothing for women, you sow. You saw to that."

Lydia's hand combed through his thick hair and tightened into a fist to tug his head back. "Would that make you feel better performing for me? If you felt pleasure at my touch again?"

She ran her tongue up the length of his neck, over his chin, then took his mouth, tasting and licking and sucking his lips and tongue into her mouth and making the most obscenely wet noises she could. She thought she heard a sound from Bruin behind her as Hann moaned, his cock twitching and growing against Lydia's skirts.

The nights they had stolen in empty cells, in dark corners, in Hann's room (never hers), came back to them, and Hann felt the sense memory of what it had meant to worship her body as one he had always wanted to worship, the relief of feeling straight and narrow...and the horror when he realized that feeling was gone, so many ashes in a witch's pyre. He slid his arms around her, hands grasping until he found her shoulders and held on tightly. Then his eyes flew open, and he wrenched his mouth away from hers, gazing in terrible realization at the grinning enchantress above him. She felt good against him, her breasts heavy on his chest and her legs firm on his hips, but that goodness was only created by her; she was the last woman in the world he wanted to want. And in this bed, too.

Lydia laughed, the sound sharp. As she straightened, her bodice began to fall away. There were no fastenings to speak of. The threads that made up its center simply unraveled, revealing her breasts, her abdomen, the hair that framed her cunt, her thighs. It slithered down her and finally settled on the floor in a black shadow. Whether he wished to or not, Hann found himself staring at her. She tossed her head back to make her tangle of dark hair spill over her shoulders and plumped her breasts for her own enjoyment.

"I can make you want me, but do not despair too deeply— I will not have you inside of me. I have no wish for it. Your humiliation is enough for me. Turn around, on your stomach," Lydia commanded.

"Why?" he asked.

She pushed herself standing on the pallet and raised her hand above him. He flipped around abruptly, cock digging into the pallet at an awkward angle that made him cry out.

"Now, executioner, you may continue with what you were doing before I arrived," Lydia said, kneeling beside Hann and stroking the muscles of his exposed back before sliding her palm over the swell of his buttocks. She slapped it none too gently, making him quiver.

Bruin looked at her, then at Hann, then back at her.

"I can make you do it," Lydia said to him. "You may have only done the thankless task for which you are paid, but you are not blameless in my persecution. I could take it upon myself to seek retribution from you as well. But in doing this, I ask nothing from you than what you already want."

He pushed her hand away from Hann then and squeezed the firm muscle of Hann's ass, watching dimples form under his great, thick fingers. Lydia ran her nails admiringly over them.

To Lydia's heated gaze, Bruin muttered, "I will not put my cock in you."

"I would not dream of it," Lydia said, looking up at him with irises almost all dark, glittering caves. "Mind if I borrow these wonderful things?" She brought his hand up to her mouth and took two large fingers into her mouth, moaning as she coated them with her saliva.

Bruin shrugged. "As long as it is not my cock, witch." His lip curled in distaste at the thought of it.

"Enchantress," Lydia said, releasing his fingers with a cold smile. "I am no mere witch." The rumble of thunder, still distant when she first entered, was now quite close, and at the end of her words, rain pounded violently on the sides of the house.

As Bruin worked saliva-slicked fingers into Hann, the poor man beneath him bit his forearm to muffle his groans. He was helpless, lost to the fervor of his lusts. Lydia's scent and plea-sure-filled fingers and the familiar intimacy of his lover made Hann feel light-headed and stupid, able to do nothing except succumb to the demands of his weak body. Thunder's vibrations thrummed through him.

He could no longer hold himself back when Bruin pressed the head of his cock against him and pushed in. He yelled, fists clutching the sheet.

"Yes, take him," Lydia commanded as Bruin sheathed himself completely. "Take him!"

Bruin grunted as he pulled out and shoved himself back into Hann. "Yes," Hann said, lost as always to the sensation. His other hand reached beneath him to stroke himself.

Lydia crawled over Hann to straddle his waist again and trap him underneath her, facing Bruin and watching him quicken his pace. Hann's ass rippled now with each firm thrust, and Lydia leaned back until her head rested between Hann's shoulder blades.

"Good god, Bruin!" Hann shouted as the repeated pounding against his prostate became too much to bear. "Need you to..."

"No," Lydia said. "Not until *I* am finished." An orange glow independent of the fire dipped under Hann's body and seeped into him to restrain him from coming. He gave a frustrated shriek, bucking beneath her, and she laughed. Her laughter mingled with the sharp, deep thunder as lightning struck not too far from the cottage and made the earth tremble.

Lydia arched and reveled atop the body of her desperate former lover. She curled her tongue in the air and moaned, moving with Hann to the rhythm of Bruin's thrusts, riding him. Finally, the taste of their frustration and need was too sweet in the warm perfume of the cottage, and she brought her hands between her legs, taking herself in wild abandon, shrieking to rival the banshee cry of the wind outside. The Oculum slid down her breastbone and rested in the hollow of her throat from the angle of her arched back. It was only when she slid down onto the bed that she ended the enchantments on Hann, letting loose a flood of orgasm over him that wracked him with the most exquisite, too brief pleasure. Holding Hann's hips in a bruising grip, Bruin grunted and slumped over Hann, overcome with his own release. Firelight glistened with an amber glow over the contours of their tangled bodies.

Lydia wiped her hands on the sheet, stretching like a wildcat. The two men were replete, but she felt energized, as though charged with the lightning that still rocked the cottage with its thunder. She climbed over them. Bruin flinched when her breasts dragged over his back, but she just patted his shoulder and stepped onto the floor. She summoned her dress, which vined up her body and sewed itself tightly against her, as though it had never been removed at all.

"Dally with whom you will," Lydia said. Her voice cut into the postcoital fog shared by the two men—Hann's eyes flew open. His pupils were still large from arousal, his face flushed and shining, but Lydia latched onto his reflexive guilt, taking it in as though it were bitter wine. "As long as you serve me."

Rain soaked half the room as she walked into the storm. When Bruin ran out with his ax, a perfunctory defense, she was gone. Rain pummeled his naked body, but although he knew Hann would be impossible for a while—from the fear of being caught and of never being with Bruin again—he thought that Lydia would not return for them. And she was no worse a master than Micah.

Lightning struck both sides of the road as the worst of the storm followed Lydia into the heart of Adal. Her hair was soaked now and rain dripped down her chest and dipped between her breasts, but her gown continued to repel all efforts to destroy it. She could have stopped the rain from soaking the rest of her, but it honestly felt good to *feel* at all—the cold, the wind, the water, the ozone, her heated skin pebbling into gooseflesh— after waiting in that in-between place.

With the king newly dead—how tragic to die as he did, not from the blade of an enemy, but struggling for speech like an infant as something in his head abruptly failed to function during his nightly ablutions—Micah was having more trouble than he anticipated turning Queen Lilac's ear with his silver tongue. He thought her more delicate and malleable than she was, but Lydia knew better. With enough care, she could be nurtured into a formidable monarch...with Lydia Eyekeeper at her right hand, of course. The only thing left was to eliminate

Micah from meddling. She *could* do as he did to her—charge him for a crime punishable by death. After all, she had a warden and an executioner in her pocket.

However, her last prophecy was set to pass. Micah would be sleeping in his luxury of a sorcerer's high tower. She could See it so clearly through her Oculum now, as she had seen it before her burning. All it would take was the shock of seeing her alive... and one good push.

THE WIDOW'S MAN

Nyla Nox

My Lady Widow,

The light is fading fast, and I don't know if there will be a morning for me.

I only know that I was the one who chose this path. Every step I took through our illustrious city, I took for you, my Lady, from the first to the last. Although I may die as a traitor, I ever was and ever will be the Widow's Man.

Would I try to flee if I could? Life is sweet. Maybe I would, but no one has made an offer.

Would I try to trade my life? Yes, absolutely. I would trade anyone and anything, my friends, my loyalty, whatever little is left of my dignity, and whatever little is left of my material possessions. But not my love for you.

You own my love, my Lady Widow, but I wish with all my heart that you would let me live for it, not die.

When the guards came to take me from my cell, I was afraid.

So far, the interrogation had been very moderate compared

to what I know is possible from my long association with the royal household. What if that changed?

But instead they allowed me to clean up. I even got to wash my hair. After so many days in the cells, I didn't mind the rough prison soap. And they gave me clean clothes, almost decent, almost my size. I will admit that hope stirred in me. I will admit that I was, by then, also afraid of hope.

Possibilities crossed my mind as they took me through the tunnels.

Was I going to see you? Or had our queen perhaps been able to turn things around? What chance would I have to persuade her again of my loyalty? Or had something gone disastrously wrong and an intimidating duke or a stern minister was waiting for me in the royal offices? I felt the lack of information like an acute hunger.

The guards took me up the stairs and into the private palace.

What a pleasure to see daylight again. It drew intricate patterns on the old stone floor.

I remembered the last time I walked down this passage, on my way to the royal bedchamber.

Our queen was in a lighthearted mood that night.

She joked and laughed as she asked for my help in taking off her elaborate dress. She had sent her maids home early, "so we would have more time."

The dress had many layers of white and cream, decorated with stylishly exaggerated flowers that looked a little menacing to me but that I was told were the envy of all the ladies at court. Our queen was thinking of taking the designer under her wing.

Perhaps, she said, there would be a need for a larger dress, particularly in a certain area...

I could not help getting confused with the hooks and eyelets when I heard that. For a moment I started to put them back together again by mistake, until my queen turned around and playfully slapped my hand.

"What are you doing?" she said. "Is this how you are going to serve me?"

My turn to laugh now, lightheartedly. "Maybe I was caught up in a dream," I said.

I was indeed. At this very moment the assassins were watching the shift change of the royal guard from the vantage points I had revealed to them.

The queen put her arms lovingly around my shoulders.

"Is it your dream, too?" she said.

Experienced as she was with the daily deceits of the royal court, she couldn't hide her sudden joy. I suppose she always felt, deep down, that something was missing in me, in spite of my imaginative attention to the details of our frequent celebrations in her bedchambers. I never had any trouble showing my admiration and respect, in every way. You taught me superb control, my Lady Widow. And I know I never said anything that could give her the slightest clue to my real passion. I never talked about it to anyone. Not even to you.

No sounds from outside. Your assassins were true experts. Or else they had been discovered and our plans destroyed. I had no way of knowing.

The queen gripped my buttocks with her strong, workman-like hands. She is no ethereal beauty like you, my Lady Widow, her body bears witness to her descent from a long line of provincial farm wives. She pulled me in as deep as she could. Had she chosen this night of all nights to make me come inside her?

In all the time I served in her bedchamber, she never replaced me with another lover, although of course, as our queen, she always had a few men on the side, a well-designed cross section of our population who kept her in touch with current thought and fashions as well as current lovemaking. She had no reason to assume that I would be anything but delighted to share even more of her life and contribute to the history of our illustrious city. What man would not love to father the queen's child?

Well, perhaps the man who, while embracing her, reassuring her with soothing words and making love to her with her precious gown still half hooked up, flowers all crumpled and sticking out in awkward places, exposing only her magnificent breasts and, if pushed up far enough, her smooth strong thighs, feeling the softness of the silk against his belly and the softness of her inner body tightly around him, knows that he has already betrayed her to her enemy and expects the assassins to enter the bedchambers any moment now using the key that he himself supplied.

In spite of all that, I obeyed.

Our queen is strong and athletic, and she likes her men to make their presence felt with a considerable amount of thrust. So I pushed my cock in as assertively as I dared. She gripped it with her well-developed muscles. After a short, fierce contest she rode me to her rhythm, laughing with delight. Then she made a more serious face, sucked me in as deep as she could, and told me to take control. I took her at her word. I could see the surprise in her red-cheeked face as I built up to a furious pace. Still on top, she was the one shaken around now, trying to keep up her response.

Then she told me to come. Inside her. She looked so vulnerable with her hopeless, groundless love on her farm-wife's face. I had to suppress my natural inclination to pull out and instead allow my body to pass the point of no return. My cock pulsated with life inside our queen's vagina. I felt sadness, but no hesitation as I took a breath, then rammed myself in all the way to the top of her cervix, letting myself swell until I felt that the pressure must tear her apart, and shot my sperm from the hot, wet head of my cock into her royal womb.

I am well aware of the irony of the situation, my Lady Widow. You own my passion and my soul. While I vigorously and dutifully fucked our queen, I was dreaming about welcoming you to the palace in victory, perhaps to these very private quarters. (I was confident that your assassins would keep everything nice and clean up here.)

But instead I was arrested for treason.

At the door of the inner office, your own private guards took over.

You had changed nothing in the room. That surprised me. I thought you would make it look more like a reflection of yourself, or perhaps I remembered the dark rooms and passages where we used to meet in secret and always in danger of being discovered. But now I saw nothing darker than the afternoon light on the highly polished furniture and the rich, muted colors of the wall hangings.

Your guards sat me down on a hard chair in front of the big desk, a desk that no one would ever change, since it is said to date from the time of our First King, your direct ancestor of course. I would expect you to wipe the queen's dirty little fingerprints from it, though, if necessary with her own blood. Or my blood?

Before today I had seen this desk only from the other side, standing behind our queen in a small circle of special advisors. But now I sat where others used to sit in fear, strangers, petitioners, enemies.

And now I was the enemy, as your guards confirmed by binding my hands together behind the chair's high wooden backrest. The bond was firm and impossible to break, but not painful. Then they stepped away.

I watched the afternoon light reach deeper into the room. It was still eerily quiet outside. Someone, perhaps you, my Lady Widow, yourself, had made sure this was a scene unwitnessed by anyone except your guards.

I drank the light in. It streamed like water through the windows, drenching every object in its path. I managed to turn my head until I could see a small slice of sky.

The door to the private offices is hidden in the paneled wall behind the desk, but I know where it is. I heard its slight squeak and I saw your long thin fingers push the frame aside.

I wanted to get up to greet you but I couldn't. So I bowed deeply. I caught a glimpse of your dress and that made me look up again. You no longer wear your mourning black, so I suppose those who say that the husband you grieve is the city, and the power that you lost with him, are at least partly right. This dress of night-sky purple with the faintest hint of rose around the wrists and neckline showed me that in your mind a new day has dawned. A day that I may not see.

You stood there for a while and let me look at you.

Maybe this is the longest time I have ever been allowed to look at you undisturbed and unhurried, my Lady Widow. I never saw your face at all in the first year of our clandestine meetings. You were either touching me from behind in some dark corner, kissing my neck and using my body any way you wanted while I drank in your scent, or your head was covered by your thick widow's veil.

But now your face looked radiant. Your dark brown eyes shone. Your hair fell freely in long black curls. You didn't smile.

Then you walked over to our queen's chair. I could hear the hem of your skirt slide across the polished floor. You took your rightful

place, sitting where our queen and her deplorable father before
her had sat so wrongfully, taking the power that should have been
your husband's and now is yours again, my Lady Widow.

Again, you gave me a mouthful of silence. I wished that time
could expand sideways, that I could be embedded in it like a
fly in amber. But, as I could see, my wishes were fast becoming
irrelevant.

"So here we are," you finally said.

"My Lady Widow," I answered, lowering my head again.

"You have been the Widow's Man for a long time," you said,
coming straight to the point as always. "When did you stop?"

"I never stopped," I said. "I am the Widow's Man today."

That brought a brief sarcastic smile to your lips.

"But not when it counted the most," you said. "Not when
we had our enemy's life in our grasp. Not when you helped her
to escape."

"I only serve you," I said. It was painful to contradict you
when all I wanted to do was to declare my devotion.

You looked at your guards who came forward, standing just
within my line of vision.

They nodded.

You leaned back into the huge carved chair on the other side
of the desk.

"I believe you have been asked this question before," you
said, "downstairs in the cells, and in more ways than one."

I admit I was afraid. I had heard of the special skills of the
Widow's private guards. Who hasn't?

"I cannot give a different answer," I said. "I am the Widow's
Man."

No one had stopped the assassins. I had done my job well.

They slipped silently into our queen's bedchamber using my

well-oiled key at a moment when both she and I were supremely occupied. Drawing her eyebrows together to help her focus, the queen wrapped herself around my penis, which stood alert again. She gave satisfied little sighs that made her magnificent breasts sway. I reached up and stroked the pink areolas around her nipples. When she shuddered and told me, "Yes," I pulled the royal nipples down and gave them a fierce twist for every time she fucked my cock. Then, with a sudden thrust, I threw her over to land on her back amidst the pretty cushions. She slapped my backside with a hard thud and I came a second time inside her, this time without waiting for permission. And this time, she was not the only one who felt a little dizzy.

Like gentlemen, the assassins waited a moment for us to compose ourselves.

I recognized one of them immediately. He was the same gentleman who organized the invitations to the carnival long ago that impressed my friends so much. So much so that they, in turn, opened many doors for me, doors that led me eventually to the bed of our queen, now struggling to sit up, trying to grasp what was happening to her.

It was also that very same carnival when I met you for the first time, my Lady Widow. A day of fate, but of course I now realize that my fate was constructed for me. By others.

I didn't bother with hauling up sheets, covering myself, making excuses, comforting the queen, engaging in small talk with the assassins and so forth. I had nothing to hide, not anymore. I calmly released our queen from my arms, moved aside to give the assassins some space and got out of bed.

I stood there naked. Completely comfortable.

The queen had seen me naked many times, and the assassins surely had seen it all.

"Your unrightful rule is over," said the gentleman I knew.

The other assassin was not a man of words. Instead, he took out a thin leather strip. I was right, they were going to keep it clean in here. That leather strip around her neck would strangle the life out of our queen.

Not that they weren't prepared to adapt the plan if necessary. They made no attempt to hide the knives they carried just underneath their cloaks, long, dark and well used.

Our queen was still sitting up in bed, still half tangled in her ridiculous flower dress, and trying to hold on to the sheets. She had not quite caught up with the end of her world.

"What is this?" she said, to me.

"My queen," I said, "these are your assassins."

I admit I did enjoy the situation, somewhat. For such a long time I had had to do the farm wife's bidding, and I didn't even love her.

Her hand went to her belly and then to her face.

The assassin with the leather garrote moved closer to the bed.

"But," she said, still looking at me, "who are you?"

"I am the Widow's Man."

"The Widow..." she said.

"...is taking back her rightful place and power," said the gentleman assassin.

I suddenly realized that he had never liked me. This man who smoothed my path to power at every turn, who arranged so many amorous meetings with you, my Lady Widow, at great personal danger to himself, and who protected me wherever I went in our illustrious city as long as I went where you sent me, felt nothing but hatred for me. And now...

He turned and looked at me. I could see that I had reached the end of my usefulness, if not for you, my Lady Widow, as I still hope, then certainly for him. He had come here to kill not just the queen but also me.

Maybe he should have communicated that intention to his fellow assassin who clearly knew nothing about it. Maybe then their mission would have been successful. Maybe.

Because in that short moment of his distraction our queen showed what she was made of.

She rolled her sturdy body over the bed sheets and jumped at the gentleman assassin, ripping her flowery dress apart, startling him out of his fixation on me. With the same strong, workman-like hands that she had used to pull me inside her she grabbed the long knife from under his cloak, raised it up in the air and, using her elevated position on the bed, stabbed him in the back with all her considerable might.

Who would have thought that a gentleman could scream like that? Like a frightened child?

He collapsed into the ruin of the ridiculous flowers, spreading his blood everywhere. So much for keeping it clean. The second assassin, although revealing himself quite obviously as an ardent admirer of her voluptuous shape, did his best to race after our queen who had managed to jump off the bed and to head for the back door.

I stood in her way. Yes, that is right. I stood in her way. I could have held her, I could have fought her down, I could have slowed her for just long enough so that the man with the garrote could do his job. Your job.

But I did nothing. I did not help her, but I also did not stop her. She pushed me aside with her strong hands, she ran past me and then she was out the door.

I don't know why. Hadn't I left her bed, just a few minutes before, to give the assassins space to do their deadly work? But something happened to me when I recognized the gentleman's true feelings toward me. I believe my world was shattered then, too.

Besides, I caught the wild after-sex scent of our queen as she

THE WIDOW'S MAN   189

slipped past me, her splendid naked buttocks brushing against
my thigh, and perhaps it crossed the more primitive recesses of
my mind that she might be carrying my child.

Still, my inaction would not have made any difference to the
outcome of this assassination if the rest of the Widow's Men,
what looked like a whole company of them, had not chosen that
very moment to enter the bedchamber.

The blood on the bed and the gentleman's messy business of
dying confused them.

"Is this not the wrong body?" they asked.

The second assassin tried to follow our queen and his
mission, but he was held back with, I am sure, the best of inten-
tions. But with unfortunate results.

I still stood there, naked, surveying the scene with something
like faint amusement.

Our queen can no longer harm you, my Lady Widow, or
interfere with your rightful rule. She and her deplorable father
were upstarts from the provinces, and not related at all to your
illustrious ancestor, the First King. Or at least not more than we
all are, linked through centuries of intricate entanglement.

I had not expected to receive you naked, and in a bed satu-
rated with the gentleman assassin's blood. But I expected you
anytime now.

Instead, there was a heated conversation at the back door and
then your men arrested me "for treason." For helping the queen
escape. For not being what I am and always will be, through
and through, the Widow's Man.

In the palace, in the quiet light of afternoon, you leaned across
the desk, resting your chin in your hands, and gave me that long
clear look that you had given me the morning you first showed me
your face, hidden in the attic of some deserted storage building

near the docks that smelled of wine and spices. Then, kneeling between your thighs, I felt that my body and soul were being weighted and that my life hung in the balance of your judgment.

Then, as now, I could not look away.

Then, as now, something happened in the silence, out of my power, just out there beyond my horizon, that determined my fate.

You said nothing. Gave me not even a nod.

Then, slowly, you waved your guards back. You got up and walked toward me. Your dress shimmered in many shades of darkness. You hesitated for a moment, supporting yourself on my side of the desk. That hesitation told me everything.

I tried to speak, to explain myself again. Maybe I could find the one thing to say that would change the world back to the way it was before, but no words came to me.

And then it was too late. You walked up close to the chair. I smelled the perfume you favor. I saw the soft swelling of your breasts under the cleavage of your rose-rimmed corset. I imagined the dark brown nipples underneath, straining against the material. I wanted to touch them so much, my arms made an involuntary movement toward you. My wrists reminded me with a sharp pain of where I was and who I was, now, to you.

You raised your hand. Over the last few days I have learned to fear a raised hand, but you just lightly touched my forehead and I felt your thin fingers run like a shadow over my hair. I was glad I had been allowed to wash it, even if it was only with a rough prison soap that many had used before.

Then you gripped the back of my neck, hard, and leaned in to kiss me.

I think I can count on the fingers of one hand the times you kissed me before.

The time you told me, in the damp passage under the canal

bridge, your great plans for this city and your return to power. The time I became, on your instructions, with the expert assistance of your gentleman assassin and, I admit, not without a certain amount of satisfaction, the lover of our farm-wife queen. The time when you sent me off to the culmination of my mission in the royal bedroom, to betray her.

And now.

Although I have tasted them rarely, I instantly recognized the exquisite flavor of your lips. I opened my mouth a little to accommodate you. I closed my eyes and shut out the world.

You pushed your tongue inside, fast and hard. I took it in.

Sensations exploded. Some people can pass out from such sensations. Maybe I hoped I would, too. But I stayed alert. Alert and alive. Then I felt your other hand inside my shirt, your thighs underneath the midnight silk pressing on mine.

I wanted to feel your full weight on my body but you only gave me a little bit. You gripped my neck more fiercely. You forced your tongue in deeper. I caressed it with my own, always careful to follow your lead, until I ran out of breath. Politely, you pulled out. I would have preferred to lose consciousness. Then I felt your lips brushing mine again.

Your scent was everywhere.

I don't know how long your kisses lasted, but by the time I opened my eyes again, the room seemed much darker.

My body responded in other ways, too. You looked down briefly and, equally briefly, ran your hand across my pants. I looked into your eyes as you tested my reaction. My cock rose to meet you. Your fingers rubbed along its length. You rolled your thumb roughly around the rim. The blood rose hot under my skin. Still looking into my eyes, you slowly stroked the head of my penis through the coarse fabric of my prison pants. It started to throb in tribute to your power. I returned your gaze.

"As always," you said, "you have perfect control."

"Control is the servant of surrender," I said. I often wanted to say that to you, because I am not sure, even now, that you understand it, but I had never been so bold. Now, I could say whatever I liked.

You kissed me one more time, sweetly and gently. And then you drew back. You leaned against the old king's desk.

"Is there a request you would like to make?" you said, and I could hear a certain sadness in your voice.

"May I ask for a piece of your clothing?" I said.

That surprised you. Maybe you thought I would ask for a girl to be sent to my cell (and from the brief test you performed on my body I would have put her to good use, that is true), or maybe you thought there was someone I wanted to send a message to. Maybe you thought I would ask for a dark drink to ease the passing.

But you quickly overcame your surprise.

With a fast, decisive movement, you tore a long strip off your sleeve. Your skin shimmered pale and delicate underneath. Then you bent over me and slowly laid the fabric around my shoulders.

The scent of your favorite perfume rose from it.

You looked down at me, hands suspended, fabric suspended. Silk would be perfect for the purpose. It is soft but it does not yield.

I looked up.

"Please," I said.

You hesitated.

I didn't close my eyes. Did I want you to do this for me?

Well, one part of me did, and another part was still not ready.

You saw that, and you pulled away.

The silk strip dropped onto my chest.

Your hands ran all the way down to my thighs.

You touched my crotch again, but nothing more.

Then you turned and walked away through the private door without so much as a backward glance.

I saw the long fingers of your hand slide it shut behind you.

The carnival, colorful costumes and intricate masks, ladies of the court and gentlemen of the bedchamber, took over the entire outer palace, and admission was very exclusive. Of course, everyone wanted to be there. This was during the time of our queen's deplorable father, whose proximity was to be avoided if one valued one's life, or at least that's what our teachers told us. But we were young, and we did not believe in personal death.

I, of all people, was the one who got invitations. They came to me through what I thought then was a fortuitous, perhaps an accidental path. Now I know that it was the long hand of history that selected me. To go to the carnival, where I first felt your breath on my neck and your silent touch from behind, and where I lost contact with my friends by falling helplessly and gloriously in love with you. To return to this prison cell, and wait for your assassin.

I don't know how it will be done. They were trying to keep it clean in the royal bedroom (and look how that turned out...) but does it matter here?

This is not an honorable death. This is not a public execution, where the condemned man gets to make a last speech and take a last stand, with all the good citizens as witness. This is the dirty little assassination of a dirty little traitor, who betrayed both the queen who loved him and you, my Lady Widow, who owns his immortal soul.

Is it right that I should die tonight?

My Lady Widow, everything you do is right by me.

All those years of life in the shadows, when I prepared myself every day to catch a glimpse of your face in the crowd or the faintest scent of your perfume in an empty room, and when many, so many days passed giving me nothing but longing, I never once wavered in my love.

With you, I have lived a life in memories, stolen moments of ecstasy, intense desire and pain. And the many joyful celebrations I experienced, first with the girls in the street, and then with the girls at court, and lastly, in your service, with our queen in her royal bed, are nothing compared to the marriage of my soul with your passing shadow.

The Reign of the Widow—how will it pan out? Will you rule us from our rightful throne? Will you be deposed again? Perhaps by your own people? Will you, too, at some point feel the kiss of the assassin on your neck, or will you leave this life as you lived it, all on your own terms? A new day is dawning over our realm, that is for sure. I would have dearly liked to see it.

Is that the assassin's soft footfall I hear outside my cell? Or is it just my own fearful heartbeat? It won't be long now.

When the assassin comes, I will take his touch as if it was yours, my Lady Widow. I wear the thin strip of silk around my neck, hoping he will favor me by using it. It will be your last embrace, the consummation that I have desired ever since that first night at the carnival. I can move my cheek just enough to feel the fabric you tore from your sleeve.

I am glad that your scent on it will not fade before I die.

JERICHO

Megan Arkenberg

He sits in a corner of the room, far away from the others. It is better this way. He can watch them flutter through the house like birds in a dark cage, swathed in damask and velvet and brocade, glittering and twirling to the music. They wear silver rings in their ears, their eyes are shadowed with kohl and masks, their lips glisten with wine like dark jewels. The men's bare necks, the women's arms and breasts and shoulders shimmer like damp silk. A bitter-smooth scent is in the air, brandy and musk and sweat.

They are his guests in this rented house and he, their charming host, despises them. He sits on the edge of a velvet chair the color of a drunken woman's mouth and watches the dancers with steepled fingers pressed against his lips. The rest of his face is hidden by a gray mask. His clothes are dark and plain. He wears a scarlet cord around his neck, and from that cord hangs an iron key.

His name is Rahab, and the key opens the gates of the city.

***

He thinks of the people camped outside the city walls.

In his head, he calls them the Golden People. That is how they seem—hot, metallic, too bright to look at. Nothing at all like the silver-twilight people dancing in the rented ballroom, begging to be stared at, to be desired. In his heart, Rahab knows he is one of these twilight people, and worse; he is a whore, and a whore in Jericho is like a city without walls.

There are walls inside the Golden People, holding them inside themselves, holding strangers out. Even the beautiful ones are hard to look at. They hide their secrets so well, it is easy to forget they are hiding anything.

Like a cheap harlot, Jericho cannot keep a secret.

The first Golden People came to his house two months ago. It was strange for foreigners to venture so far across the city, where the streets became mazes and bridges ran between houses overhead, and young women would stand in the bridges' windows with one shoulder bared and masks over their eyes. Rahab's house, a dark sinuous thing with many windows, leaned against the city wall like a girl drowned in absinthe. It smelled like absinthe, the sweet anise scent of brothels.

The Golden People smelled like sunlight, sweat and molten metal. The man had been distant, dispassionate, watching everything with a smile that did not reach his eyes. But the woman's hair was soft between Rahab's fingers, and her hands when they touched his face were as hot as gold worn against skin.

It was already dawn when the woman came into his room at the top of the house, where early sunlight hemmed the windows in ruby. She closed the door softly and slipped into his bed, the old mattress creaking with her solid weight. She was naked beneath her black silk robe.

"My name is Tamar," she whispered, her breath hot on his ear. One warm hand pressed across his lips, and he smelled metal on her fingertips, gunpowder beneath her nails. Her other hand traced a slow line down his throat, across his muscled chest and firm abdomen, and curved around him down below. He swallowed a gasp. Her grip was hard, her strokes rough and demanding. Soon her mouth replaced her hand, the tip of her tongue unbearably harsh against the most delicate skin.

Rahab gasped again, breath catching in his throat like something solid, and she rewarded him by taking him deeper, her fingers stroking and caressing and tormenting. There was something indescribably wonderful about her rawness, her inexperience. He came with a moan and Tamar hesitated, unsure whether to swallow. He looked down at her, meeting her dark golden eyes, and she swallowed with a smile that chilled his blood.

She slid up beside him, resting her forehead against his temple. Her hands were stroking his hair, stroking his cheek, as though she wanted to make her touch on him visible to the world. He could barely hear her speaking over the pounding of his pulse. "It's morning," she was saying. "I have to return to camp."

"Take me with you."

He turned his face to hers and saw her firm lips tighten in uncertainty. A glistening pearl drop still clung to the corner of her mouth, and he brushed it away with his thumb.

"I can't," she said. "Rahab, I—"

He silenced her protest with a kiss, deep and lingering. Her mouth tasted of wine and salt and him. "Then stay here. For as long as you can."

They stayed in his house for three days and three nights.

***

The second time he welcomed the Golden People, it was the same man but a different woman. He knew at once that she would not desire him. She was brighter and harder than the others, and the walls inside her were older, more fiercely maintained.

"I am here to thank you," she said, though she seemed too proud to be thankful. "In the days you kept Achan and Tamar in your house, the soldiers searched for them in the city. Your hospitality saved their lives, and for that you have my gratitude."

The word "soldiers" brought dim memories to his mind; damp alleys, cold hands, biting rings. Rahab hated the soldiers of Jericho and was pleased to know the Golden People were their enemies.

"I have another favor to ask of you," the woman said. He had begun to think of her as the Leader, for clearly she was one. He did not realize until later, much later, that the Golden People were soldiers, too.

All soldiers want the same thing from whores.

Rahab fingers the cord around his neck. He remembers the Leader's words as she slipped it over his head: *This is how we will know you.* He wonders at that. Among the shimmering twilight-people of Jericho, his dark eyes, plain clothes, the strands of silver in his dark hair make him conspicuous. The Leader must be blind indeed if she needs a chain, the mark of a prisoner, to find her allies.

Jericho's key hides inside his open collar, cold against his skin. It was not hard to find. He smiles to remember the girl, daughter of Jericho's gate-master, who answered his card at one of the extravagant park-side restaurants where caged birds

sang in the smoky rooms and anything at all could be negoti-
ated.

"Who will be there?" she had asked, leaning over Rahab's
table.

He laughed and ran his fingers through her brittle hair.
"Everybody," he said. "Anyone worth meeting. Though I do
have a small price—a token of worthiness, if you like."

She blushed prettily. "That's ridiculous," she said, sounding
uncertain.

Very gently, Rahab wrapped an arm around the girl's waist
and drew her down to her knees. "Completely ridiculous," he
said. "But worth it, I promise you." He gave her a quick kiss,
sweet and fleeting.

The girl was the first guest to arrive, holding the city key in
her pocket.

One of the glistening birds detaches herself from the flock and
flutters toward Rahab in the corner. Sweat makes her white
shirt stick to her back and the silky skin between her breasts.
Her braids unravel around her black mask, little stands of
sunlight beside the night sky.

"I think I've danced enough for the evening," Rahab says,
as she perches herself on the arm of his chair. He takes her
hand and kisses it, tasting salt and spilled wine.

The woman tightens her fingers on his. "So have I," she
says. "Come upstairs."

Rahab raises his eyebrows, glancing at the other guests. The
Golden Woman laughs and pulls him to his feet. He follows her
up the winding staircase, her laughter ringing in his ears.

He pulls her into the first bedroom they come to. Its walls are
smooth and dark blue, its floorboards bare. Cobalt and silver
fabrics hang over a wide bed. The Golden Woman ignores it,

leaning against a wall and dragging Rahab toward her by the
red cord around his neck.

"This is it?" she asks, fingering the iron key.

"Yes," Rahab says.

She finds the clasp and slides the key from its cord. One
hand lifts her cigarette case from her pocket and tucks the key
inside while her other tangles up through Rahab's hair. She
finds the wire that holds his mask in place and breaks it with a
flick of her finger.

"You've very beautiful," she says as the gray silk floats to
the floor. "Somehow I didn't expect that."

Her skin tastes like hot metal beneath his tongue.

Before the Golden People came, Rahab would walk along the
walls of Jericho in the cool hours before dawn, watching the
lights waken or die in the city below. Jericho, city of the moon,
city of twilight, city of stone shadows and arabesques. It seemed
fragile enough to crush between his fingers.

It is only the walls that defend Jericho. Not the soldiers, slipping into alleyways with the cheapest of whores. Not the gates,
whose key can be bought with a kiss. Jericho prides itself on
the ceremonial beauty of its warriors in their dark uniforms,
the masterful workmanship of its gates, but it does not look at
its walls. Its walls were not made to be looked at.

Before the Golden People, Rahab was like the twilight city,
fragile and dark and undefended. It is dangerous in Jericho to
be secretive, to let others see that you have secrets. The treasure
precious enough to hide is the only treasure worth stealing, the
saying goes in Jericho, and this is a city of thieves.

Rahab wonders if the Golden People have heard this. They
are so eager to rip down the walls of Jericho, to get at the sweet
treasure inside. But without its walls, Jericho is nothing.

**

The Golden Woman leaves her mask on.

The rest comes off in a rush of white silk and silver ribbon, clutching and tearing, the rich fabric drifting to the floor like snowfall. Her body is lean and hard like Tamar's, her skin tanned deep brown, almost darker than the small red-tinged nipples that stiffen beneath his tongue. He wonders, for a moment, if the Leader's body is like this. He is not sure if it is that thought or the masked woman's deft caressing hand that makes him hard.

He carries the masked woman to the bed. They hardly make it. She twists in his arms and pushes him flat across the pillows, sheathing him in her moist heat with a harsh moan. She clutches his hips, her fingernails biting. Their pounding makes the whole bed shake and creak.

The masked woman's climax ripples through her, tearing a gasp from her soft lips. Rahab rolls on top of her and buries his face in the curve of her throat. She wraps her legs around his waist, drawing him deeper, and he comes a moment later. They collapse across each other, gasping for breath.

The masked woman whispers something.

"What?" Rahab can barely lift his head. She shifts beneath him until his head is pillowed on her breasts, and he can hear the words echoing through her skin.

"Tamar asked me to tell you," she says, "that her tent is the blue and gold one at the edge of camp. If you still want to leave Jericho. If you think you can."

He looks up at her, but her face behind the black velvet mask is as smooth and unreadable as her voice. She presses a dry kiss on his forehead. A moment later she rises to dress, drapes the city key around her neck and is gone.

**

After the Golden Woman returns to the ball, Rahab remains
in the bedroom, smoking at the foot of the bed. It is one of the
Golden Woman's cigarettes, and it has her taste, dry and sweet.

His mask is on the floor near the doorway. He closes his eyes,
feeling again the roughness of the Golden Woman's fingertips
along his cheek, the fragile skin of his eyelid. How safe she had
seemed behind her mask, how impenetrable, until the velvety
sigh broke from her throat.

It is not good, he thinks, for the Golden People to wear
masks. It leaves them unguarded. Undefended. Conquerable.

He looks at his pocket watch, lying open-faced on the pillow.
She has been gone for half an hour—enough time to leave his
house, to go down to the edge of the city and the gates, to
slip Jericho's key to the Leader. Enough time to build the fires
within the city that will bring down the walls.

Rahab grinds the fire from his cigarette and goes down to
the ballroom to join the birds.

Some of the Golden People are like the sharpest knives, the
knives that cut so deep and so smoothly that there is no pain.
The Leader is not one of them.

"Jericho will fall," she said the day she gave Rahab the
scarlet cord. She seemed so hard, so certain, as if her knowledge came from the gods themselves. "The question is whether
you will help us break it, or if you will fall with the rest."

"Do you not trust me?" he asked.

"I trust you." The Leader smiled quickly, brutally. "You're
good at what you do, Rahab. And you know where your best
interest lies."

"Whores are known for keeping secrets," the Golden Man
murmured.

"You forget, Achan, that we are in Jericho," the Leader said. "You can have secrets here, but you can't hide the fact that you have them."

When her back was turned, Rahab caught Achan by the wrist. He let his long nails sink into the soft flesh. "A good whore knows how to be conquered," he hissed.

"Or how to pretend to be," Achan said.

In the ballroom, the birds are reeling drunkenly, stumbling over each other's gowns and landing in laughing tangles on the carpet. The gate-master's daughter is lying on a couch, her head in the lap of an eminent composer, while an actor and playwright disappear for a moment into the shadows beneath the stairs. Rahab keeps his distance, leaning against the door frame. The damp-lilac smell of the room is making him sick.

The composer stands and goes to the organ. She smiles at her audience and begins to play one of her celebrated themes. The notes sound wet and deflated, but the audience laughs and applauds.

Rahab pushes his way out onto the ballroom balcony. The night air is bitingly cold, and the sound of high-pitched laugher and the scent of lilac follow him out. A spidery silver bridge runs from one corner of the balcony to his own house across the street. The house where the Leader promised that he would be safe.

With a last spiteful glance at the guests in the rented house, Rahab crosses the bridge.

Three hours after midnight, the drums begin.

For seven days the Golden People have marched around the walls. Some in Jericho believe they are doing it on the orders of gods; others say they mean to be frightening. And they are frightening, silent and gleaming in the brutal sun.

But Rahab knows the truth; the Golden People have been digging beneath the walls. And tonight, when the Leader slips through the city gates, she will find the fires that have been kindled along walls where the tunnels end. She will pour something on the fires, something that smells of sulfur and saltpeter.

The drums are like the marching—a distraction. It is fire and earth that will break the walls of Jericho.

And when the walls have fallen, the slaughter will begin. The Golden People with their swords and with their knives will break down the doors and shatter the windows and crush the bridges and bring down the roofs, and the streets where fruit vendors gathered and pretty girls walked will soon run with blood. Rahab imagines the sticky red trails staining the walls of the rented house, imagines corpses piled on the wide beds. He thinks of the gate-master's daughter, too much of a child yet to carry a knife.

Anyone in his house will be spared, the Leader promised. But there is no one in Jericho that Rahab wishes to save.

Four hours after midnight, in the first veiled light of morning, the walls come down.

When it is over, the Leader comes to Rahab's house. She carries no sword, but her clothes and hair and the bare skin of her hands are drenched in blood. There is a long streak of it beneath her left eye, like a scarlet tear.

Rahab holds his hand out to her, and to his surprise she takes it and kisses it. "Jericho is yours," he says, with a smile calculated to melt a woman's bones.

Her other hand slips to his knee. He feels the awful heat of her skin through the fabric of his trousers. "Yes," she says. Only that.

Rahab tightens his grip on her wrist, tightens it until it must hurt her, though she is good at hiding her pain. He is not used to asking for things—to begging, for there is no uglier or more accurate word for what he is about to do—and his tongue sticks to the roof of his mouth. The Leader is not a child to trick, a girl to entice, a lover to demand things of. Her face when she looks at him is like a wall of stone.

"I want to fight for you," Rahab says finally. "Wherever you go next, whoever waits for you there, I want to go with you."

"You are not a soldier," she says.

"Then I will become one."

The Leader smiles, and suddenly the walls in her eyes are down, and he sees the naked thing behind them, bloody and starved. "Let me give you a secret, Rahab. I'm not a soldier, either."

He opens his mouth, but she lifts her bloody hand from his knee and presses it over his lips. "I took Jericho, yes. I leveled her walls. But what I want—what I desire, yes, more than I've desired any man—is to raise those walls again. I want a home, Rahab. I want a city for my sons and daughters. I want to live my life behind walls."

He tries to stand, but she drops to the floor and wrenches him down beside her, envelopes him in the smell of blood.

When she is asleep, he carries her up the stairs to his bed. Her hands have left finger-trails of blood on his skin, and his lips have left smooth red circles on her shoulders and neck. When he lies down beside her on the white sheets, their bodies leave bloody stains.

The Leader sleeps deeply and still as stone. Rahab traces the firm muscles of her shoulder, her hard waist, the solid curve of her hip, and thinks of what Jericho will make of her. She has been hardened by wind and sun and rain, the cold and the heat, the brutal light of day. She built walls within her because she had no walls without.

She will become soft in Jericho if she raises the walls again. Soft and sweet and drunken, mellow in her desires, vulnerable in her beauty. He imagines her as one of the girls on the bridges, her face hidden behind a mask, her soul naked. The thought makes him sick.

She was supposed to free him from Jericho. She cannot become trapped here herself.

He kisses her neck, and when she does not stir, he whispers into her ear.

"Cursed be the man who raises the walls of Jericho," he says. "He shall lay her foundation in the grave of his firstborn, and in the grave of his youngest shall he set her gates."

He kisses her again. "You are meant to break walls, Hoshea, not to raise them."

Tamar is waiting for him at the Golden People's camp, smelling of coriander and cardamom and the ashes in her hearth. Her children play in the dust outside her gold-and-cobalt tent, building fortresses of pebbles and leaves and kicking them down again. They stop when they see him coming. By the time he reaches the tent, Tamar has a cup of tea and a plate of spice cakes set out for him on the low table.

"She tells us we are to leave," she says. "She says the gods told her that the city is cursed and we are to take nothing from it. But you will come with us, won't you?"

He looks down at the paper-thin cup in his hands, at the tea leaves crusting the surface like a sharp-edged moon. "Do you want me to?" he asks.

"Yes," Tamar says. Only that.

But it is enough.

THE LAST SACRIFICE

Zander Vyne

*T*he cursed statue had stood in my valley long before even the Druids vanished. It might have crumbled into harmless myth had it not been for the last sacrifice, for all those who came before had walked into death's lair.

I could blame her for everything that happened, but blame is a very human fixation, one they value far too much.

Only time will tell how anyone's story will end, no matter the choices they make. Mine is no different.

I did what I could. My role will have little impact on the outcome. Still, the world is on fire and, though it is not my fault, man will blame me. They always blame the dragon.

The casting of lots decided which girl would become an offering for the basilisk, but never before had the name of a princess been chosen.

The King and Queen, not having the power to stop the ritual sacrifice, grieved her loss alone, for the people of the Haven cheered when the crier read their daughter's name. Most almost certainly suspected, as I had, that royals' names were not entered into the lottery.

Princess Aerten—unlike her parents and all the girls who had been sacrificed before her—had not shed tears, begged for mercy or screamed in terror over her fate. "You need not bind me with chains. I go gladly, giving my life so another may live," she said when the Scarlet Knights made to seize her.

Though her words were a dagger to my heart, for I could not imagine a world without her in it, I was there when they took her away—the only one who dared accompany them from the safety of the Haven's protective stone walls into the forest-without-end.

Aerten rode with only a small saddle covering my back and a plain, single rein bit. Nothing fancy for her, she always said, shooing away the stable lads who thought a princess's mount should be fitted with a royal caparison and a gold bit decorated with fancy bosses.

Today the knights had seen to it anything of value was left behind. They had not even allowed her a cloak. Her slippered feet curved against the warmth of my ribs, giving my sides a slow caress.

"You are a fine beast, Taran." Her hair had come undone. The long glossy tendrils wound through my mane as her voice tickled my ear.

One of the Scarlet Knights laughed. "Look at 'er, whispering to tha' courser like the horse is going to talk right back!"

"Mayhap she thinks it will sprout wings and fly her over the forest-without-end, to a land far, far away," the other knight said.

"Or grow a unicorn's horn to stab the beastie to death before it can devour her!"

Only the Princess knew how close their jests were to my reality, for only she knew my secrets, and even she did not know them all.

Aerten did not answer them, though her fingers tangled tighter in my mane, her weight shifting subtly with the rising of her back and the tightening of her thighs. My Princess—proud to the last.

Listening to the knights' taunts, thinking ahead to what waited, I had few regrets, though I felt remorse for my parents' hurt when they discovered I had stacked the lottery to make up for all the years my name had not been entered.

Taran nickered, as if reading my troubled thoughts.

"Settle. We will be there soon, and all is well in my heart." I repeated the words like a spell meant to soothe us both, "All is well. All is well."

The Scarlet Knights picked up our pace. As the sun sank behind the Mystic Mountains, we reached a clearing where tall stones curved around the mouth of a ravine, each one carved with ancient symbols that meant nothing to me. Bones of those who had come before, the remains of the dragon's yearly feast, littered the forest floor.

In the center of it all stood a huge statue, rust and moss covered, almost hidden by vines and brambles. Still the shape of some sort of hound could be made out. From its neck hung chains and manacles. How odd, I thought, to find such a thing here, so far from the Haven. Had it been another occasion, I might have asked the knights what they knew of it, but I had other worries this night.

Before the knights could dismount, I slid from Taran's back. "I would meet the dragon unchained."

"You will be the beast's meal either way." The older of the

two knights spoke with a confidence belied by the darting of his gaze to the fast-sinking sun.

From within the mountain could be heard a deep rumble. The air was acrid and bitter on my tongue. Tendrils of smoke lapped at my feet and flirted with my skirt.

"We canna' leave her thus. She is sure to run," the other knight said, though he too remained atop his mount.

"Even if I could make it to the Haven before full night falls, I would not be welcome. Running would mean death. Dinner for the wolven."

"Stand in the circle, by the statue, and I will consider my duty ended. 'Tis the least we can do, but be quick about it. Night comes." His gaze darted to the fast-darkening, twilight-blue sky.

I saved myself further torment, avoiding Taran's expressive equine eyes as I passed his reins to the knight. "Thank you."

Pungent smoke seeped from the fissure in the mountainside. A skull stared blindly up at me from the forest floor. Terror drove me to my knees. Despite my previous intention to go nowhere near the thing, I reached for the statue that had held so many before me as offering for the dragon. Its thorns bit my fingers, sending me to my haunches sucking pinpricks of pain from their tips.

Gloom had overtaken the forest, and creatures crept with skittering claws over dry, fallen leaves in the darkness all around me. I struggled, barely able to resist the urge to run. I knew what terrible things wolven could do. The dragon was a thing of mystery, for no one who ever met it returned to tell any tales. Mayhap a death at its whim would not be as dreadful.

"Come out, come out...wherever you are." A hysterical giggle erupted.

"Only you would offer yourself up to a demon and then goad

it with laughter," Taran said, stepping into the clearing.

No matter how many times I saw him first in one form, then the other, it still gave me a jolt. As a stallion, he was midnight black with rippling muscles. As a man, he was tall and just as powerfully built. Both guises shared the same animated brown eyes and black, silky hair. He wore no clothing, and could not have been more beautiful. My heart and my body reacted to him, flooding with warmth and emotions.

"You came back!" I rushed into his arms wishing I could feel his bare flesh through my gown. I had only seen him naked once before, on a day that now seemed so far away. I had kissed him then, long and slow. Touched him and loved him. Ached for more ever since.

"Of course." He pressed his lips to my forehead.

"Foolish." Burying my nose in the curve of his shoulder, I inhaled his familiar smell—leather, horse, sandalwood soap. Man or beast, I loved him all the same.

"That remains to be seen." He set me gently away from him.

"The dragon will come, and I will die. If you have any sense, you will go now before he comes for me." I entwined my fingers with his to keep myself from giving in to the temptation of his naked body, my lust almost more than I could bear.

"Are you prepared to die?" His voice was gruff.

Shame, and the love I saw in his expressive eyes, prodded me into confessing, "I did it because I was angry. Angry with my parents for continuing the lottery, though surely they could have found a way to stop it. Angry they tried to spare me. Trapped, like all of us, only waiting for the wolven or the dragon to grow strong enough to kill us all. Angry with you for tempting me with things I cannot have. Things you refuse to give me." I closed my eyes, unable to bear the bitter resentment in my heart when I looked at him.

Once, and only once, Taran had held me close, made love to me and told me his secrets. They were many, and they were shocking, but the only one that truly mattered was his ability to leave the Haven and return to a safe, beautiful place far, far away, occupied by gods like himself. Many times since, I had asked him to take me there. Many times, he had refused.

"Will you do it now?" I asked, though the question in my heart was, "Do you love me enough?"

"Do you love me?" Aerten had asked, on a day that now seemed so far away.

Above us the sky was robin's-egg blue. Atop lush, green grass, on a blanket upon the meadow, warmed by the sun, danger seemed impossible. "As much as I have ever loved, I love you," My fingers played in her unbound hair.

"Always the riddles. You must have loved many. You *are* very old."

I teased the tip of her nose with the fuzzy end of a stalk of grass. "You would know no peace if you knew."

She gasped, laughing, and punched my arm as she rolled onto her stomach. "That many?"

"Is it not enough that I am here, that I choose to be here with you?" Though I should not have done it, I placed a kiss upon the dimple of her chin.

She sighed, her breath sweet upon my mouth. So innocent, my Princess, so full of youthful yearning for things she thought she lacked. In truth, I had never loved another the way I loved her. She had made many long years of suffering in exile worth the price paid.

"I want...more," she said, sliding her fingers under my tunic, cupping her palm over my heart, smoothing the flat of her hand over my belly and under the waist of my trousers. "More," she whispered, her lips moving over mine, her fingers dancing on my skin.

"No," I said as my body betrayed my base desires with flesh that swelled and said, "Yes, yes, yes," despite the denial on my lips.

Now, after all that has happened, I have to ask myself if things would have been different had I not given in that day. But those are worries for another time. My choices have been made, and there is no turning back.

I let lust consume me as I taught her the pleasure to be had with our mouths and our hands, skin touching skin. She was an eager pupil, swollen and wet under my fingers and tongue with her own desire.

Under the summer afternoon sky, I made love to her and found a peace unlike any I had felt since being sent to the Haven. I forgot everything but her and I fell in love, deep and true.

Drunk on lust, I let down my guard. Though stories were coming more frequently of wolven striking people in full daylight, I was not prepared. Rubbing myself between the squeeze of her slippery thighs, arm wrapped around her curvy hip, fingers buried in her sex, I did not see them coming until they were upon us. Snarling teeth snapped at empty clothing. Their confusion over finding only cloth in their muzzles is what saved us. As the enraged wolven shredded our clothes, I changed from man to horse to save her. I did it without thought, breaking one of the only rules the gods had given me, leading me into telling her afterward almost all of my secrets, giving her my trust as well as my heart.

"Will you do it now?" she asked, the question in her eyes, *Do you love me enough?*

"I should never have told you I can leave the Haven."

She came to where I sat, kneeling on the ground at my feet, clasping my tightly tucked fingers in her own. "Take me to your true home. Save me from the dragon!"

"They've never failed to give him his due. If you leave now, what then?" The bitter taste of shame twisted my mouth. Until now I had given no thought to my duty to the Haven's inhabitants.

"Maybe they will not realize we have gone, and no one will have to die at all this year."

I shook my head. "I *must* remain."

"You said you could go!"

"Not at my will or yours."

"More riddles. If you do not leave, we both shall die." She rose from her knees, brushing the dirt from her gown.

"I will do anything possible to save you, but I cannot take you away." My duty was to watch over her people, but my heart ached at my failure to give her that which she desired most. Even if I prevented her death now, I knew not where I could keep her safe. I could not take her to my home or hers. She had nowhere to go.

"If you cannot save me, then love me, Taran. Love me before I die. Just once. Give in to it. Just once."

I held out my hand to her and, may the gods help us all, there was no going back.

I ran to him before he changed his mind. Into his arms I came, standing between the spread of his thighs as his fingers worked the tiny buttons of my dress. I dared not speak, lifting my arms to help him pull each piece of cloth from my trembling body.

My emotions were beaches, like the ones he had described, with opposing shores. The moon of my desire fought with my innocence for the water's caress.

"Still, calm," Taran said.

My fingers trembled, but his were sure as he rolled me to rest like the sacrifice I was, prone upon the slab of stone. All around us, smoke swirled, but even the fear faded when we touched.

Lying beside me, he traced my skin with gentle fingers, kissing me until I spread my legs eagerly when he parted my thighs and ruffled the hair covering my most sensitive place.

Against my hip, I felt the press of him, long and hard. I had only seen horses mating. Hiding behind the stable, thrilled by the forbidden sights and sounds as the grooms had led an eager stallion to a mare, I had been horrified and excited. The great male horse had reared and pranced, snorting as his mate turned her rump to him, tossing her black mane. Out of the sheath under the steed's belly shot a tube of flesh, easily as long as my arm and as thick as a small tree. This he plunged into his mate, pawing the air above her head, biting at her neck in his frenzy. When he was finished, though the grooms tried to prevent it, his glistening appendage slid from the mare and sent his seed gushing over the hay in a torrent.

Now as I felt the press of his hard flesh on mine and my thoughts brought me back to that memory, excitement coursed through me. Though I was frightened, I knew he was not as large as the horse had been, despite his dual nature. I turned slightly so I could take it in my hand, and knew at once that I had done the right thing for he sighed, his muscular thighs quivering as I ran my hand over the velvet surface. Like steel beneath silk he was. I grew drunk on a power I might never have the chance to use again. Already my mind conjured memories of his taste on my tongue, his hands on my flesh. This time I knew there would be more. I would have it all.

It was as my mother had told me when I had come of age as a maiden. "You will know what to do. Your body will show you the way to your man's pleasure." She had not spoken of the delight I might find, but I felt it now.

I thought again of the stallion and mare; the flesh between my legs tingled with want. The buds of my breasts rose to peaks begging for the warm suckle of his mouth. Each pull of his lips, each scrape of his teeth against my sensitive flesh sent me higher, closer and closer to something wondrous. "Show me," I begged, knowing the wisdom in my mother's words as my legs parted farther of their own accord and he came between them.

His answer was to slide into me, slowly but firmly. Pain was a dull sword in my belly, soothed by the sweet rubbing of our bodies as he moved within me. Soon I knew only fullness and beauty and once again climbed to that place he had shown me before, that I had longed for since. It was love, I thought as I came undone with the exquisiteness of our joining. True love.

After, he held me close, kissing the sore place between my thighs, wiping away the droplets of blood I had shed with my chemise and virginity.

Had we been able to stay just like that until our heads cleared, maybe we would have had a chance, but just like on the day the wolven attacked, we were enraptured by each other and taken completely by surprise.

A voice rang out, "Virgin blood, upon the sacred stone, taken by one charged with doing the humans no harm!"

Aerten screamed. I pushed her behind me as a giant of a man, clad from head to toe in armor the likes of which I had never seen, appeared in the smoke-filled clearing. Expecting a terrible dragon, my confused mind could not reconcile this man's presence or his strange words.

Flame shot from the dragon's lair and the beast slithered into the clearing at last—every bit as fearsome as I had imagined him. Covered in emerald scales like battle shields sharp enough to flay a man alive, with jack-o'-lantern teeth filling a jawbone so full it could not close and orange eyes that burned like the fires of Hades; he was the stuff of nightmares.

Never had I been more stunned when the dragon roared, "Aye, the terms have been met. Be gone!"

"The sacrifice is still mine!" The warrior's growl sent bats flying from the trees. In the forest, wolven howled.

His metal-gauntleted hand knocked me aside as easily as a man swatting a fly. Catching Aerten's arm, he lifted her clear from her feet hauling her up to eye level, scowling through the slit in his helm as his gaze met hers just before she fainted. Tossing her over his shoulder, he stepped into the forest's darkness. They were gone before I could even find my feet.

"You cannot track him down low," the dragon said. The harshness had gone from his voice and the fire had faded from his eyes.

"Who is he?"

"Lord Wulfgar, ruler of the wolven. Do you know the legend?"

"No."

"Wulfgar was a man once, a fierce and arrogant warrior. His ego caught the attention of the gods, who sent down their finest fighter, challenging him to a fight, promising eternal life and rule of the wolven if he could best their champion."

"He lost?"

"No!" the dragon roared. "He tricked the gods' champion, defeating him but earning their anger. They gave him eternal life, as promised, but as a statue of iron, alive only once a year unless his spell was broken."

"For how long?" If he turned back into iron, it was only a

matter of waiting, unless he fed Aerten to the wolven before he went.

"You and the sacrifice are responsible for breaking the spell! Now he will bring war to your gods and her people. If he wins, he gains true eternal life."

For the first time I noticed the statue that had stood in the clearing had vanished.

"Why now? Why Aerten?" *Why on my watch*, I wanted to scream.

The dragon sighed. Wisps of smoke curled from his snout. "I am old, I am tired, and I am very, very hungry. Go now. They headed for the top of the mountain."

"Can I defeat him?"

"In truth, you would be best served carrying a warning to her people and to the gods. Sacrificing her to save many is the wise, but more difficult choice."

The dragon was right. It was all I had waited for, all these years. My one true purpose—to alert the gods should war threaten the humans. I had to go home.

I woke with an aching head and a heart torn asunder. Upside-down, hanging over the warrior's enormous shoulder, I knew Taran was dead, for he would not have let the beastly man take me without a fight had he lived.

Up and up we climbed, into the rocks and ruts of the mountainside. Was this my penalty for being such a foolish girl, willing to risk everything to taste a bit of life, a morsel of freedom, forbidden things?

When I stacked the lottery stones, I had been prepared to die in the dragon's valley. Anything to force Taran to take me away with him. Now I would give anything to take it all back, to save Taran, even the pleasure found beneath him. How thoughtless I had been. How selfish.

My captor stopped his climb, tossing me to the ground where I huddled, naked and afraid.

I expected to see sharp claws when he stripped off metal gauntlets, and huge teeth in a monster's maw when he removed his helm. Instead he revealed strong, capable-looking hands and a handsome face. In the Haven, he would have set any young girl's heart aflutter with his good looks and mine was no different. My cheeks flushed hot.

"Not what you anticipated?" He smiled, showing perfectly normal, white teeth.

"You, and indeed this entire night, have held naught but surprises." My fingers closed on a stone. I hid it behind my back, lifting my knees, shielding my body from his devouring gaze with my hair, which fell in tangles around me.

"What use will rumination on the past do? Better to move forward, into the now we find ourselves in." His blue eyes twinkled.

Handsome, well spoken and a philosopher? I could not reconcile the riddle of him, and was more than a little disturbed by my attraction to him. "What *now* then?"

We had come to a place on the mountain where the trees were thin and stubby, the landscape made up of black flint stone, boulders and dirt. I was reminded of my father as I watched him perch a mail-covered foot upon a large rock and survey the forest below us as a king would his kingdom. The howls of the wolven had grown closer, and now seemed to come from all sides.

"I could eat you or fuck you," he said, the growl in his voice matching the hunger in his words.

I shivered, wrapping my arms about myself. "I am very thin, surely not fit for a meal."

"Pity. Skinny *and* no longer virgin." His gaze dropped, seeming to see right through the protective veil of my hair.

"Hardly worth your time." I inched away from him.

"Still, it has been an entire year since I felt the pleasures to be had in the arms of a wet, willing woman." He took a step closer to me and, despite my fear, I felt myself begin to respond to him.

"I would hardly be called willing."

"I watched you fucking him. Touch you just right and you'll be willing all right, as willing as they come." He reached out and brushed the hair back from my cheek, and my nipples hardened and proved his words true. "Fucked by a man who knows a few things your tender young lover hasn't learned yet. Things about what women really want."

What could I say in reply? I had become a wanton in Taran's arms, and the thought of doing the same with the powerful and handsome stranger had indeed made my body tingle, setting my mind to visions of things I might be made to do by him.

"There is to be a war. The only thing you need concern yourself with *now* is whether you will be my queen and bedmate, or food for my minions. What shall you choose?"

My fingers itched to throw the stone at his arrogant head. "Our Haven is not worth a war."

"While your people busied themselves behind their walls, they have been watched keenly and closely by those who put them there to start with. The gods are the ones bringing the war. I only defend my own. As my queen, you will become a goddess when we defeat the gods."

"I see no god in you!"

"I see a frightened girl who has a choice before her! Queen and willing little fuckmate or meal to the wolven?" he growled.

The wind screamed and from above us came a great flurry of sound unlike anything I had ever heard. Falling from the night sky came an extraordinary beast—an enormous, black, winged horse whose flailing hooves struck my captor, knocking him to the ground.

The Pegasus horse landed in the clearing. His nostrils flared with the breath he sent over my fingers, still lifted in fear until his familiar, equine gaze found mine and he came to a knee before me.

"Taran!" My man of mystery and riddles had kept this last secret to himself.

Behind him, the stricken warrior came to with a mighty roar. I jumped upon Taran's back, holding tight to his mane as he flew into the night.

Below us the warrior bellowed, whirling like a dervish in his anger, kicking up flint stones that sparked. The wind caught showers of glowing orange embers, sending them dancing over the treetops below us, setting the rain-parched forest aflame like kindling wood. Fire raced down the mountainside.

The wind and smoke tearing my eyes, I gave thanks to the gods for Taran. I would never tell him about the choice I had been about to make when I thought all had been lost, or of my shameless fantasies about my captor.

"Some things a woman must bear for her man," my mother had taught me and, in this, I believed she was right.

I had made difficult choices this night. There would be thorny questions to answer, decisions to atone for and a war to fight.

My Princess is finally getting her wish—I am taking her home.

What is man's greatest strength? I cannot answer. Love, however, is mine. I hope it is enough.

ABOUT THE
AUTHORS

PIERS ANTHONY was born in Oxford, England in 1934. His family was doing relief work in Spain during the Spanish Civil War, so Piers spent a year in Spain. The new fascist government expelled the family from Spain, and Piers had his sixth birthday on the ship to America. He was not a great student, taking three years and five schools to make it through first grade because of his trouble learning to read. Yet in due course he became a writer, making his first story sale in 1962 and going on to have twenty-one novels on the *New York Times* bestseller list. Today he lives with his wife on their tree farm in backwoods Florida. He is still writing stories and novels.

MEGAN ARKENBERG is a student in Wisconsin. Her work has appeared in *Fantasy Magazine*, *Beneath Ceaseless Skies*, *Clarkesworld*, *Strange Horizons* and dozens of other places. She edits the fantasy e-zine *Mirror Dance* and the historical fiction e-zine *Lacuna*.

JANINE ASHBLESS is a multi-published author of fantasy and paranormal erotica. Her stories have been published by—among others—Spice, Black Lace, Nexus, Xcite, Ellora's Cave, Samhain and Cleis (including the anthologies *Red Velvet and Absinthe* and *The Handsome Prince*). She lives in England and blogs at janineashbless.blogspot.com.

M. H. CRANE is a writer and artist in Arizona. She won Silver Honorable Mention and Honorable Mention in the Writers of the Future Contest and appeared in the spec fiction anthologies *Such a Pretty Face* and *Past, Present, Future 2011*. Her science fantasy novel *Blackfire* won a finalist award in the 2011 Suvudu.com Writing Contest sponsored by Random House.

ERIC DEL CARLO's (ericdelcarlo.com) erotic work has appeared in numerous Circlet Press anthologies, as well as with Loose Id and Ravenous Romance. He also contributed to the Cleis Press collection *Beautiful Boys*. His mainstream sci-fi and fantasy have been published by *Futurismic*, *Talebones* and many other magazines, and is upcoming at *Asimov's* and *Redstone Science Fiction*. He lives in California's wine country.

AURELIA T. EVANS is the author of several erotic short stories in such anthologies as Amber Dawn's *Fist of the Spider Woman* and Kristina Wright's *Fairy Tale Lust*. When she isn't writing, she attends school, makes jewelry and watches horror movies. She lives in Dallas, Texas.

SACCHI GREEN's stories have appeared in a hip-high stack of publications with erotically inspirational covers, and she's also edited and coedited eight erotica anthologies, including *Girl Crazy*, *Lesbian Cowboys* (winner of the 2010 Lambda Literary

Award for lesbian erotica), *Lesbian Lust, Lesbian Cops* and *Girl Fever,* all from Cleis Press. Her alter ego Connie Wilkins writes and edits science fiction and fantasy.

KIM KNOX (kim-knox.co.uk) brews sex, magic, darkness and technology in a little corner of northwest England. She writes erotic science fiction and fantasy romance for Carina Press, Ellora's Cave and Samhain Publishing.

ASHLEY LISTER (ashleylister.co.uk) is the pseudonymous author of more than two dozen erotic fiction titles and countless short stories (one of which appeared in Mitzi Szereto's *Red Velvet and Absinthe: Paranormal Erotic Romance*), as well as two nonfiction titles exploring the secret lives of the United Kingdom's swinging community. Aside from working as a performance poet, he currently teaches creative writing in northwest England.

ANNA MEADOWS is a part-time executive assistant, part-time Sapphic housewife. Her work appears on the Lambda Literary website and in nine Cleis Press anthologies, including *Red Velvet and Absinthe: Paranormal Erotic Romance*. She lives and writes in Northern California.

MADELINE MOORE has published three novels: *Wild Card, Amanda's Young Men* and *Sarah's Education*. Her stories have appeared in many anthologies. The Erotic Awards 2011 declared Madeline "Story Teller of the Year" for "Get Up! Stand Up!" from the anthology *The Cougar Book*. Madeline lives near Toronto, Ontario.

NYLA NOX is author of the story "Heart of the Desert"

(*Needles and Bones*) and the essay "The Midnight Moralist," a winner of the 2010 Seven Fund international competition. In 2007 she was shortlisted for a UK first novel prize. She is a magazine columnist in Southeast Asia.

ZANDER VYNE (zandervyne.com) can find something erotic about most situations, so she writes about it. Her macabre story, *La Belle Mort*, was a reader favorite in Mitzi Szereto's anthology, *Red Velvet and Absinthe: Paranormal Erotic Romance*. She lives in Chicago and is currently writing her second novel.

JO WU (jowu-timeispoisoned.blogspot.com) is a UC Berkeley student, an aspiring novelist, and the author of two columns for UC Berkeley's *Caliber Magazine*.

ABOUT
THE EDITOR

MITZI SZERETO (mitziszereto.com) is an author and anthology editor of multi-genre fiction and nonfiction. She has her own blog, Errant Ramblings: Mitzi Szereto's Weblog (mitziszereto.com/blog) and a Web TV channel, Mitzi TV (mitziszereto.com/tv), which covers the quirky side of London. Her books include the controversial Jane Austen sex parody *Pride and Prejudice: Hidden Lusts*; *Red Velvet and Absinthe: Paranormal Erotic Romance*; *In Sleeping Beauty's Bed: Erotic Fairy Tales*; *Getting Even: Revenge Stories*; *Wicked: Sexy Tales of Legendary Lovers*; *Dying For It: Tales of Sex and Death*; the *Erotic Travel Tales* anthologies and many other titles. A popular social media personality and frequent interviewee, she has pioneered erotic writing workshops in the United Kingdom and mainland Europe and lectured in creative writing at several British universities. Her anthology *Erotic Travel Tales 2* is the first anthology of erotica to feature a Fellow of the Royal Society of Literature. She divides her time between England and the United States.